Harlan Page Beach

Dawn on the Hills of T'ang

Missions in China

Harlan Page Beach

Dawn on the Hills of T'ang
Missions in China

ISBN/EAN: 9783337327316

Printed in Europe, USA, Canada, Australia, Japan

Cover: Foto ©Andreas Hilbeck / pixelio.de

More available books at **www.hansebooks.com**

孔夫子

K'ung Fu - tzŭ.

REDUCED FAC-SIMILE OF A RUBBING FROM A MARBLE SLAB
BEHIND THE TEMPLE OF CONFUCIUS AT CH'IU-FU HSIEN.

OR

MISSIONS IN CHINA

BY

HARLAN P. BEACH

FORMERLY MISSIONARY IN CHINA; MEMBER OF THE AMERICAN
ORIENTAL SOCIETY; EDUCATIONAL SECRETARY OF
THE STUDENT VOLUNTEER MOVEMENT
FOR FOREIGN MISSIONS

NEW YORK
STUDENT VOLUNTEER MOVEMENT
FOR FOREIGN MISSIONS
1898

EXPLANATORY

THE somewhat peculiar form of this little volume is due to the fact that it is one of a series of text-books prepared for Mission Study Classes, found mainly in higher educational institutions, though many have been carried on by young people's societies and women's missionary organizations. A book which gives the main points in as brief a form as possible, and which makes ample provision for further study by class members, is demanded for such a use; and the satisfaction of such demands has been aimed at in the preparation of this volume. That this form of text-book is appreciated is evidenced by the fact that more than ten thousand copies were sold to study classes during last year.

Experiments extending over three years have led to the peculiarities of typography, found in these pages. The heavy-faced **Clarendon type** indicates the main divisions of the chapter; numerals indicate subordinate divisions; and paragraphs, or Italics, mark subtopics under the latter. Those preparing the lesson usually group their facts about these words in special type, and class leaders employ them as the basis of questions. At the request of many, an analytical index has been prepared—see pages 167 to 173, and can be used after the lesson has been carefully read over to ascertain how much has been remembered. It also brings the thoughts of the chapter before one with great clearness and at a glance.

As the text-book is but an outline, it is expected that classes will supplement its meagre statements by outside readings. A collection of such readings will be found on pages ix. to xvii. While only a small portion of the very full bibliography of this field has been entered in the list, a far larger number of references has been printed than can be used, for the reason that if only a few readings were suggested, libraries to which access was possible might contain none of them. With a comparatively large number listed, the chance of finding at least some readings is increased. It is not usually advisable to assign more than three or four additional readings to be reported upon at any one class session.

It will be noted that no missionary periodicals are found in this list except _The Chinese Recorder_ and _The Missionary Review of the World_. The reason for this is that the two periodicals excepted are interdenominational, and the latter is easily accessible. Moreover, as over fifty boards labor in the Empire, it would be obviously impossible to refer to their official organs. In the book itself, practically nothing has been said concerning the work of any one society. An attempt to do this would have resulted in a volume too large for class use, as well as being too expensive. The hope of the author is that missionary societies using it for class work will supplement it by pamphlets issued by their board. In two cases provision has already been made for such classes. The Board of the Methodist Church in the South has a special edition for its own use, containing an additional chapter, written by Bishop Galloway, upon the work of their Church in China. Similarly, Mrs. Professor Barbour and Miss Huntington, of the Episcopal Church, have prepared a special pamphlet to accompany the text-book, in which full details concerning the Missions of the American Episcopal Church in China are admirably summarized. Doubtless other boards can make a like arrangement. Suggestions for the study of the work for any given board may be found in Appendix C.

The special map prepared for the book, while not perfect, is more nearly so than any missionary map of the Empire hitherto published. The index accompanying it makes it easy to find any place occupied at the present time by missionaries.

Many will criticise the orthography of proper names, both on the map and in the body of the book. In defense the author would say that scarcely any map of China is consistent in its Romanization of geographical names, and the same is to some extent true of personal names in works on this country. The attempt has here been made—though some exceptions will be found—to follow a uniform system of Romanization. But if this is desirable, what system is to be used ? The one followed is that of Sir Thomas Wade, which is increasingly employed in the latest dictionaries, lessons for beginners, etc. To say that it is a system peculiarly adapted to the Pekingese, and hence should be discarded, is like objecting to Parisian because it does not correctly represent the pronunciation of southwestern France. While Sir Thomas Wade's system does not properly reproduce the sounds of southern China, no system is universal, and Wade's is the standard for Northern Mandarin, which is understood by more persons, perhaps, than any other Chinese dialect. An approximate key to this system is found on page xviii.

September 1, 1898.

CONTENTS

	PAGE
BIBLIOGRAPHY,	ix
KEY TO PRONUNCIATION OF CHINESE WORDS,	xviii
I. THE WORLD OF THE CHINESE,	1
II. CHINA'S INHERITANCE FROM THE PAST,	15
III. "THE REAL CHINAMAN,"	32
IV. RELIGIONS OF THE CHINESE,	52
V. PREPARATION AND BEGINNINGS,	75
VI. THE PROTESTANT OCCUPATION OF CHINA,	95
VII. THE MISSIONARIES AT WORK,	116
VIII. THE DAWN,	134
APPENDIX A. PROVINCIAL DIVISIONS,	153
APPENDIX B. PROMINENT EVENTS OF THE HISTORIC DYNASTIES,	159
APPENDIX C. SCHEME FOR STUDYING DENOMINATIONAL MISSIONARY WORK IN CHINA,	162
ANALYTICAL INDEX,	167
MAP INDEX,	175

BIBLIOGRAPHY.

ADDITIONAL READINGS FOR CHAPTER I.

BARNES, I. H.: Behind the Great Wall (1896), ch. I.
Chinese Recorder for 1896, pp. 170–174.
CUNNYNGHAM, W. G. E.: Young People's History of the Chinese (1896), ch. II.
CURZON, G. N.: Problems of the Far East (1896), ch. VIII.
DAVIS, J. F.: The Chinese (1851), vol. I., ch. V.
Encyclopædia of Missions (1891). Article, China.
General Encyclopædias. Article, China.
GRAY, J. H.: China (1878), vol. I., ch. I.; vol. II., ch. XXXII.
HART, V. C.: Western China (1888), chs. VI.–XIII.
HENRY, B. C.: Ling-nam (1886). Especially ch. XXVII.
KEANE, A. H.: Asia (1896), vol. I., pp. 245–361.
Kleine Missions-Bibliothek (1880), vol. III., pt. III., pp. 1–13.
MORRIS, T. M.: A Winter in North China (1892), ch. VII.
NEVIUS, J. L.: China and the Chinese (1882), ch. I.
Nouveau Dictionnaire de Géographie Universelle (1897). Article, Chine.
ROCKHILL, W. W.: The Land of the Lamas (1891), chs. I., II., VII.
THOMSON, J.: Through China with a Camera (1898).
WILLIAMSON, A.: Journeys in North China (1870), vol. II., ch. II.
WILLIAMS, S. W.: Middle Kingdom (1882), vol. I., chs. I.–III.
WILSON, J. H.: China (1894), chs. III.–V.

ADDITIONAL READINGS FOR CHAPTER II.

BOUGHTON, W.: History of Ancient Peoples (1897), pt. II., ch. II.
BOULGER, D. C.: A Short History of China (1893).
Chinese Recorder for 1896, pp. 233–242, 284–292, 336–342, 589–592.
DAVIS, J. F.: Sketches of China (1845), ch. IX.
DAVIS, J. F.: The Chinese (1851), vol. I., ch. VI.
DE LACOUPERIE, T.: Western Origin of the Early Chinese Civilization (1894), chs. II., III.

DOUGLAS, R. K. : China (1882), ch. I.
Encyclopædia of Missions (1891), vol. I., pp. 251-252.
FABER, E. : China in the Light of History (1897).
FERGUSSON, T. : Chinese Researches (1880), pt. I., ch. I.
General Encyclopædias. Article, China.
Kleine Missions-Bibliothek (1880), vol. III., pt. III., pp. 15-27.
LEGGE, J. : The Chinese Classics (1865), vol. III., pt. I., ch. V.
MACGOWAN, J. : History of China (1897).
MAYERS, W. F. : Chinese Reader's Manual (1874).
MEDHURST, W. H. : China; Its State and Prospects (1838),
   ch. I.
MORRISON, R. : View of China for Philological Purposes (1817),
   pp. 4-60.
MOULE, A. E. : New China and Old (1892), ch. I.
WILLIAMS, S. W. : Middle Kingdom (1882), vol. II., ch. XVII.
WILLIAMS, S. W. and F. W. : History of China (1897).

ADDITIONAL READINGS FOR CHAPTER III.

BALL, J. D. : Things Chinese (1893), pp. 91-101.
COCKBURN, G. : John Chinaman (1896).
DAVIS, J. A. : Choh Lin (1884), chs. I.-XI.
DAVIS, J. F. : Sketches of China (1845), ch. XV.
DOOLITTLE, J. : Social Life of the Chinese (1865).
DOUGLAS, R. K. : China (1882).
DOUGLAS, R. K. : Society in China (1894).
E. M. : The Chinese; Their Mental and Moral Characteristics
   (1877).
Encyclopædia of Missions (1891). Article, China.
FIELDE, A. M. : A Corner of Cathay (1894).
FIELDE, A. M. : Pagoda Shadows (1884).
General Encyclopædias. Article, China.
GRAY, J. H. : China (1878).
HENRY, B. C. : The Cross and the Dragon (1885), ch. III.
HOLCOMBE, C. : The Real Chinaman (1895).
HOSIE, A. : Three Years in Western China (1889), ch. XIII.
HOUGHTON, R. C. : Women of the Orient (1877), chs. V., VIII.
KEANE, A. H. : Asia (1896), vol. I., pp. 361-383, 432-439.
MACGOWAN, J. : Pictures of Southern China (1897), pp. 316-
   320.
MARCH, D. : Morning Light in Many Lands (1891), chs. X., XI.
MEDHURST, W. H. : The Foreigner in Far Cathay (1873), es-
   pecially chs. XII., XVIII.
Missionary Review of the World (1895), pp. 84-89.
Mission Stories of Many Lands (1885), pp. 173-219.
NEVIUS, J. L. : China and the Chinese (1882), chs. II., XVII.,
   XIX.

SMITH, A. H. : Chinese Characteristics (1894).
SMITH, A. H. : Proverbs and Common Sayings of the Chinese (1888).
WILLIAMS, S. W. : Middle Kingdom (1882), vol. I., chs. V., VII., IX., XIII., XIV.
WYLIE, A. : Notes on Chinese Literature (1867), pp. i-xiii.

ADDITIONAL READINGS FOR CHAPTER IV.

BARROWS, J. H., Editor: World's Parliament of Religions (1893), vol. I., pp. 374-439; vol. II., pp. 1355-1358.
BEAL, S. : Buddhism in China (1884).
BETTANY, G. T. : The World's Religions (1891), pp. 102-166.
China Mission Hand-Book (1896), pt. I., pp. 1-31.
DAVIDS, T. W. R. : Buddhism (1890), chs. VIII., IX.
DOOLITTLE, J. : Social Life of the Chinese (1865), vol. I., chs. VIII., XI., XIV.
DOUGLAS, R. K. : Confucianism and Taouism (1889).
DU BOSE, H. C. : The Dragon, Image, and Demon (1886).
EDKINS, J. : Early Spread of Religious Ideas (1893), chs. V.-VII.
ELLINWOOD, F. F. : Oriental Religions and Christianity (1892), lect. VII.
Encyclopædia of Missions (1891). Articles, Confucianism, Taoism.
FABER, E. : The Mind of Mencius (1897).
General Encyclopædias. Articles, Confucius, Confucianism, Taoism.
GRANT, G. M. : Religions of the World in Relation to Christianity (1894), ch. III.
GRAY, J. H. : China (1878), vol. I., chs. IV., V.
HENRY, B. C. : The Cross and the Dragon (1885), chs. IV.-VII.
HUC, E. R. : A Journey through the Chinese Empire (n. d.), vol. II., ch. VI.
JEVONS, F. B. : Introduction to the History of Religion (1896), see China in Index.
LEGGE, J. : Chinese Classics, Translated into English (1887), vols. I., II.
LEGGE, J. : Chinese Classics [with Chinese text] (1893), vol. I., the Prolegomena.
LEGGE, J. : Chinese Classics [with Chinese text] (1895) vol. II., the Prolegomena.
LEGGE, J. : Religions of China (1881).
LEGGE, J. : Sacred Books of the East, the Texts of Taoism (1891), especially vol. I., pp. 1-44.
MATHIESON, G. : Distinctive Messages of the Old Religions (1894), ch. III.

MENZIES, A.: History of Religion (1895), ch. VIII.
Missionary Review of the World, 1894, pp. 80–89; 1896, pp. 96–100.
MOULE, A. E.: Four Hundred Millions (1871), ch. I.
MOULE, A. E.: New China and Old (1892), chs. VI., VIII.
NEVIUS, II. S. C.: Our Life in China (1868), ch. III.
NEVIUS, J. L.: China and the Chinese (1882), chs. III., VI.–XII.
Present Day Tracts—Non-Christian Religions (1887), Christianity and Confucianism.
Progress for October, 1897, pp. 103–107, 112–150.
Records of the Missionary Conference, Shanghai, 1877, pp. 62–75; pp. 367–387.
SCOTT, A.: Buddhism and Christianity (1890), lect. VI.
Student Missionary Appeal (1898), pp. 93–100; 336–338.
WILLIAMS, S. W.: Middle Kingdom (1882), vol. II., pp. 188–266.

ADDITIONAL READINGS FOR CHAPTER V.

ARNOLD, T. W.: The Preaching of Islam (1896), ch. X.
BALL, J. D.: Things Chinese (1893), pp. 419–430; 294–299.
China Mission Hand-Book (1896), pt. I., pp. 31–45.
Chinese Recorder for 1891, pp. 263, 264; 354–358; 377, 378; 401–405; 545–553; for 1892, pp. 57–60; for 1895, pp. 251–260.
DAVIS, J. F.: The Chinese (1851), vol. I., ch. I.
DOOLITTLE, J.: Social Life of the Chinese (1865), vol. II., pp. 394–403.
Encyclopædia of Missions (1891), vol. I., pp. 264, 265.
FOSTER, A.: Christian Progress in China (1889), pp. 247–255.
HAINES, C. R.: Islam, as a Missionary Religion (1889), ch. VI.
HUC, E. R.: Christianity in China (1857–58).
MARSHALL, T. W. M.: Christian Missions (1863), sections on China.
MARTIN, W. A. P.: A Cycle of Cathay (1896), pt. II., ch. IV.
MARTIN, W. A. P.: The Chinese (1881), pp. 287–306.
NEANDER, A.: General History of the Christian Religion and Church (1871), vol. IV., pp. 45–59.
NEVIUS, J. L.: China and the Chinese (1882), ch. XXVI.
Records of the Missionary Conference, Shanghai (1890), pp. 196–202.
WILLIAMS· S. W.: Middle Kingdom (1882), vol. II., pp. 266–318.

ADDITIONAL READINGS FOR CHAPTER VI.

BERRY, D. M.: The Sister Martyrs of Ku Cheng (n. d.), ch. XXII.

BLISS, E. M.: Concise History of Missions (1897), pt. II., ch. VI.

BUTLER, W. F.: Charles George Gordon (1889), ch. III.

Centenary Conference on Foreign Missions, London, 1888, vol. I., pp. 220–238.

China Mission Hand-Book (1896), pt. II.

CHRISTLIEB, T.: Protestant Foreign Missions (1880), pp. 189–209.

COBB, H. N.: Far Hence (1893), chs. XX.–XXVII.

Conference on Foreign Missions, Mildmay (1878), pp. 168–179.

CREEGAN, C. C.: Great Missionaries of the Church (1895), chs. VI., VII.

CUNNINGHAM, A.: History of the Szechuen Riots (1895).

Encyclopædia of Missions (1891), vol. I., pp. 265–271.

FAGG, J. G.: Forty Years in South China (1894), chs. V., XI.

GRAHAM, J. A.: Missionary Expansion of the Reformed Churches (1898), pp. 139–160.

GRUNDEMANN, R.: Neuer Missions-Atlas (1896), maps 24, 25.

GUINNESS, M. G.: Story of the China Inland Mission (1894).

GUNDERT, H.: Die Evangelische Mission (1894), pp. 334–355.

Historical Sketches, Presbyterian Missions (1897), pp. 39–65.

HORNE, C. S.: Story of the L. M. S., 1795–1895 (1895), ch. V.

In Lands Afar (1897), pp. 207–264.

LAWRENCE, E. A.: Modern Missions in the East (1894), pp. 57–70.

LENKER, J. N.: Lutherans in all Lands (1893), vol. I., pp. 639–644.

LEONARD, D. L.: A Hundred Years of Missions (1895), pp. 307–332.

LOVETT, R.: James Gilmour of Mongolia (1893), ch. II.

LOVETT, R.: Primer of Modern British Missions (n. d.), ch. V.

LYON, D. W.: Sketch of the History of Protestant Missions in China (1895).

MABIE, H. C.: In Brightest Asia (1891), chs. V.–XII.

MACCRACKEN AND PIPER: Leaders of Our Church Universal (1879). Life XXXVI.

McLEAN, A.: Circuit of the Globe (1897), chs. XIX.–XXIX.

Missionary Review of the World (1896), pp. 87–96; 1897, p. 123.

MOOREHEAD, M. W., Editor: The Student Missionary Enterprise (1894), see index, p. 366.

MOULE, A. E.: China as a Mission Field (1891), pt. II.

MOULE, A. E.: New China and Old (1892), ch. X.

NEVIUS, J. L.: China and the Chinese (1882), pp. 300–331.

Picket Line of Missions (1897), chs. IV., V.

REID AND GRACEY: Missions and Missionary Society of the Methodist Episcopal Church (1895), vol. I., pp. 409–485; vol. II., pp. 9–177.

Reports of the Boards of Missions of the Provinces of Canterbury and York on the Mission Field (1894), pp. 260–283.

RONSON, W.: Griffith John (n. d.).

STACY, T. H.: In the Path of Light Around the World (1895), ch. VI.–VIII.

TOWNSEND, W. J.: Robert Morrison (n. d.), especially ch. X.

WALSH, W. P.: Modern Heroes of the Mission Field (1881), ch. IV.

WILLIAMS, F. W.: Life and Letters of S. Wells Williams (1888), especially chs. III.–X.

WILLIAMS, S. W.: Middle Kingdom (1882), vol. II , pp. 318–371; chs. XXII., XXVI.

YOUNG, R.: Modern Missions, Their Trials and Triumphs (1884), pp. 100–138.

ADDITIONAL READINGS FOR CHAPTER VII.

BAINBRIDGE, W. F.: Around the World Tour of Christian Missions (1882).

BRYSON, M. I.: Fred. C. Roberts of Tientsin (1895), chs. VII.–XII.

BRYSON, M. I.: John Kenneth Mackenzie (n. d.).

Centenary Conference on Foreign Missions, London, 1888, vol. II., pp. 266–272; 308–315.

China Imperial Maritime Customs, Medical Reports, 1886–1890.

Chinese Recorder for 1892, pp. 199–209; 362–367; 556–563; for 1894, pp. 21–30; 66–72; 167–170; 172–174; 369–375; for 1896, pp. 62–72; 116–124; 107–115; 331–334; 374–384; 432–440; for 1897, pp. 563–569; for 1898, pp. 51–69; 227–233.

COLTMAN, R.: The Chinese (1891), chs. VIII.–X.

Conference on Missions at Liverpool, 1860, pp. 275, 276.

DAVIS, J. A.: Leng Tso (1886).

DU BOSE, H. C.: Preaching in Sinim (1893), chs. IV., V., VIII.–XII.

DUDGEON, J.: The Diseases of China (1877).

DUKES, E. J.: Along River and Road in Fuh-kien (n. d.), chs. VI., IX., XII., XIII.

FOSTER, A.: Christian Progress in China (1889), pp. 104–246.

HENRY, B. C.: The Cross and the Dragon (1885), chs. XII.–XXI.

HODDER, E.: Conquests of the Cross (n. d.), see Index in vol. III.

JEWETT, F. G.: Luther Halsey Gulick (1895), ch. XXVIII.

JOHNSTON, J. : China and Formosa (1897), ch. XIX.
LOCKHART, W. : The Medical Missionary in China (1861), chs. VI.-IX.
LOWE, J. : Medical Missions (1887), ch. V.
MATHEWS, G. D., Editor : Alliance of the Reformed Churches (1892), pp. 151-156.
MEARS, W. P. : Preservation of Health in the Far East (1895).
Missionary Review of the World, 1894, pp. 371, 372.
Mission Press in China (1895).
NEVIUS, H. S. C. : Life of John Livingstone Nevius (1895), especially ch. XXXV.
NEVIUS, J. L. : China and the Chinese (1882), chs. XXII.-XXV.
NEVIUS, J. L : Methods of Mission Work (1895).
Records of the Missionary Conference, Shanghai, 1877.
Records of the Missionary Conference, Shanghai, 1890.
Second Triennial Meeting of the Educational Association of China (1896), pp. 178-180 ; 243-253.
SPOTTISWOODE, G. A. : Missionary Conference of the Anglican Communion (1894), pp. 213-221.
STEVENS AND MARKWICK : Life, Letters and Journals of the Rev. and Hon. Peter Parker, M.D. (1896), ch. VIII.
STOTT, G. : Twenty-six Years of Missionary Work in China (1897).
Student Missionary Appeal (1898), 331-335.
WILLIAMSON, I. : Old Highways in China (n. d.).

ADDITIONAL READINGS FOR CHAPTER VIII.

BARROWS, J. H., Editor : World's Parliament of Religions (1893), vol. II., pp. 1137-1144.
BROOMHALL, B. : Evangelization of the World (1887).
China Mission Hand-Book (1896), pt. I., pp. 83-92.
Chinese Recorder for 1891, pp. 371-373 ; for 1894, pp. 194-200 ; for 1895, pp. 151-161 ; 436-438 ; 501-508 ; for 1897, pp. 27-33, 67-71 ; 580, 581 ; for 1898, pp. 78-87, 161-169 ; 260-265 ; 311-320.
Conference on Foreign Missions, Mildmay, 1886, pp. 94-107.
CURZON, G. N. : Problems of the Far East (1896) chs. IX., X.
DENNIS, J. S. : Christian Missions and Social Progress (1897), vol. I., pp. 80-86.
DENNIS, J. S. : Foreign Missions after a Century (1893) pp. 76-85.
Evangelization of China (1897).
GRAVES, R. H. : Forty Years in China (1895).
GUINNESS, G. : In the Far East (1889), ch. XV., XVI.
GUNDRY, R. S. : China, Present and Past (1895), chs. IV., V., X.
HENRY, B. C. : The Cross and the Dragon (1885), ch. XXV

KELTIE AND RENWICK: Statesman's Year-Book (1898), pp. 422–429.

LIGGINS, J.: Great Value and Success of Foreign Missions (1888), pp. 55–70.

MARTIN, W. A. P.: A Cycle of Cathay (1896), pt. II. chs. XI.–XV.

MARTIN, W. A. P.: Hanlin Papers, Second Series (1894), ch. XVII.

Missionary Review of the World, 1892, pp. 81–91; 1896, pp. 100–106; 372, 373; 510–512; 1897, pp. 95–102; 116–120; 764–769; 1898, pp. 52–55; 127–132; 678–680; 684–688.

MOTT, J. R.: Strategic Points in the World's Conquest (1897), ch. XV.

MUIRHEAD, W.: China and the Gospel (1870), chs. VIII., IX.

NEVIUS, J. L.: China and the Chinese (1882), chs. XXVII., XXVIII.

REID: Glances at China (n. d.). chs. XXVIII., XXXIV.

RICHARD, T.: The Awakening of China (1897).

RUDDLE, T.: Samuel Thomas Thorne (1893), ch. XVI.

Second Triennial Meeting of the Educational Association of China (1896), pp. 33–39.

SMITH, A. H.: Chinese Characteristics (1894), ch. XXVII.

Records of the Missionary Conference, Shanghai, 1877, pp. 352–367.

Records of the Missionary Conference, Shanghai, 1890, pp. 11–22.

SPEER, R. E.: Missions and Politics in Asia (1898), lect. III.

Student Missionary Appeal (1898), pp. 336–345.

TAYLOR, J. H.: China's Spiritual Need and Claims (1887).

WILLIAMSON, A.: Journeys in North China (1870), vol. I., chs. I.–VI.

WILSON, J. H.: China (1894), ch. XXI.

ARTICLES ON CHINA IN RECENT SECULAR PERIODICALS.

Blackwood's Magazine: The Crisis in China, February, 1898.
    The Chinese Imbroglio, April, 1898.
    The Yellow Peril, June, 1898.

Catholic Review: John Chinaman, January, 1898.

Chambers's Journal: The Mineral Riches of China, March, 1898.

Chautauquan: Who will Exploit China? January, 1898.
    Europe in China, and the Great Siberian Railway, May, 1898.

Contemporary Review: How China may be Saved, May, 1898.

Cosmopolitan: The Land that is Central, March, 1898.

Edinburgh Review: British Policy in China, July, 1898.
Fortnightly: Germany in China, May, 1898.
Forum: China and Chinese Railway Concessions, January, 1898.
Harper's Monthly Magazine: The Situation in China, June, 1898.
National Review: The Coming Partition of China, March, 1898.
    Great Britain's Future Policy in China, July, 1898.
New Century Review: Life in China, April, 1898.
Nineteenth Century: The Partition of China, January, 1898.
North American Review: America's Interest in China, February, 1898.

KEY TO PRONUNCIATION OF CHINESE WORDS

The system of Romanizing Chinese words followed in this book is that of Sir Thomas Wade as adapted to the Mandarin of Peking. While it is impossible to accurately pronounce Pekingese without the aid of a native, and though it would be useless to pronounce accurately in China, if the tones were not acquired —as is still more impossible without a teacher—an approximation is here offered that the prevalent atrocious pronunciation of Western lands may be modified and that a correct Chinese pronunciation may be more nearly attained. Only those letters and combinations of letters occasioning difficulty are given; others are pronouuced as in English. We would repeat that the suggestions here made will only enable the reader to gain *an approximate pronunciation* of the Peking Mandarin, the Parisian of China. Only English equivalents or partial equivalents are given. Those who would gain a more accurate idea of Chinese pronunciation are referred to Wade and Hillier's "Tzŭ Êrh Chi."

a as in f*a*ther.
ai as in *ai*sle.
ao as *ow* in n*ow*.
* *ch* as *j* in *j*ar.
ch‘ as in *ch*ange.
ê as in p*e*rch.
e in *eh*, *en*, as in y*e*t, wh*e*n.
ei as *ey* in wh*ey*.
* *hs* as *hss* in *hiss*ing, when the first *i* is omitted.
i as in ma*chi*ne, when it stands alone or at the end of a word.
i as p*i*n, when in before *n* and *ng*.
ia as *eo* in g*eo*logy.
iao as *e ou* in m*e out*.
ie as in s*ie*sta.
* *ih* as *er* in ov*er*.
iu as *eu* in J*ehu*, when h is omitted.
* *j* as the first *r* in *r*egular.
* *k* as *g* in *g*ame.
k‘ as *k*.
ng as in si*ng*.
* *o* as *oa* in b*oa*-constrictor.
ou as in s*ou*nd.
* *p* as *b*.
p‘ as *p*.
rh as *rr* in bu*rr*.
ss as in hi*ss*.
* *t* as *d*.
t‘ as *t*.
* *ts* as *ds* in pa*ds*.
ts‘ as in ca*ts*.
* *tz* as *ds* in pa*ds*.
tz‘ as *ts* in ca*ts*.
u as *oo* in t*oo*.
ua as *oe o* in sh*oe on*.
uai as *o ey* in tw*o eyes*.
uei as *way*.
ui as *ewy* in scr*ewy*.
* *ŭ* as final *a* in Americ*a*.
* *ü* as French *u* or German *ü*.
* *üa* as French *u* plus *a* in *a*n.
* *üe* as French *u* plus *e* in y*e*t.

* Those thus marked have no close English equivalents. Consonants followed by an aspirate (‘) are almost like the same in English; the same consonants without the aspirate are more difficult to correctly pronounce.

DAWN ON THE HILLS OF T'ANG

I

THE WORLD OF THE CHINESE

Scope of the Text-book.—The first missionaries to China, men of the Buddhist faith, called the land Chin-tan, or Dawn. Centuries later, when the rulers of the T'ang dynasty had made the Empire the most polished nation of the world, the Hills of T'ang became the popular name for the whole land, a designation still frequently used in regions south of the Yang-tzŭ Kiang. This little volume does not pretend to discuss fully either the land or the people of China. All that is attempted is to furnish a glimpse of the hills and men of T'ang, and to sketch, in outline, the Christian dawn as it is touching mountain and plain, city and hamlet, throughout this most populous empire. It should further be stated that, inasmuch as there is so little missionary work attempted among the sparsely settled Chinese dependencies, attention will be restricted to missions within China Proper, Shĕng-ching, in southern Manchuria, being regarded as a nineteenth province.

"What's in a Name?"—Of ten thousand Chinese hearing the word China, probably not more than one would have any idea that it referred to his native country. Their own names for the Empire and the designations by which it has been known in history demand a moment's attention.

1. *Early occidental names* applied to this land seem to have varied according to the direction from

which it was approached. When reached by the
northern land route, it was known to the ancients
as Seres, and to the Middle Ages as Cathay. The
Latin word Seres may have been derived from the
Chinese character for silk, *ssŭ*, and seems to have
come into use in the Han dynasty, as it was a name
familiar to the Augustan poets. Cathay, the mediæval designation, is from Khitán, a race of Tartar con-
querors, who subjugated the northern provinces during the tenth and eleventh centuries, and thus gave
to North China the name Khitáï.

Travellers by the southern sea route knew the Empire, or its people, by the terms Sin, Sinæ, Chin,
China, and Tsinistæ. The occurrence of the name
China in the Laws of Manu and the Mahábhárata
may indicate that the Hindus had intercourse with
the Chinese at an early period, though other peoples
may have been referred to under this name. The
apparently cognate Hebrew word Sinim (Isaiah
xlix. 12) is regarded by many exegetes as referring to
China. It is probable that this group of names finds
its origin in the dynastic appellation of Ts'in or
Ch'in, a family which, in 221 B.C., subdued all
China. This sept had been powerful from its rise,
more than six centuries earlier, especially in the
western half of the country.

2. *Native appellations* are various. *Hua Hsia*, Flowery Hsia, *T'ang Shan*, Hills of T'ang, and *Ta Ch'ing
K'uo*, Great Pure Kingdom, are phrases derived from
celebrated dynasties of the past and present, while
the commonest name, *Chung Kuo*, Middle Kingdom,
points back to the time, more than 3,000 years ago,
when the Chou dynasty called the royal domain—
located in modern Ho-nan — by that name, because
it was in the centre surrounded by its feudal states.
Ssŭ Hai [all within], the Four Seas, and *T'ien Hsia*,
Beneath the Sky, are very ancient appellations, while
Chin-tan, Dawn, and *Tung T'u*, Land of the East—
a Mohammedan name—are of comparatively recent
date. Our phrase, the Celestials, comes from *T'ien*

Ch'ao, Heavenly Dynasty, meaning the kingdom which is ruled over by the dynasty appointed by Heaven. *Chung Hua Kuo*, Middle Flowery Kingdom, does not so much refer to a land of flowers as to the fact that the Chinese regard themselves as among the most polished and civilized of nations (cf. our word flowery in its rhetorical sense).

China's Place in Asia.—A glance at the map will show the favorable position occupied by the Empire. To the north lies comparatively barren and largely frigid Siberia. To the west and southwest are the dry regions of Central Asia, Afghanistan, Baluchistan, Persia, and Arabia. India and southeastern Asia are fruitful and populous, but their inhabitants are subject to the enervating influences of the tropics, while the Asiatic lands of the Bible are less favored than is China. Japan and Formosa and portions of Korea are as fortunately located as she, but are of very limited extent. What is the significance of China's natural advantages as they affect Asia? With a sea-coast upward of 2,000 miles in length, with a soil of remarkable fertility, open to the ocean winds and watered by noble rivers, with a territory lying almost entirely within the temperate zone, and containing beneath its surface mineral wealth of untold value, China has not only been able to maintain a large population during past millenniums, but in all probability she is also destined to be in the future the home of Asia's most numerous and influential inhabitants.

Areas with Some Comparisons.—Owing to uncertainty as to a portion of its boundary and to inadequate surveys, areas are only approximate; consequently the estimates of different authorities greatly vary.

1. According to the "Statesman's Year-Book, 1898," * the *area of the Empire*—including China

* Unless otherwise stated, the statistics of population and areas contained in this chapter are taken from this standard work.

Proper, and its dependencies, Manchuria, Mongolia, Tibet, Jungaria, and East Turkestan—is 4,218,401 square miles.   It is thus equal to that of the United States, the provinces of Ontario and Quebec and all of Mexico to a line a little beyond the Isthmus of Tehuantepec combined.   Applied to the map of Europe this area would include every country with the exception of about one-fourth of Russia, while on the map of Asia it equals all its southern portion from Cochin China to the Mediterranean, and a strip extending north to include Turkestan, together with the Japanese Empire on the northeast.   It should be remembered that within this last-named region lies the so-called "Continent" of India, if one would realize the vast extent of the Chinese Empire.

2. The *area of China Proper* is not much more than one-third of the total extent of the Empire, measuring 1,312,328 square miles.   Compared with familiar standards, it is equal to nearly one and a half times that part of the United States lying east of the Mississippi.   Its territory would furnish more than enough material for ten United Kingdoms, there would be unused land after France had been laid down upon it six times over, and India without Burma would extend beyond China's limits only by a slight fringe.

An idea of the *corresponding latitudes and longitudes* bounding China Proper can be gained if we suppose it superimposed on the United States.   The city of Mukden, in the remote northeast, may be placed on Boston.   Its southernmost island will then lie upon Yucatan, Havana roughly corresponding in position with Canton.   Its southwestern boundary will almost touch the Mexican coast to the north of Tampico. Kansas City will be near the northwestern boundary, if the extension of the province of Kan-su be neglected, and the northern frontier will thence pass through Chicago and Detroit back to Boston again.

Striking Physical Features. — Sloping to the eastward and to the southeast from the lofty "roof of the world " in Central Asia, the territory is seen to be alternately furrowed by extensive river systems, and divided up by mountain-ridges and hills, which cover the country save in the northeastern quarter, where there is an immense delta plain, one of the most noticeable features of the Empire.

1. The numerous *rivers* and many canals of China form its frequented highways. The two largest of these rivers—ho is the term commonly used for river in the north, as kiang (chiang) is in the south—are the Huang Ho, Yellow River, and the Kiang River, less properly called the Yang-tzŭ, or Son of Ocean, as its incorrectly written form is translated.

The *Huang Ho* receives its name from the yellow clay deposit which it takes up in its course through the loess region of the provinces of Shan-hsi and Shen-hsi, the same deposit giving its color and name to the Yellow Sea also. As it reaches the Great Plain, this clay silts up the river-channel until its bed is in some places almost as high as the surrounding country. Naturally, in times of unusual freshets, the illy constructed dikes are broken through, the populous low-lying plain is overwhelmed with ruin, and occasionally—ten times in the last 2,500 years—the river opens a new channel to the sea. Its right to the appellation of " China's Sorrow " will be granted when it is remembered that every such outbreak means the wholesale destruction of crops, the melting down of numberless adobe houses, and an enormous loss of human life—millions having perished in the overflow of 1887, for example.

Far more useful is the *Yang-tzŭ*, called " the girdle of China," because of its central position and the number of provinces through which it passes. Rising in Tibet, not far from the sources of the Huang Ho, this mighty river stands first in the world for arrangement of subsidiary streams which make its entire basin accessible from the sea. Ocean steamers readily reach Nanking ; river steamers can ascend as far as I-ch'ang, and a small steamer has just passed through the rapids into the heart of Ssŭ-ch'uan; while native boats navigate it as far as remote Yün-nan. The opening up of this river—whose basin, with its 12,000 miles of navigable waterway, occupies nearly one-half of China Proper—to the trade of the Occident is an important factor in China's future development. These and other smaller yet very important rivers are her glory, and "no country can compare with her for natural facilities of inland navigation."

2. The *lakes* of the Empire are unimportant, though in some sections they are very numerous, as in Koko-nor, known by the Chinese as the "Sea of Stars," because of its many lakelets. They are usually quite picturesque and support a large aquatic population, whose fleets of boats thickly dot their waters. The largest one, T'ung-ting Hu, is about the size of our Great Salt Lake, and lies in the centre of China, giving its name to the provinces Hu-pei and Hu-nan—"North of the Lake" and "South of the Lake."

3. The various *mountain ranges* cannot be spoken of in detail. In general it may be said that starting from the Central Asian mountain system they traverse the western and southern provinces, decreasing in height as they approach the coast. Naturally, with this difference in elevation the rugged sides and snowy summits of the western ranges give place to the wooded tops and carefully cultivated terraces of the southeastern hills. Roughly speaking, that portion of China lying west of the longitude of Canton is mountainous, while the region lying east of that same meridian and south of the Yang-tzŭ River is hilly.

4. *The Great Plain* occupies the remaining northeastern section of the Empire, and forms its richest portion. Extending from a point somewhat north of Peking to a short distance below the Yang-tzŭ, with an average breadth of two hundred miles in its northern portion and four hundred miles in its southern,

it contains an area equal to that of the New England and Middle States, together with Maryland and Virginia. This plain is simply the slowly accumulating delta of the Huang Ho, aided somewhat by the Yang-tzŭ. If historical statements can be trusted, the former river is encroaching upon the Yellow Sea at the rate of from seventy to one hundred feet per year.

The significant fact concerning this plain is the *vast population* which it supports, it being estimated that one hundred and seventy-seven millions live upon that little strip of country, an average of nearly eight hundred and fifty per square mile. The states named above as its equivalent in area, though among the most densely populated in America, had in 1890 only a little over twenty million inhabitants, or an average of less than ninety-one per square mile. Bengal, the most thickly inhabited province of India, has four hundred and seventy-one per square mile, while the density of Belgium's population, which leads in European statistics, is but five hundred and seventy-one per square mile. Thus the Great Plain, with its mountain spur in eastern Shan-tung, is more densely settled by far than any other equally large portion of the world.

5. The fertility of this Plain is largely accounted for by the *loess formation* which is characteristic of the northern provinces, adding fertility to the soil and grotesqueness to the topography. Though many competent geologists have styled the loess " the most difficult geological problem," its appearance and characteristics are thus accurately described by Baron von Richthofen : " The loess is a solid friable earth of brownish-yellow color, and when triturated with water, not unlike loam, but differing from it by its highly porous and tubular structure ; these tubes are often lined with a film of lime, and ramify like the roots of plants. . . . It spreads alike both over high and low ground, smoothing off the irregularities of the surface, and its thickness often consid-

erably exceeds 1,000 feet. It is not stratified, and has a tendency to vertical cleavage. . . . It is very fertile, and requires little manure." This last characteristic has made it possible for farmers to raise two excellent crops year after year on the same plot of ground for many centuries. In the mountainous regions of the northern frontiers it furnishes comfortable homes to many thousands, who excavate rooms in the side of loess cliffs, and live more comfortably in them than do the troglodytes of any other land.

Two serious drawbacks arising from the loess formation are the dust-storms, which occur quite frequently in the winter, and the bad roads, due to the friable nature of the soil. The writer has journeyed over highways in northern Shan-hsi that were narrow canyons nearly fifty feet in depth, formed by the pulverization of the soil by cart traffic, the dust being swept away by the first strong wind or heavy rain.

6. *Chinese scenery* is as varied as a tropical and a cold climate, lofty mountains and low-lying hills, elevated plateaus and monotonous plains rising only a few feet above the ocean, parched and sterile areas and fertile districts bathed in moisture, would lead one to expect. While the gorges of the great rivers and the scenery of the western highlands are the most striking scenic features, there is a quiet beauty no less attractive as one gazes upon the terraced and carefully cultivated hills of the southeast, and the matchless mosaic formed by differing crops of the multitudinous farms of the Great Plain, which serve as a setting for adobe hamlets embowered in elms, willows, and the so-called date-trees.

Most striking to the occidental traveller are the massive walls of China's more than 1,700 walled cities, often overgrown in the south with roses and honeysuckle, and reminding one everywhere of dreams of the mediæval period in European history. Almost equally impressive are the evidences everywhere present in the littoral provinces, and in those bordering on the Yang-tzŭ, of a " country overburdened with a population which swarms about you wherever you go. The fields are everywhere full of laborers; in the mountainous districts you will see scores of terraces, rising above one another to the height of 500 or 1,000 feet, and the hills cultivated in many places to their very tops. Pedestrians are everywhere seen in the roads and by-paths; the rivers and numerous canals are filled with boats, and a great variety of busy artisans ply their crafts in the noisy streets of the cities and villages."

Climatic Conditions.—1. The *temperature* varies greatly, but its average is lower than in any other country of the same latitude. The isothermal line of 70° F. as the average for the year, passing north of Canton, runs through New Orleans, which is eight degrees north of it. That of 60° F., passing through Shanghai, is the same as the isotherm of St. Louis and San Francisco, while that of Peking passes through Philadelphia. "Canton," Williams writes, "is the coldest place on the globe in its latitude, and the only place within the tropics where snow falls near the seashore. One result of this projection of the temperate zone into the tropical is seen in the greater vigor and size of the people of the three southern provinces over any races on the same parallel elsewhere, and the productions are not so strictly tropical."

2. The *rainfall* in the north does not average much over sixteen inches, in Canton it is seventy inches per annum, while in the remote west it is prevailingly dry. Almost all of the eastern half of the Empire has a wet season of two months during the summer, the rest of the year being almost rainless. In the north the winters are superb. Cloudless skies, except for the dust-storms, and bracing cold act as a tonic to the foreigner.

3. Missionaries and other Occidentals find China *fairly healthful*. While cholera, small-pox, and fevers are common, and local diseases, like the leprosy of the south and the bubonic plague of Hongkong and Canton affect many natives, foreigners are rarely

attacked, and with proper precautions may safely dwell in every province.

Wealth of the Empire.—1. The Chinese are for the most part agriculturists, and derive their sustenance from a *fertile, wisely tilled soil*. They can scarcely be called farmers, as land is occupied in such small holdings that gardening and fruit-culture are the result. An incessant use of the hoe, an application of every particle of fertilizer obtainable, even to refuse hair from the barber's razor, and unstinting irrigation, when required, insure abundant crops. All the cereals, most of the vegetables common in America, a variety of fruits, including some of tropical character, can be had, while the opium poppy, the mulberry for silk raising, and the tea-shrub are largely grown also.

2. Along the water-courses and on the lakes are found populations numbering many millions, who thrive on the *aquatic resources* of the Empire. Fish swarm in the seas and rivers, and are found even in pools. Wild water-fowl are netted or shot; frogs are ingeniously caught in large numbers, and the duck-boats, accompanying along the rivers artificially hatched ducklings, are a source of great profit.

3. The *mineral wealth* of China is enormous, but thus far has hardly been touched, largely because of superstitious regard for *fêng-shui*—wind and water. All the common metals, except platina, are found, but coal and iron are most important. The coal measures are twenty times more extensive than those of Great Britain, and are conveniently distributed throughout the provinces. Not only are these fields exceptionally rich, but, owing to the thickness of the seams and their horizontal position, they can be more readily worked than the mines in any other part of the world. Professor Keane does not go beyond facts when he says that "next to agriculture the main resource of China lies in the ground itself, which harbors supplies of ores and coal sufficient, some day, to revolutionize the trade of the world."

4. All the above-mentioned sources of wealth are made effective by an *abundant supply of patient and willing labor.* The English navy and British sailor may be unexcelled by any of their class in the world, the patent-devising Yankee may not find his equal in other lands, Germany may stand pre-eminent in point of laborious and exhaustive scholarship, but China will not yield the palm to any nation in the matter of ability to labor in field and water and mine under the most exhausting and unfavorable circumstances ; and herein lies a secret of the prophecy of her fitness to survive through all the future.

Chinese View of the World.—1. To the average Chinese, *the world* is a synonym for China, as the names T'ien Hsia, All beneath the sky, and Ssŭ Hai, All between the four seas, indicate. Concerning this territory he ought to know very exactly, for no country has so many carefully written local topographical works as China possesses. As a matter of fact, however, owing to lack of facilities for rapid intercommunication, their love for home, and their failure to teach geography in schools, even literary graduates are wofully ignorant of remote provinces. Since the Jesuit missionaries, in 1708–18, surveyed the Empire, corrections have not been made in their maps to correspond with changes in provincial boundaries, so that it is impossible for even the most interested to gain accurate information concerning the Chinese world. Still, the wild ideas of their own country, so far as the marvellous is concerned, could be easily remedied, if such local geography as they have were taught.

2. Ask a well-read native, living in the interior, about *the extra-Chinese world,* and he may give you the most fantastic answers, derived from Chinese works on foreign geography written a century or more ago.

Ordinary maps are a sight to behold. Beyond their own frontiers, islands, kingdoms, and continents are promiscuously distributed, with important omissions and equally remarkable exaggerations. "The two Americas and Africa are entirely omitted on most of them, and England, Holland, and Portugal, Goa, Luçonia, Bokhara, Germany, France, and India are arranged along the western side, from north to south, in a series of islands and headlands. The southern and eastern sides are similarly garnished by islands, as Japan, Lewchew, Formosa, Siam, Burma, Java, the Sulu Islands, and others, while Russia occupies the whole of the northern frontier of their Middle Kingdom."

Common ideas about these countries— where any ideas at all are present — are equally bizarre. The earth is an immense stationary plain. "In some parts of its surface," says Williams, "they imagine its inhabitants to be all dwarfs, who tie themselves together in bunches for fear of being carried away by the eagles ; in others they are all women, who conceive by looking at their shadows ; and in a third kingdom all the people have holes in their breasts, through which they thrust a pole, when carrying one another from place to place."

3. *Foreigners at close range* are not discriminatingly understood by the Chinese. They hold that opium was forced down their throats at the mouth of English cannon, and hear from their countrymen in America of the injustice and persecution often endured by them there. Sailors from Christian nations roam through Chinese ports in a state of lawless intoxication, and encourage impure women to walk the streets in a most brazen-faced manner, so that native officials of Shanghai, some years ago, entered at foreign consulates a formal protest against such open violations of morality. Stereoscopic and other views of the most obscene character are bought from foreigners by peep-show men and penetrate hundreds of miles into the interior.

And when they come in contact with foreigners in commercial or diplomatic circles, the fame of the Shanghai horse-races makes many feel that the for-

cign devil has come to establish such races in their
city. A game of cricket or lawn-tennis is a profound
mystery to them; why should men so laboriously
exert themselves, unless it is a new and most profitable form of gambling, or a contention for stakes?
A morning constitutional is interpreted as a search
for gold, an excursion for the purpose of planting
little men, or a religious duty, inasmuch as walking-
sticks are carried and are often aimlessly waved in the
air. A foreigner walks arm-in-arm with his wife, or a
party of both sexes dine together, and Chinese ideas
of propriety are shocked beyond measure, especially
if the ladies are in evening dress or possess a wasp-
like waist.

What wonder, then, that the missionary in a new
locality is a living interrogation point in their minds.
He is carefully watched, and it is reported that his
wife has light hair; why does she not use ink, to
cause it to conform to the orthodox color? How can
she be so unfilial as to be living in China, when her
rightful mistress, her mother-in-law, is a myriad of
miles away? Her garments, too, are so odd, and her
husband's coat has buttons on the middle of the back,
and they have a stove, with no one knows how many
lumps of coal burning in it all at once! Rumor says,
moreover, that there are unmarried ladies in the mission station; how account for women having reached
the age of thirty and being single yet? Probably the
reason for this is that they had such bad tempers that
no would-be mother-in-law was found heroic enough
to consent to the marriage; or perhaps a more sinister
reason is suggested, if the male missionary frequently
calls upon them. Even the wonder-working medical
missionary does not escape the tongue of the gossip-
monger. He works great cures—yes, but do you not
know that he also gouges out eyes and digs out
hearts? No marvel that with good Chinese hearts
and eyes to aid them, foreigners can compound magic
medicines and construct heaven-piercing telescopes.
And so on endlessly.

4. If one would understand the views concerning their own superiority and the great inferiority of the other nations, prevalent among even Chinese scholars, the facts above mentioned must be borne in mind. Their *prejudice against foreigners* is quite largely due to ignorance.   Happily, the increase of mission schools, in which Western geography is taught, the establishment of higher government institutions for training in the Western sciences, the increasing number of readers of Christian and scientific books and periodicals among the literati, and above all wider contact between China and the Western Powers—rendered necessary by wars and growing international complications—are rapidly transforming their crude and grotesque views, and the consequent prejudices are disappearing, especially in the coast and Yang-tzŭ provinces.

CHINA'S INHERITANCE FROM THE PAST

Character of Chinese Historical Records.—
1. *Credibility.* Like most nations whose existence
dates from remote antiquity, China's early history
fades away through the legendary into the mythical
realm. Yet the Chinese historian does not claim for
these early ages any genuine historicity. He mentions them just as modern writers speak of the Ho-
meric legends in writing of Greece, or of Romulus and
Remus in treating of Rome. It must be admitted,
however, that their historians have gone back further
into the mists of antiquity than most Western scholars
care to follow them. So famous a writer as Chu Hsi,
e.g., begins his history with Fu Hsi, 2852 B.C., while
other native histories commence their chronology
with the sixty-first year of Huang Ti, 2637 B.C.

When once they have reached genuinely historic
times, which can safely be put in the Chou dynasty,
founded earlier than the reign of David and Solomon,
Chinese historians are more trustworthy than those
of most other nations; though some discredit is
thrown upon annals preceding Shih Huang-ti, the
Great Wall builder, two centuries before Christ, owing to the fact that he ordered a wholesale destruction
of books.

2. *The material* for compiling Chinese history
comes from four main sources, the Bamboo Books, the
ancient classics, especially the "Books of History,"
and the "Spring and Autumn Annals," local annals
and dynastic records. *The local annals* classify under
twenty-four headings everything that can be known
concerning even the smallest district in the Empire,
as well as each province.

Dynastic histories are officially prepared by historians of the right hand, who record the facts of the reign, and those of the left hand, whose duty it is to report imperial speeches, charges, etc. Their instructions require these state historiographers to accompany the Emperor at all times, noting and dating everything, and at the end of each month these records are sealed up and deposited in a desk, whence, at the end of the year, they are transferred to the care of the Inner Council. Not until a given dynasty ceases, and a new line assumes the imperial yellow, are these records taken from the iron safe and given to the world. Fearless and faithful annals are thus provided for, though absolute accuracy is not always secured, even with such admirable precautions.

3. *The literary character* of these writings is decidedly disappointing. Like the compilers of Protestant church history who prepared the Magdeburg Centuries, Chinese historians write under categories, thus producing a monotonous set of formulæ, so to speak, with blanks filled in as facts require. Dynastic historians carefully refrain from any reflections or comparisons; they make simple statements only, after the manner of Confucius in his "Spring and Autumn Annals." The minuteness and exhaustive prolixity of their historians may be judged from the fact that the Bureau of Military History reported that their account of two rebellions occurring in our century fills 360 volumes, while the local history of the city of Su-chou has forty volumes, and that of the province of Kuang-tung is in 182 volumes.

China's Prehistoric Dawn.—If this age is subdivided into a mythological and a legendary period, it is not strictly prehistoric; for doubtless much that has been written of the legendary period is true history.

1. *The mythological ages* cover from 45,000 to 500,000 years. Though this is absurdly long, it is as nothing compared with the kalpas of India, "whose highest era, called the Unspeakably Inexpressible,

requires 4,456,448 ciphers following a unit to represent it."

Within this period lies *Chinese cosmogony* with its theory of a *T'ai Chi*, or Great Extreme—the ultimate immaterial principle of Chinese philosophers—and of the dual powers, yin and yang. *P'an Ku* first appears after heaven and earth are separated, and begins his eighteen thousand years' task of chiselling out of formless granite, floating in space, the sun, moon, and stars. Companions with him during these ages are China's famous fabulous animals, the dragon, phœnix, and tortoise, "progenitors with himself of the animal creation."

After his death, in which every portion of his body accrues to the benefit of his universe—even to the parasites, which become men—*three great sovereigns* or families of brothers, possessed of monstrous form, rule the world for from 18,000 to 432,000 years. Following the Celestial, Terrestrial, and Human Sovereigns, come two monarchs, one the Nest-having, who may have invented nests or abodes for his subjects, and the other Fire Producer, a Chinese Prometheus who brought down fire from heaven for man's use.

2. *The legendary period* is universally regarded as beginning with the monarch Fu Hsi, but its later limit is questioned, some saying that it ceases with the beginning of the Chou dynasty, 1122 B.C., and others limiting it by the accession of Yao, 2357 B.C., or by the year 781 B.C.

Between Fu Hsi's reign and that of Yao, the Chinese place nearly all the inventions and the formulation of those ethical and governmental theories which have distinguished the life of China from the earliest times. Yet it is not until we reach the reign of Yao and his successor Shun that we find Confucius and Mencius making any great use of Chinese history. If, with Dr. Legge, we regard Yü as the founder of the Empire—as he was of the Hsia dynasty in 2205 B.C.—we still find ourselves surrounded with legend-

ary mists which do not clear away until T'ang, the
Successful, established the succeeding Shang dynasty
in 1766 B.C.—nearly as long before the Christian era
as our Declaration of Independence dates after it.
The reason that may possibly have led Confucius and
Mencius to place their Golden Age earlier than this
in the reigns of Yao and Shun—who were doubtless
real and able rulers, but whose history is deeply tinged
with legendary coloring—is thus stated by Dr. Williams : "Whatever was their real history, those sages
showed great sagacity in going back to those remote
times for models and fixing upon a period neither
fabulous nor certain, one which prevented alike the
cavils of scepticism and the appearance of complete
fabrication."

3. *The residuum of fact* underlying the story of
this prehistoric and legendary period proves that
China possessed culture and civilization at a time
when only the Egyptian, the Chaldean, and the Hittite
had risen above the level of surrounding nations.
Forty centuries ago—nearly a thousand years before
the earliest assured event in Greek history, the Dorian
invasion, and a century before Abraham was born—
we find in North China, in the modern province of
Shan-hsi, a people with institutions, government, and
religion, with a fairly well-developed literature and a
knowledge of sciences and arts.

This much is generally agreed to by scholars; but
there is greater diversity of opinion when the questions are asked, *Whence came the Chinese? From
what source was their culture derived?* Whether the
question is answered by the record found in Genesis,
chs. ix.-xi., or by the researches of archæologists, the
usual reply to the first query is, that the Chinese
originally came from the region lying below the
Caspian Sea, and entered China from the northwest,
settling along the banks of the Yellow River.

The origin of Chinese culture is a more difficult
problem to solve. The main answers given are, the
plain of Shinar, Egypt or an Egyptian colony,

Scythia, India, and a denial of any Western origin. As some eighty eminent Sinologues, Assyriologists, and Orientalists assent to the main conclusions elaborately argued for by Professor Dr. Terrien de Lacouperie, the prevalent verdict may be said to point to Babylonia and Elam as the springs whence China's early culture flowed.

Key Characters in Chinese History.—The student desirous of understanding China's past, must make himself familiar with certain characters whose names and deeds are well known to every scholar, and some of which are household names.

1. *The ruler* practically, though not theoretically, stands first in order among men. One must know the accepted history, partly legendary, no doubt, of the early rulers *Yao, Shun,* and *Yü,* and of the historic kings *Wên* and *Wu,* as well as Duke *Chou.* These are worthy of double honor, since they are accounted sages as well as rulers. From an occidental rather than a Chinese stand-point, one must learn the true position of the much maligned *Shih Huang-ti,* of wall-building and literature-destroying fame, who has been called the Napoleon of China. The second T'ang sovereign, *T'ai Tsung,* who after death was styled the Literary-Martial Emperor, must be known ; for he " may be regarded as the most accomplished monarch in the Chinese annals—famed alike for his wisdom and his nobleness, his conquests and good government, his temperance, cultivated tastes, and patronage of literary men." His dominions, moreover, extended as far west as the Caspian Sea. Nor must one be ignorant of the *Empress Wu,* wife of the son of the famous T'ai Tsung, who during the last two decades of the seventh century made herself famous as well as infamous ; though it is doubtless true that to support their favorite thesis that women ought not to meddle with government, native historians have unduly blackened her character. No one who has tasted Marco Polo's story of *Kublai Khan* will be in danger of neglecting that hero of the Yüan dynasty,

though here again the Chinese do not so much ad-
mire their foreign sovereign as Occidentals are likely
to do. *K'ang Hsi*, the second Emperor of the present
dynasty, is more celebrated than almost any other
Asiatic sovereign, rivalling if not surpassing T'ai
Tsung. His record is of the utmost interest to Chinese and foreigner alike. And, of course, no friend
of China will care to be ignorant of the reigning Emperor, *Kuang Hsü*, Succession of Light, and of the
scarcely less famous rulers of the Empire during his
minority, the *Empress Dowager*—one of the most remarkable of Manchu women—and *Li Hung-chang*.

2. We do not need to speak of the sages, as most
of them pose also as rulers, and have been already
mentioned. Of the *philosophers and noted literary
men*, *Lao-tzŭ*, the founder of the Taoist sect, is first
in point of time, and though contemporary with Confucius, he was perhaps a keener thinker and a more
enlightened man than his more famous compeer.
"The throneless King" is no empty title for K'ung
Fu-tzŭ, Philosopher K'ung, Latinized into *Confucius*.
Probably no one has exerted a more extensive influence among men than this last officially recognized
Chinese sage. His *alter ego* is *Mencius* or Mêng-tzŭ,
though he lived nearly two centuries later. He is to
Confucius very much what Plato was to Socrates.
Chu Fu-tzŭ, who flourished 700 years ago, is perhaps
China's greatest philosopher and teacher, and it is
his interpretation of the Classics that constitutes
present-day Confucianism. These are the commonly
mentioned names among a host of great philosophers
and teachers, but Western readers will find more to
their taste, perhaps, the works of the heretic *Micius*,
who laid it down as a duty "to love all equally," or
those of *Chuang-tzŭ*, the great Taoist philosopher,
mystic, and magician, "whose writings have been described as ' a storm of dazzling effects.'"

The student of Chinese *general literature* must
become acquainted with China's Herodotus, *Ssŭ-ma
Ch'ien*, the scarcely less illustrious Han historian, *Pan*

Ku, and *Ssŭ-ma Kuang* of the Sung dynasty, who was statesman as well as historian, and the author of " General Mirror to Aid in Governing." Nor can one afford to be ignorant of the heptameters of the famous T'ang poets *Li T'ai-pai* and *Tu Fu*, or of the one hundred and fifteen volumes of the Sung poet, *Su Tung-p'o*. Less weariness is experienced as the foreigner takes up *Ch'in Shou's* " History of the Three States," replete as it is with graphic descriptions of plot and counterplot, battles, sieges, and retreats, character delineations and episodes, all composed in a style known to the Chinese vulgar as *jê nao*, hot racket, or most interesting. Dr. *Li*, author of the " Herbal," must be a familiar name to the medical missionary, as also that of the Æsculapius of the Chinese Pantheon, *Hua T'o*. Modern Dry-as-dusts will desire to know *Ma Tuan-lin*, the author of " Complete Antiquarian Researches," in three hundred and forty-eight chapters. " No book has been more drawn upon by Europeans for information concerning matters relating to Eastern Asia than this." This work, the first to deserve the name of encyclopædia, introduces the occidental student to an illustrious line of encyclopædists. Thus, the third emperor of the last dynasty, Yung Lo, " Eternal Joy," appointed a commission of two thousand members, who prepared a manuscript encyclopædia of 22,937 chapters, while the second emperor of the present dynasty, K'ang Hsi, appointed another commission, who, after forty years, finished with volume 5,020 the " Imperially Ordered Complete Collection of Ancient and Modern Literature, with Illustrations."

3. *Illustrious women* of China gain fame for the most part by methods decidedly unique. There are in the Empire more outward evidences of feminine renown than of the greatness of Chinese statesmen, warriors, and scholars. These usually take the form of honorary portals, erected by Imperial rescript in honor of distinguished women. Dr. Faber estimates that they may average one to every million women

during the past 2,500 years, and mentions three chief
reasons for their being so honored by the Emperor :
suicide, committed because of attachment to parents
or husband, or through fear of shame ; *living as a
widow* in mourning to the end of life ; *filial devotion*,
exhibited by remaining unmarried that she may serve
her parents, or refusing to marry again after her husband's death, that she may minister to her parents-
in-law, or the cutting out of a portion of her own
flesh to be used as a tonic for sick parents or parents-
in-law.   Imperial orders bearing on such cases are
frequently appearing in the " Peking Gazette."

If we ask what causes have made those women famous or notorious, who have become so through the
voice of the people, the high authority just quoted
gives, as the reasons suggested in a large number of
native works consulted, the following categories :
filial daughters, devoted sisters, young women who
had something to say or do in the matter of securing
a husband, famous courtesans, women skilled in in-
trigue, renowned empresses, good wives, bad wives,
good mothers, bad mothers, widows, authoresses,
artists, artisans, supernatural females, and goddesses.

While the foreigner will not care to read the rather
voluminous literature relating to illustrious women,
he will be aided in his understanding of the people
by a knowledge of the reasons leading to the existence of honorary portals and the slabs mounted on
the backs of stone tortoises erected in their honor in
his district.   It will also prove interesting to learn
details about the Empress Wu and the present Empress Dowager, Tzŭ Hsi (plus fourteen other words
contained in her recently conferred title).   Of the
many *authoresses* who are worth knowing, perhaps
the most influential is Pan Chao, a sister of the Han
historian, Pan Ku.   On her brother's decease, she
was appointed state historiographer, and at her death
was honored by the Emperor with public burial and
the title of Great Lady Ts'ao.   It was she who wrote,
soon after the death of St. Paul, " the first work in

any language on female education," and her "Female Precepts" has been the basis of many succeeding books on that topic.

Present-day Survivals of China's Past.— We must pass on to this topic without naming China's great warriors, like the famous generals of the Three Kingdoms, Ts'ao Ts'ao, and especially the Chinese Mars, Kuan Ti, who reappeared in the heavens forty-two years ago, *à la* Castor and Pollux, and gave the battle to the Imperial cause, when their antagonists, the T'ai P'ing rebels, were fighting under the Christian's God. For this signal service the Emperor raised him to the rank of Confucius, and he has become the patron deity of the present dynasty.

1. Some of these survivals exist in material form after the lapse of millenniums. Thus, *the Great Wall*, extending across China's northern frontier, existed in some of its detached sections some time before Shih Huang-ti, in 214 B.C., ordered it to be added to and consolidated into one mass of stone, brick and earth, stretching over a distance as great as that between Philadelphia, Pa., and Lincoln, Neb. Counting its sinuosities, its length is nearly or quite 1,500 miles. The magnitude of this undertaking grows upon one, if, like the writer, one walks along parallel with it for ten days at an average of thirty miles a day, and then remembers that one has seen only a fifth of this mountain-scaling rampart of past ages.

The Grand Canal, or Yün Ho, though no longer either grand or a canal scarcely, was in its day one of the most useful artificial waterways in the world. While the famous Mongol Emperor, Kublai, ordinarily has the credit of excavating it, it existed in some of its parts from the Han dynasty, while the Sui and T'ang emperors likewise did much toward its extension and improvement. The design was to artificially connect lakes and rivers, so that an inland passage for junks might extend from Peking to Canton. Changes of the course of the Yellow River, one of its great feeders, the silting up of its bed, and the introduction of coasting steamers, account for its present dilapidated and partially useless condition.

Some of the *roads and bridges* of ancient times still exist, mostly in North China, though in a sad state of repair. The excruciating stone road between Peking and its junk-port, T'ung Chou, was centuries ago almost equal to the royal roads of the Roman Empire. A more conspicuous work of the ancient road-builders is seen in the great highway, dating from the third century, A.D., and leading from Peking to Ssŭ-ch'uan, in the remote west. In the mountain regions this called for a pathway "which for the difficulties it presents and the art and labor with which they have been overcome, does not appear to be inferior to the road over the Simplon." "At one place on this route, called Li-nai, a passage has been cut through the rock, and steps hewn on both sides of the mountain from its base to the summit." The narrow roads or paths over the passes in Fu-chien and Kuang-tung are less ancient, but hardly less useful. Some have claimed for China the invention of chain *suspension bridges*. They certainly possessed them from ancient times. Archdeacon Gray describes one in Knei-chou, built in A.D. 35.

Other *minor survivals* of the past are some bells of the Chou dynasty and the famous stone drums of Peking, commemorating a royal hunt, 827 B.C. The so-called inscription of Yü on a mountain-peak in Hunan is ancient in spite of the fact that it may have been a fabrication of the Han dynasty or of many centuries later. Copper cash by the thousand are genuine remains of at least a three thousand years' coinage. The writer, when in Mongolia, exchanged a Christian booklet costing less than half a cent for a coin minted during the reign of King Saul.

2. Far more numerous than these actual specimens of China's ancient handiwork are *institutions and*

inventions of past ages. While it may be true that a large majority of the three hundred and seventy items of culture—mentioned by Professor de Lacoupcrie as derived from Anterior Asia and Western India during the 2,500 years of China's early history—may have come from those sources, it still remains true that China has uninterruptedly possessed those elements of civilization during the succeeding centuries, though all Asiatic nations, save India, have lost most of them and lapsed into semi-barbarism, if indeed they have not become extinct nations. It should also be remembered that there is in China much civilization that is indigenous.

Her *government*—a combination of the patriarchal and imperial form—its codes of laws and scheme of civil-service examinations, and China's system of territorial divisions, have existed for centuries almost unchanged, making her people law-abiding and capable of progress when other nations were in darkness.

As one reads the *Erh Ya*, Ready Guide, and notes the close resemblance of its pictures to objects used in the arts and trades of to-day, one can hardly believe that it is the oldest philological work extant, claiming to be the work of Duke Chou, 1100 B.C., though it was largely added to by a disciple of Confucius and again in A.D. 280. Some of these ancient tools and implements are very ingenious and serviceable.

Three of the greatest agencies in the progress of the race were used in China long before they became known to Europeans. Thus the invention of the *compass* is attributed to Huang Ti, who was said to have constructed a chariot for indicating the south and used it to direct his way in a fog some 2,600 years B.C. It is explicitly mentioned in a Chinese dictionary of A.D. 121, and seems to have been used by mariners more than fifteen centuries ago. *Gunpowder*, according to Grosier, was known at or before the Christian era, though it is quite probable that it was not employed as an agent of warfare until

the twelfth century. Mayers, on the other hand,
contends that it reached China from India or Central
Asia in the fifth century A.D. Full credit may be
given the Chinese for an invention second only in
importance in the realm of thought to the formation
of alphabets, the art of *printing*. Reproducing copies of a writing from an engraved block dates from
the sixth century, but "the honor of being the first
inventor of movable type undoubtedly belongs to a
Chinese blacksmith named Pi Shêng, who lived about
A.D. 1000, and printed books with them nearly five
hundred years before Gutenberg cut his matrices at
Mainz." These were porcelain type set in an iron
frame, and could be reset and used indefinitely.

Two of China's principal manufactures should be
mentioned, as their originality has never been successfully contested, those of silk and porcelain.
Aristotle to the contrary, Europe undoubtedly obtained the secret of *silk manufacture* from China,
even if it were through the links of Greece and Persia. From the earliest historic time, sericulture has
been a highly honored Chinese occupation, with the
Empress as a living and active patroness. Of *porcelain*, James Paton writes : "It is to the Chinese that
the world owes the manufacture of porcelain ; and in
strict chronological sequence, in antiquity of the
industry, in skill and resource in working raw ma-
terials, and in richness and variety of the finished
products the Chinese ought to have the first place.
When the Greeks were making their terra-cotta vases,
the Chinese were manufacturing porcelain ; they had
mastered the secrets of that most difficult of ceramic
tasks 2,000 years before it was accomplished by Europeans."

3. China's most precious heirlooms from the past
are her *literary treasures*. Her spoken language remains in essentially the same simple monosyllabic form
of 4,000 years ago. Its marvellous written characters
put to shame the hieroglyphs of every nation, and serve
a purpose which nothing else could fill, if a nation is

to have a copious and clearly understood vocabulary expressed by monosyllables. Chinese literature is voluminous and ancient in spite of its fiery *auto da fé* 2,100 years ago. Its antiquity, however, only adds lustre to its strongly ethical character and its fitness for governmental uses to-day, not only in China, but in other nations which desire an ethical idealism as the basis of law. In a later chapter this topic will be dealt with more fully.

It must not be forgotten that education, which has been almost deified in China, and which has made her a nation of scholars from before the Christian era, has, until this decade, depended almost solely upon a literature that antedates that of Rome and nearly all of Grecian literature. This is but one item of many that might be cited to show that the Chinese Empire differs from every other existing nation, India not excepted, in the fact that it is dominated to-day by the life, the processes, and the ideas of a past which is mainly antique.

Some Secrets of China's Protracted Existence.—A review of Chinese history would be incomplete, if no explanation of her unequalled antiquity were attempted. The Hittites have left scarcely a trace of their former greatness; Chaldea exists only as a name and on clay tablets; Egypt of the Exodus remains in brick and mummy and hieratic hieroglyphs; ancient Greece and Rome have left to the world only their precious pearl-bearing shells; even Vedic India has fallen from her lofty height to the god- and caste-ridden myriads of modern Hinduism. China, on the contrary, is to-day stronger, perhaps, than she has ever been after an unbroken existence of nearly forty centuries. How account for this marvellous anomaly ?

1. China has always possessed that fundamental element of perpetuity, *protection from foes without.* The loftiest mountains in the world, and the broadest ocean swept by armada-destroying typhoons, the bulwarks of deserts and barren soil, supplemented by

the greatest artificial rampart ever raised by man—
these have been an ample defence against China's
enemies.

Scarcely less formidable is the barrier of an isolat-
ing monosyllabic *language* which has made China a
sphinx among her Asiatic neighbors. It has at once
prevented the Chinese from learning from others, and
has practically forced all who came within her boundaries to forsake their own tongue and learn hers.

Add to these barriers the hopelessness of attempting to overcome such *vast masses of humanity* as are
contained within the Empire, and one can readily see
that the task could not be successfully undertaken by
the sparsely settled regions surrounding China on all
sides save on the populous Indian quarter against
which God thrust upward for miles into the sky His
snow-capped towers and insurmountable battlements.

2. Some *national characteristics* have doubtless
tended to China's perpetuity. Ignorance of anything
better beyond her confines would make her satisfied
with her own rich endowment. Physical strength,
hostile to decay, which the Chinese, dwelling in the
temperate zone, have enjoyed to a remarkable degree,
partly accounts for her survival. Industry, neces-
sitated by physical environment and competition, has
left little leisure for discontent and organized plotting
against the powers that be. A contented perseverance
in the midst of difficulties makes the Chinese abide
in their callings as few nations care to do. Love of
home keeps the population from coveting and striving
for the possessions of those more remote, whether
within the Empire or outside its borders. To a people possessed of a notoriously phlegmatic temperament
and of a conservatism amounting to almost uncon-
querable inertia, the above characteristics would
prove both a centripetal and a conserving force of
great strength.

3. The *internal resources* of the Empire in point
of natural wealth, fairly easy intercommunication,
salubrious climate, and facilities for the cultivation of

the mind, have, until recent centuries, been such that no inducement has offered to emigrate, nor has any desire been felt to allow to come within the Empire outside barbarians who might disturb this desirable prosperity and tranquillity.

4. Unlike most extinct nations, China has contained within herself *safeguards against internal conflict and decay.* Rebellions and revolutions, which have wiped out other peoples, have affected China but little, since her sages have taught that when a dynasty so far forgets itself as to disregard the desires of Heaven, Heaven will smile upon their armed protest and appoint a new vicegerent who will rule righteously. Hence rebellion quickly accomplishes its object, and peace reigns again. Ambition for martial renown has struck the death-blow of many a nation; but in China her crowned kings are her canny men, and ambition finds its highest rewards in the conquests of knowledge and the triumph of academic victory.

Against tendencies to decay are pitted some of the items already named in paragraph numbered 2, and a temperance which has been phenomenal until this century of grace has forced upon an unwilling people the destructive appetite for opium. A system of ethics, second only to the Christian system, has been taught in every school-room for 2,000 years, and in its important society-preserving elements has been insisted upon by local officials for an even longer period. Filial piety, which so many historians and preachers of the arm-chair type have considered to be the secret of China's long existence, may have failed in many respects, but it has been the means of engrafting on the nation a sense of obedience and subordination that has checked revolt and anarchy. Hoary old age, before which even the mighty Emperor K'ang Hsi stood in reverence, is an influential Chinese Ecclesiastes, which cries out to libertines and spendthrifts, " Vanity of vanities." High officials do not encourage a desire for luxury, since they serve for a limited time in a given place, and that away from their own home, so that there is little inducement to live luxuriously. Private wealth must hide itself, lest it arouse the cupidity of official underlings, and the almost universal nearness of want makes luxurious decay impossible.

5. *Government and laws* are often responsible for a nation's perpetuity or destruction. China's code is remarkable in many respects and its paternal theory makes it popular. Officials are civic fathers and mothers, while the Emperor, Son of Heaven, prays and sacrifices to the heavenly powers when his children suffer from great calamity. That this government should have long survived is quite natural ; for it supports by its strong sanction the authority of rulers on the one hand, while on the other it authorizes resistance to glaring evil in high places. Moreover, all official positions in the Empire save the Imperial ones are open to any man in the land—except certain wisely debarred persons—provided he has the requisite ability. As every family has in its membership some noted official, Chinese clan-spirit supports the system.

The laws are, in the main, very equitable, and in the villages, where the majority of Chinese dwell, they are largely in the hands of village elders, who dispense them as befits so nearly a republican form of administration. The corruption found in city courts of justice also tends to obedience to law ; since lawsuits mean bribery, torture and loss, even if the case is won.

6. To the Christian who sees the *purposes of God in history,* His hand is beneath the Chinese throne and this wonderful Empire has been continued through the ages to accomplish His will. That a nation of such marked strength has existed for 4,000 years is an indication of its future survival, and we may be sure that God has reserved it for some gracious and world-influencing purpose. It is, then, the privilege and duty of every child of God to co-operate

with Him in helping Sinim to know its Maker and to accomplish His great designs.

The Dawn of a New Era.—For the reasons above given, China's great age has benefited few beyond her own subjects. Seated on a throne of selfish isolation she has ruled "all within the four seas," and cared nothing for the nations without.

But to-day conditions have radically changed. China's open ports are filled with the merchantmen of the world. Railroads are beginning to be built ; telegraphs extend to most of her provincial capitals ; her mineral wealth is coveted by the nations, and has become an object of importance to her own prosperity. Contemporaneously with the removal of ignorant prejudice against foreigners, and the emergence of her new importance to the world, has come the rude awakening caused by the imperious knocking at her doors of the great European Powers. Port Arthur, Wei-hai-wei, Kiao-chou Bay, the Yang-tzŭ valley, the territory bordering on the possessions of France, have been invaded and isolation is at an end. Even anti-foreign Hu-nan has an open port, and missionaries preach within her territory. China's garnished house has been swept clean from effective opposition and prejudice. But who is to enter in through her open gates—the Church of God with her ministration of mercy and salvation ? or Western avarice and land-hunger, occidental vices and materialism ? The latter forces are entering ; shall not Christianity enter with equal stride as a conserving factor in this period of national transformation ?

III

ONE who would understand the Chinese and the work which the Church and Western civilization are called upon to do for them, must carefully consider Chinese character and the social and industrial environment found in the Empire. So important is the moral and religious life of the Chinese, that it will form the topic of a separate chapter.

Numbers and Distribution.—A reference to the statistics given under the provinces in Appendix A will reveal these facts in detail. According to " The Statesman's Year Book, 1898," the total population of the Eighteen Provinces is 383,253,029. China is, therefore, the most populous nation of the world, containing as it does more than five times the population of the United States, and fully one-fourth of the inhabitants of the globe. Other authorities vary from 300,000,000 and even less to over 400,000,000. The census of 1812, regarded by authorities as the most trustworthy of Chinese enumerations, gives a population of 362,447,183.

Reasons for such wide differences of opinion are found in the facts that the *mên pa'i*, or registration tablets, supposed to be found on every householder's door, may be altered according as the registration is for the object of securing persons for public service or for purposes of taxation ; or, on the other hand, for learning how many " mouths " may need to be fed at public expense in time of famine. Moreover, as a yearly record of population is required by the government, many officials doubtless save themselves trouble by adding or subtracting a certain percentage

32

on the basis of the previous reports. In one case testified to by Dr. Dudgeon, of Peking, a foreign minister received from the proper board a total population which had been deliberately reduced by one-third, because "the officials sought to check missionary zeal by this considerable reduction of the population. In the following year, as no abatement of missionary immigration seemed to follow, the [subtracted] figures were again added to the records."

A glance at the accompanying map will show *where the population is densest*, and where most sparse. The coast provinces and a belt across the centre of the Empire along the Yang-tzŭ are the populous sections, while in the northwest and southwest are the sparsely inhabited regions.

Characteristics of the Chinese.—A Chinese proverb to the effect that the summer insect will not speak of ice, nor a frog in a well discourse on the heavens, is forgotten by many writers who study the Chinese in our laundries, or in Chinese ports, where contact with the vices of a Western civilization let loose for a lustful holiday has had a baneful effect on a much tempted and abused people. Merchants who live in the treaty ports, travellers along the coast with no knowledge of the language, and the average steamer captain with the vicious life of the port from which to gain his data concerning the Chinese and missionary effort, are not to be wholly trusted as witnesses concerning the natives and missions among them.

As foreign customs-officials have mainly to do with the seamy side of Ah Sin's nature, and as diplomatic representatives of the Occident consort largely with the official classes, the missionary has thus far come into closest contact with the typical Chinese, and hence is best fitted to pronounce on their character.

1. While the races of China Proper are remarkably homogeneous, the Miao-tzŭ excepted, they *differ physically* so much as to deserve separate mention.

The *Tibetans* are found only in small numbers on

3

the western border. "They are short, squat, and broad-shouldered in body, with angular faces, wide, high cheek-bones, small black eyes, and scant beard." Physically they are a cross between the Mongols and the Hindus.

The *Mongols*, *i.e.*, Brave, are quite abundant along the northern frontier, especially north of the Great Wall. They are essentially nomadic and pastoral except inside the Wall, where they are found transporting goods on their camel-trains or engaged in trading. They are generally "a stout, squat, swarthy, ill-favored race of men, having high and broad shoulders, short, broad noses, pointed and prominent chins, long teeth distant from each other, eyes black, elliptical, and unsteady, thick, short legs, with a stature nearly or quite equal to the European."

Scattered through the southern and southwestern provinces are many large communities of *Miao-tzŭ*, or aboriginal tribes, differentiated by the adjectives "Savage" and "Subdued." "They are rather smaller in size and stature, have shorter necks, and their features are somewhat more angular. . . . An examination of their languages shows that those of the Miao-tzŭ proper have strong affinities with the Siamese and Annamese, and those known as Lolo exhibit a decided likeness to the Burmese."

The present rulers of China, the *Manchus, i.e.*, Pure, though perhaps derived from the same stock as the Mongols, are hunters and agriculturists in Manchuria, and in China are distributed in various parts of the Empire, often in garrisons, as supporters of the reigning dynasty. They "are of a lighter complexion and somewhat larger than the Chinese, have the same conformation of the eyelids, but rather more beard, while their countenances indicate greater intellectual capacity. . . . They have fair, if not florid, complexions, straight noses and, in a few cases, brown hair and heavy beards." Dr. Williams regards them as "the most improvable race in Central Asia, if not on the continent."

"The physical traits of the *Chinese* may be described as being between the light and agile Hindu, and the muscular, fleshy European. Their form is well-built and symmetrical; their color is a brunette or sickly white . . . ; in the south they are swarthy but not black. . . . The hair of the head is lank, black, coarse, and glossy; beard always black, thin and deficient; scanty or no whiskers; and very little hair on the body. Eyes invariably black and apparently oblique. . . . The cheek-bones are high and the outline of the face remarkably round. The nose is rather small. . . . Lips thicker than among Europeans. . . . The height of those living north of the Yang-tzŭ is about the same as that of Europeans." In physical endurance the Chinese rank very high, and can undergo extreme hardship in the frigid or torrid zone better than almost any other nationality. This is the race that constitutes almost the entire population of China Proper, the other races being comparatively few in number.

2. In what some ethnologists call *emotional characters,* the Chinese rank almost as high as in their physical excellencies. They are remarkably *industrious* when there is sufficient motive, and were it not for the opium vice, recently contracted, they would rank high among the nations of the world for *temperance,* a trait largely fostered by their use of tea. Early and almost universal marriage prevents outward indications of *sensuality,* though in the ports one sees abundant evidence of it, as also in the catamites of the inns, and in the Adonises kept by many officials and men of wealth. The swarm of eunuchs in the palace and the Emperor's extensive harem are happily not duplicated elsewhere, and polygamy does not extensively prevail. The abnormal development of the vocabulary of obscenity is a sure index of depraved imaginations, though its common use may be as thoughtless as the oaths of habitual swearers among us. Except within clan and family lines, the Chinese are not a very *sociable* people, nor does

their idea of the privacy of home life permit of
much *hospitality* outside of those who may legiti-
mately be received as guests. Though naturally peace-
able, *quarrels* are extremely common and the voca-
tion of peacemaker is an awkward necessity. Among
women quarrelsomeness frequently results in a rage
which so excites the individual that it brings one-
half the cases among women patients to many mission dispensaries ; while not infrequently do men as
well as women *ch'i ssŭ liao, i.e.*, die of anger, as they
say. *Bravery* is not so characteristic of the Chinese
as of Mongols and Manchus ; yet in war, if they have
confidence in their leaders, they well deserve the
name worn on their breasts, Brave. *Politeness and
ceremonial* are most prominent features in Chinese
intercourse, so that some have called the educated
classes the most dignified and polite people of the
world, the French and Japanese not excepted.
Indeed, life is little else than ceremonial and politeness for those in high station, and among the lower
classes it prevails on the required days and in certain
relations of society. *Filial piety* may be only exter-
nal, but it is omnipresent on state occasions and is a
dominating factor in Chinese life. *Conservatism* is a
most noticeable trait of their character; yet it has, on
the whole, been of advantage, since almost invariably
it has resulted in their conserving that which is best
for the nation, as they regard it.

3. *Intellectually* the Chinese rank high among the
races. In *cranial capacity* the ideal Mongolic type
falls short of the ideal Caucasic by only 100 cubic
centimetres, being from 1,200 to 1,300. It is thus
considerably above the average racial skull capacity.

While in the opinion of some writers, the present
simple and nearly primitive form of the *language* is
an argument against their intellectual power, it
should be remembered that the strongest reason, perhaps, for such an arrested development lies in their
possession, at a very early period, of a large body of
worthy literature, the wide use of which has satisfied

them. Moreover, no nation using hieroglyphs, not even Egypt, has begun to elaborate such a form of writing to the extent and with the ingenuity of the Chinese, as witness the almost 45,000 characters in the Imperial Dictionary of K'ang Hsi. The mere arrangement in a dictionary of such a mass of ideographs, so that they can readily be found, though there is no alphabet to arrange them under, is a triumph of genius. So, too, are the introduction of tones, the use of numeratives, the collocation of synonyms and the use of enclitics to prevent the ambiguity which necessarily arises in a monosyllabic tongue, with its extremely limited number of words—only 420 different syllables or words are used in Pekingese. Fancy our utter bewilderment if our thoughts needed to be expressed through the medium of 420 syllables representing 45,000 words, many of which are pronounced the same, but written differently, as rite, right, wright, write, for example. It would be impossible for us through an alphabet to accomplish what the Chinese have, when every one of the 105 characters—which on an average have the same sound, though not the same tone—possesses a form as perfectly distinct as the four English words in the illustration above. It is safe to say that no nation could have more satisfactorily solved the problem of homophony in a monosyllabic tongue than has China.

A no less certain indication of their intellectual power is the supreme place and honor given to *education*. If it be granted that the subjects on which they are examined for degrees are antiquated and that the memory rather than the logical powers have received cultivation, this does not prove that they are lacking in intellectuality, but indicates rather an error in method. A piece of personal testimony may here be in place. The writer taught for two years in one of our best preparatory schools, Phillips Academy, Andover, and compared carefully nearly a dozen picked Chinese students, sent to America by the Educational Commission, with students

from our best American families. The Chinese sur-
passed in diligence our own young men, but seem-
ingly failed because of their lack of logical power.
As a result, the Faculty regarded them as somewhat
inferior to our students. Later the writer was connected with what is now the North China College,
near Peking. The students there were of about the
same age, but from ordinary Chinese families ; yet
being taught through a perfectly understood medium,
their native tongue, and by missionaries who appreciated fully the intellectual weaknesses of their pupils,
they far outstripped the ordinary American student.
There were two men out of eleven in the last class
with which he had to do, who would have ranked
higher as students, if they had had like access to
Western literature, than anyone in his own class of
more than 130 members at Yale. It is quite generally admitted that with a right method of instruction
and an enlarged access to the literature of the West,
the Chinese will be close rivals with the New Japan
and with Germany for the first place in the scholarship of the twentieth century. Heredity—for every
Chinese family contains noted scholars within a
generation or two—a genius for patient, scholarly
plodding and a memory which retains, almost without
effort, practically all the data it has ever learned,
may make up in this rivalry for the present lack of
imagination, so essential for working hypotheses, and
of ingenuity, equally necessary in an age when so
much is learned in laboratories.

When asked for *the product* of Chinese mind, only
a meagre report can be given in the realm of science,
though, as already shown, China antedates the Occident in some important inventions and arts. Arith-
metic was taught from a very early period and one
T'ang dynasty arithmetician offered a reward of a
thousand tæls of silver to anyone who could discover an error in his work on solid mensuration.
Hindu algebra was early known and Chinese scholars
have willingly learned the higher mathematics from

Europeans, since they ascribe our advance in the exact sciences to them. Astronomy has always been a favorite study also, though beyond the observation and recording of eclipses and other celestial phenomena and the regulation of the calendar, they have known little until taught by the Occident. As already seen, they have been lamentably ignorant of geography, and in medicine they have held equally incorrect and ludicrous ideas, though it should be added that they have made some good use of herbs. Dr. Martin has tried to show that the Chinese have anticipated some important modern discoveries, such as biological evolution, unity of matter and motion, conservation of energy, and the existence and properties of elemental ether. Yet it must be said that any such allusions and discussions are not very clear.

In *the arts* the Chinese have done little of solid worth. Drawing and painting are conventional and are weak in perspective. Music is deficient in its theory and ear-torturing in execution, especially when produced by an orchestra or by shrill falsetto singers. One rather admires Chinese architecture, with its gracefully curved roofs, modelled perhaps after the sloping sides of their ancestral tents, and the towering pagoda, so characteristic of Chinese scenery. Landscape gardening in a few instances reaches the point of absolute genius, especially when limited space is made to appear ample by the planting of dark-foliaged tall trees in the foreground and smaller and lighter foliaged ones toward the background. In other ways also the landscape gardener produces living effects, much as our best scene painters do it artificially.

Sociological Environment of the Chinese.— Differences in various parts of the Empire make it impossible to give a faithful picture of this environment; yet some general ideas may be of value.

1. The *home and clan life* is scarcely known by any other foreigners than the missionaries. Like that in India, this life is spent by the majority in

villages and not in the 1,700 walled cities of the
Empire, nor in isolated houses, as in Western country villages.   In some cases not a person lives in this
village who does not belong to a given clan, and in
other villages it is quite common for the oldest surviving head of a family to have in the same court-
yard with himself, his sons and grandchildren, his
daughters having been obliged to marry into a family
of a different surname and so living elsewhere.   The
power granted by law and custom to these family or
clan heads makes village life in China quite patriarchal.

A *village* is a collection of low, one-story adobe,
wooden, or brick houses closely adjoining, surrounded, it may be, with an adobe or mud wall for
defence against brigands, and overshadowed by trees.
Centrally located is the village well, and often near by
is seen the little temple, with its shabby array of
local deities.   Unless large, there is scarcely a shop
to be found, as frequently recurring fairs at a larger
adjacent town supply the simple outside wants of the
villagers.   From their homes issue at an early hour
the men and boys en route for the fields, where man-
power rather than that of beast is mainly employed.
Thence they return to get the first meal of the day at
eleven o'clock, after which they again go to work, not
coming back until six or seven for supper.   The
women meanwhile, if they have not gone to the fields,
have been busy with their children and with cooking,
spinning, weaving, caring for the family wardrobe,
and gossiping or quarrelling.   And so the life goes
on, without any knowledge of a Sabbath, and allevi-
ated by only a few holidays, chief among which is the
New Year.

As to *food*, rice and vegetables are the staff of life in
the central and southern parts of the Empire, while
in the north, wheat flour or millet takes the place
of rice.   Chinese cookery is ingenious in its ability
to give flavor to the tasteless rice or boiled wheat
flour by a multitude of inexpensive relishes.   Pork

and chickens are occasionally eaten, beef is not often
so used, save in the north, while dog-meat, rats, and
cats are indulged in much as horse-flesh is in Paris.
So poor are many of the people that food is eaten by
weight, so many ounces for each person, a practice
alluded to in Scripture as a symbol of famine.   To
have all that one desires to eat and a correspondingly
ample figure, are, according to Chinese ideas, infalli-
ble proofs of great happiness.

The sumptuary laws of the Empire are most
minute and rigid; yet, as Hallam has testified concerning Europe, it has not been easy to enforce them
in China.   In village life they mainly affect clothing,
though the walking-stick regulation is also commonly regarded.   Missionaries often offend unwit-
tingly by carrying canes in middle life, or even in
youth, and by constructing houses contrary to their
sumptuary laws, a proceeding far more harmful in
villages than in cities.   Blue cotton cloth is the
commonest material for *the clothing* of both men
and women.   In the winter this may be wadded or
lined with sheep-skin.   A species of shirt and coat,
drawers and trousers, stockings and shoes are not
very different for the two sexes, though a gentleman
would never appear in public without a long gown
reaching to the ankles.   His garments, moreover,
would be of silk or broadcloth, of blue, lavender,
plum-color, or gray.   Caps are commonly worn by
men in the winter and doffed in the summer, unless
replaced by a broad-brimmed hat.   Ladies are permitted to wear gowns, instead of trousers merely,
and they often dress quite elaborately.   Were it not
for their highly rouged faces and goat-like bound
feet, some of them would look very handsome.

The great events in family life are, as with us, births,
marriages, and deaths. . If *the infant* is a girl, her
coming is not welcomed and she is often quietly despatched, not so much through heartlessness as because
the family is too poor to support her until marriage-
able, and unwilling to sell her to be a domestic slave

or for a life of shame. A boy's advent is a source of
great gladness, as in him are the sinews of family
strength and of service to parental post-mortem
necessities. *Marriages* do not follow betrothal at
the early age common in India, yet girls often become mothers at too early a period for their off-
spring's physical good. The ceremonies are naturally joyful to a company who usually pay a good
fee and expect to get their money back through
feasting. As for the bride, this ceremony ushers her
into a life made bitter by bondage to a notoriously
stern and capricious mother - in - law. Thousands
commit suicide either just before marriage or after a
few days of service under such a vixen. *Death* and
its subsequent funeral are, *par excellence*, the events
of Chinese experience. A wedding is a quiet performance in comparison. For days—forty-nine, if
the family can afford it — priestly howlings, music
from a pandemoniac band, feasting and revelry
reign, and then comes the funeral procession with
its many bearers and beggars, its mourners clothed
in white sackcloth, and the demon-appeasing ceremonies. This experience plunges a family in debt,
often for years, but through fear of the now powerful spirit, no one dares spare in this crisis of filial
piety.

2. In *the cities* the environment varies somewhat
from the above. A high, often crenellated wall
pierced by great gates, which are surmounted by
watch-towers or defended by a semicircular enceinte,
shuts out from the traveller's view everything except
a few flag-poles marking temples and official ya-mêns.
Mounting this wall one sees great expanses of tile-
covered roofs, threaded by narrow streets and shaded
by many trees or summer mattings. As one goes
through the main streets, bustle and industry are
everywhere apparent. Itinerant vendors of various
commodities frequent the side-streets, and shout out
the articles sold or indicate them by a variety of
instruments of percussion, so that modest women may

come to their gates and buy.   At night the manifold
noises of day fade out into the stridulous quarrelling
of women and the voice of the peacemaker, and soon
after nine o'clock silence reigns, save for the barking
of dogs, the shouts of private watchmen, the rattles
and gongs of the police, and the monotonous cry of
the cake-seller as he visits the opium dens of a sleeping city.

City homes are usually of brick or adobe, and contain within a single large court a number of buildings divided up into family rooms.   There is thus a
one-story tenement-life problem there, unless the
court is occupied by a large family or part of a clan.
Some of these abodes are luxurious, but the majority
have only beds or brick platforms for sleeping, a few
chairs or tables, one clock perhaps, or several if they
can be afforded, some wall scrolls, red boxes containing clothing, a few vessels for cooking, and recep-
tacles for flour, rice, etc.

The city is likewise the habitat of two numerous
classes of social parasites.   The *beggars* are often an
organized fraternity, working according to fixed rules
under a beggar king.   Howling most lugubriously
in stores or private hall-ways, or following one on
the street, they cannot well be disposed of until the
usual dole is given ; and woe betide the person who
mortally offends one of them, for he can wreak dire
vengeance on his enemy by committing suicide or
seriously injuring himself at the offender's gate.
The thief is a terror to the unarmed citizen, and as the
police and watchmen announce their whereabouts by
much noise, he is rarely captured, and so proceeds to
dig through walls and terrorize a street by raids,
often repeated many nights in succession.   Unfortu-
nately for them, when serious crime of any sort cannot be ferreted out and a victim to the majesty of the
law is needed, the head thief-catcher usually selects
his victim from their ranks.

Blind beggars, lepers in the south, and cripples of
every degree, also abound in the cities, though they

can hardly be classed as social parasites. For these and other unfortunates, *asylums* are established in many populous centres. While foundling institutions in their best estate somewhat resemble ours, their other asylums are mainly shelters from which the inmates go forth by day, sometimes in bands, to beg a precarious living. The financial support of such places depends largely upon persons who thereby lay up merit for themselves, or who expect through their charity to receive an honorary title or literary degree, and upon levies paid by the salt - merchants. No native asylum for lunatics exists ; if violent, they are kept manacled in inner rooms at home, or left lying by the highway, bound hand and foot. The harmlessly insane, whether men or women, are allowed to roam abroad, sometimes in a nude condition. Government aid is often furnished to the poor in times of famine, or when rebellion drives villagers into cities, as lawlessness is thus diminished. It also aids many aged persons to earn a livelihood by granting them the right to vend salt without a license, thus underselling the holders of the government salt monopoly. Charity also takes the supposedly very meritorious form of furnishing coffins for dead paupers.

3. The *government and laws* of China are, in the main, well calculated to secure peace and the ends of justice; this, however, is true theoretically rather than in fact. The Emperor, who is the Son of Heaven and father of his subjects, daily meets his Grand Cabinet between four and six A.M. Business is passed down by this Cabinet to the boards of Civil Office, Revenue, Ceremonies (including religion), War, Punishment, Works, Admiralty, and Foreign Affairs, or Tsung-li Ya-mén. Thence so much of it as is necessary proceeds through a perfect network of greater and lesser officials to the provinces; districts, and hamlets of the Empire. Theoretically regarded, the government is an absolute monarchy; yet because of the universal knowledge of the principles of gov-

erning contained in Confucian literature, the influence of the literati, and the alertness of the Censors,
this power is greatly limited.

Administrators of law, except in small villages—
and often there also—are graduates who have passed
the civil-service examinations, and so constitute an
aristocracy of learning. Special fitness to rule is not
considered. Office is rather the goal toward which,
from the day that the boy began to *nien shu tso kuan*
—study books to become an official—he has for long
years been struggling through first, second, and most
likely third degree examinations, with their gradations of buttons and much coveted honors. This
ordeal passed, he finds himself in office with a small
salary, many hungry subordinates, and prevalent corruption through which to pay expenses and become
wealthy. What wonder that, backed by a host of
underlings, known as his "claws," taxes speedily
increase, the court, in which he is judge and jury,
becomes the scene of bribery and torture, and the
"hell"—prison—to which he sentences obdurate or
poverty-stricken litigants loosens its grasp only to
surrender its victims to the grave. The Chinese soon
learn the moral : Avoid lawsuits, submit to petty
extortion without a murmur, be a man of peace, and
as for vengeance, trust to the proverb, "One life as
an official [is sufficient to condemn to] seven lives of
beggary [in the future world]."

Industrial Life of the Empire.—1. While caste
is unknown in China, there are *gradations in society.* A native writer has thus described these gradations : "First the *scholar :* because mind is superior to wealth, and it is the intellect that distin-
guishes man above the lower orders of beings, and
enables him to provide food and raiment and shelter
for himself and for other creatures. Second, the
farmer : because the mind cannot act without the
body, and the body cannot exist without food ; so
that farming is essential to the existence of man,
especially in civilized society. Third, the *mechanic :*

because, next to food, shelter is a necessity, and the
man who builds a house comes next in honor to the
man who provides food.   Fourth, the *tradesman :*
because, as society increases and its wants are multi-
plied, men to carry on exchange and barter become a
necessity, and so the merchant comes into existence.
His occupation—shaving both sides, the producer
and consumer—tempts him to act dishonestly ; hence
his low grade.   Fifth, the *soldier* stands last and
lowest in the list, because his business is to destroy
and not to build up society.   He consumes what
others produce, but produces nothing himself that
can benefit mankind.   He is, perhaps, a necessary
evil."

In addition to the above gradations, one should
remember that the descendants of Confucius constitute a species of nobility, and that the Manchus of
rank, especially members of the Imperial clan, are
also held in honor.   Neither of the above classes,
nor, much less, the priesthoods of the prevailing
religions, attempt to hold the people in subjugation;
hence the Chinese possess a freedom that is remarkable.

2.   The *industries* of the Empire are carried on with
a good assortment of tools, but with few machines.
This means that manual labor is everywhere pre-
dominant, though in agriculture and transportation,
beasts are often used, animals of different sorts, or
animals and men or women, sometimes uniting their
forces to draw ploughs or vehicles.   In mining, shafts
were sunk only to slight depths until recently, partly
because it was thought that it would incense the
dragon and disturb the terrestrial influences.   That
modern mining methods introduced by foreigners do
not bring disaster, is a severe blow that is helping
to destroy superstition.

Wages are naturally low and competition severe.
From six to ten cents will hire an ordinary laborer
for a day, while artisans can be had for from twelve
to twenty-five cents.   As nearly every adult is mar-

ried and has children, economy of the strictest sort must be practised, and Western machines and means of transportation are sorely dreaded in consequence. The "dried-meat money" of a graduate teacher—one must not speak of salary to such a personage—is $100, more or less, per annum.

3. *Trade guilds and unions* are more pervasive than in the Occident, extending even to beggars and thieves. Anyone caught stealing who does not belong to the guild is doubly punished; and no member would think of entering a house that had been insured by the union against larceny for a suitable premium. Non-unionists in any trade are often suppressed by the bamboo, while the guild cares for its own members in life and death, often against the strong though ineffective opposition of magistrates. Yet with such combinations of labor and with over-crowded "multitudes ever on the brink of destitution, China has no lapsed masses in her teeming cities, nor agrarian outrages in her country districts."

Amusements and Festivals.—1. "Climbing a tree to hunt for fish" describes the attempt to discuss the *amusements* of many Chinese whose life is "all work and no play." Still, even the busiest John occasionally unbends, especially in winter. Children play at hop-scotch, kick marbles about, spin a sort of humming spool in the air and use a thousand and one different games and toys. Women amuse themselves by playing cards and dominoes, gossiping, and visiting. Kite-flying, a species of battledore and shuttlecock, the feet being the battledore, acrobatic performances and juggling, cricket and quail-fights, and two forms of chess afford men their chief amusements. The whole community is fond of theatrical exhibitions, drawn out for three days and nights sometimes, Punch-and-Judy shows, and gambling in multitudinous forms. Feasts are restricted to men, and the itinerant story-teller rarely has others in his booth. Athletic sports are regarded as a doubtful and difficult way of amusing one's self, though candidates for military degrees are often very well trained.

2. Entire absence of a hebdomadal division of time with its regularly recurring Sabbath of rest, has its partial compensation in the many *festivals* of the Chinese, only the most prominent of which can be mentioned. *New Year* is *the* holiday of the Empire and the universal birthday, when everyone adds a year to his age. In preparation for it accounts have been squared, houses cleaned, new clothes bought or hired for the day, and doors adorned with mottoes of happy omen, giving the town the appearance of being painted red. On the day itself carts or chairs rush through the narrow streets carrying well-dressed men intent on " worshipping the year " through calls of ceremony, and for once the sounds of trade and business are utterly hushed. Next in importance is the *ch'ing ming*, or festival of tombs, falling usually in April. Ancestral graves are put in order by the family, who go in pilgrimage thither to offer food, money, and servants, made of paper, to the shades of the deceased. White streamers flutter from the tumuli and burning incense envelops the landscape with a filmy haze. The *dragon boat festival*, on the fifth day of the fifth moon, is the boatmen's holiday, when amid the beating of drums and gongs gayly decked boats are rowed up and down the rivers and their occupants indulge in racing, while the crowds along shore cheer and reward the victorious crews. The seventh moon witnesses the feast of *"All Souls,"* when clothes, food, and drink are offered to hungry ghosts, who have no male descendants to minister to their needs, and also a festival in honor of the *Seven Sisters*, or Pleiades, the patron saints of women. The *fifteenth of the eighth month* is sacred to the moon, and on that night all China is ablaze with every conceivable variety of lantern, moon-cakes are exchanged between families, and everywhere are fire-crackers and candles galore. The ninth of the ninth moon concludes the *kite-flying feast*. While during

the days preceding the sky has been flecked with clouds of tailless kites provided with Æolian-harp strings and the children have looked upon it as sport merely, graybeards have been doing their best to so manipulate their kites as to cut the string and cause all the family ill luck to soar away with the kite.

The Chinese as Painted by Themselves.— Their proverbs furnish the most trustworthy portrait of the Chinese, as in the Orient such sayings are regarded as axiomatic statements of indisputable truth. In selecting these, we have not "in painting a snake added legs," *i.e.*, exaggerated traits of common life ; we have simply "allowed the sick man to furnish his own perspiration."

1. *Children.* The value of boys *vs.* that of girls is expressed by the proverb, "Eighteen Lohan [goddess-like] daughters are not equal to a boy with a crooked foot." Once born, struggle is demanded from parents, as "A child but a foot long requires three feet of cloth" for its earth-trousers. Yet they gladly endure their added cares ; for "What fastens to the heart-strings and pulls on the liver are one's sons and daughters." As children advance in years, remember the saying, "If you love your son, give him plenty of the cudgel ; if you hate him, cram him with dainties." Unluckily this discipline is spasmodic as shown by the definition, "Cloudy day—leisure to beat the children." Discipline persevered in, however, has its reward ; "As the twig is bent, the mulberry tree grows."

2. *Looking out into life.* The parent planning for the boy's future sees two possibilities, learning and manual labor. In favor of the scholar's life, he recalls the maxim, "Better not be, than be nothing," and also that "No pleasure equals the pleasure of study," since "Thorough acquaintance with the Four Books and Five Classics procures for the family emolument from heaven." If this course is chosen, his son must not be a pedant, "Gnawing sentences and chewing characters ;" much less a B.

4

A., who is "A mere bag of false characters," since the superficial scholar is "Like a sheep dressed in a tiger's skin." "To make a man of yourself, you must toil; if you don't, you won't."

If the boy is to be a laborer, let him remember that "By perseverance one may grind an iron anchor into a needle," and that "Any kind of life on earth is better than being under ground." He must expect little respite from toil, since "No-work is two fairies," and "To be entirely at leisure for one day, is to be for one day an Immortal." If he labors without skill, he will be unsuccessful, "A blind fowl picking at random after worms."

3. *Marriage and family life.* "When sons are paired and daughters mated, the principal business of life is accomplished" by parents; not to so dispose of a daughter is dangerous, since "When a daughter is grown up, she is like smuggled salt"—liable to be seized. As "Nine women in ten are jealous," and as "It is impossible to be more malevolent than a woman," the husband manages her on the principle that "Nothing will frighten a wilful wife but a beating." Should either party die, "A widow does not stay so more than a month," and as for the widower, "A wife is like a wall of mud bricks; take off one row, and there is another beneath it." Indeed, if left childless remarriage is necessary inasmuch as "There are three things that are unfilial, and to have no posterity is the greatest of these." Notwithstanding these facts and the saying that "Nobody's family can hang up the sign, Nothing the matter here," it is still true that while "Customs vary in every place, there is no place like home."

4. *Moral maxims.* According to the proverb, "Good men are scarce." Some are "Lying machines," others "Black hearts and rotten livers," while everyone must confess at night that "In passing over the day in the usual way, there are four ounces of sin." Has one been impure? "Of ten thousand evils lewdness is the head." Is he hypo-

critical? "He has the mouth of a Buddha, the heart of a snake." Avoid "The three great evils, lechery, gambling, and opium-smoking." Do not say "The truth is another name for stupidity," nor excuse your wrong-doing, if poor, by the proverb, "The poorer one gets, the more devils one meets."

Remember, rather, that "The best and strongest man in the world finds that he cannot escape the two words, No continuance," and that "An upright heart does not fear demons." "Good men have fire three feet above their heads ; evil spirits will do well to avoid it." Then "Relying upon Heaven, eat your rice," and "Pray to the gods, as if they were present."

IV

WHILE the Chinese commonly speak of "The Three Religions" of the Empire, meaning thereby Confucianism, Buddhism, and Taoism, one must not imagine that all their religion is included under these names, nor yet that any person is an adherent of any single one of these systems to the exclusion of the others. Each sect has borrowed from the other two, and all have appropriated much from primitive religions existing from the earliest times. In discussing the topic, the order followed is a chronological one, though Taoism precedes Confucianism solely on the ground of Lao-tzŭ's superiority in age, and not because it was fully developed before Confucianism had become well established. Mohammedanism, though widely held, is reserved for the next chapter.

Nature-worship.—1. That *fetiches* are powerful and prevalent is evidenced by charms of various sorts, stones,—especially from the holy mountain, T'ai Shan, —sacred trees and fountains, and the employment of wormwood and sedge, as the rowan-tree and woodbine were formerly used in England. If convinced that any object is *ling*, possessed of some mystic potency, no amount of reasoning is likely to prevent the possessor from seeking its assistance, or devoting to it some paltry offering.

2. Many features of *totem worship* are noticed in connection with special trees and animals, but the clearest case of such reverence is that shown to the dragon, the grand totem of the Empire, notwithstanding the fact that he is only an imaginary being. These creatures—there are three prominent dragons,

one of the sky, another of the sea, and a third of the marshes—may have found in the fossil iguanodon their prototype. The only truly orthodox species, that of the sky, "has the head of a camel, the horns of a deer, eyes of a rabbit, ears of a cow, neck of a snake, belly of a frog, scales of a carp, claws of a hawk, and palm of a tiger. On each side of the mouth are whiskers, and its beard contains a bright pearl ; the breath is sometimes changed into water and sometimes into fire, and its voice is like the jingling of copper pans." He is all powerful and is associated in thought with the Emperor, who sits on the dragon throne, has as his ensign the dragon flag, and at death "ascends upon the dragon to be a guest on high." But the common people are also deeply influenced by him, as féng shui depends upon the right relation of celestial and terrestrial influences presided over by the dragon and the tiger. Hence they pay him homage in caves, which are his favorite places of resort, worshipping in lieu of him a lizard caught in the cave, or images of gods placed there for the purpose.

Another apparent case of totemism is found in the cyclical designation of years, twelve animals, the dog, pig, rat, ox, tiger, etc., being used in rotation five times to indicate the sixty years of a cycle. A frequent way of asking one's age is to inquire to what animal one belongs. This custom is not totemistic, however, but is useful in fortune-telling and indicates that persons born during the year denoting the specified animal should not be present when certain events are to transpire, lest some deadly influence should be visited upon them. Obviously, also, it would be highly unfortunate for a man born in the year of the rat to marry a woman belonging to the dog, as in the Chinese view they would have "a rat and dog time of it," and the husband be worsted. After death a man's relation to his animal seems to be truly totemistic, as the dead must carry to the lower world a chest of money to propitiate this animal, in order to prevent it from making him carry the animal about.

3. *Animal worship* outside of totemistic lines is very prevalent. Aside from the dragon, who dominates the scaly race, two other imaginary creatures, the lin, a sort of cross between the stag and unicorn and head of hairy animals, and the fêng, or phœnix, pre-eminent among the feathered race, are highly reverenced. To complete the quinary system of ancient Chinese naturalists, the representative of the shelly tribe, the tortoise, and man, sovereign of naked animals, must be added ; these also are reverenced. Other animals worshipped are the following : The monkey, known as "His Excellency, the Holy King ;" the fox, worshipped by mandarins as having the seals of high office under his control, and reverenced by the people because of his supposed relation to some diseases ; the tiger, worshipped by gamblers for good luck under the name, "His Excellency, the Grasping Cash Tiger," and by mothers in behalf of sick children ; the dog, worshipped before childbirth by women who were born in the year belonging to the dog ; the hedgehog, regarded as a living god of wealth ; and snakes, certain of which are deemed divine. While not worshipped, the magpie, crow, cat, hen, swallow, bat, and owl are creatures of good or ill omen, and are, therefore, to be carefully watched.

4. The *worship of ancestors*, forming the backbone of Confucianism in its practical outcome, is the Gibraltar of Chinese belief, before which Christianity stands almost powerless. *Its central position* is thus described by J. Dyer Ball : "Ancestral worship is filial piety gone mad. True to their practice of retaining customs and habits for centuries and millenniums, the Chinese nation has not given up this most ancient form of worship ; and the original worship of ancestors, like the older formations of rocks on the earth's surface, is strong as the everlasting hills, and, though overlaid by other cults, as the primary rocks are by

other strata, it is still at the foundation, nearly all the other methods of worship being later additions and accretions. The worshipping of ancestors thus underlies most of their religion, and many of their every-day acts and deeds. 'Social customs, judicial decisions, appointments to the office of Prime Minister, and even the succession to the throne are influenced by it.' . . . This worship is the only one that is entitled to the name of the National Religion of China, as the dead are the objects of worship of poor and rich, young and old, throughout the length and breadth of this immense Empire."

The basis of Chinese ancestral worship is found in the belief that a man possesses three souls, which after death reside in the ancestral tablet, in the tomb and in Hades respectively. These souls have the same needs after death as before, the satisfaction of which rests with survivors, especially the eldest son of the deceased. To satisfy these needs, clothing, household articles, money, etc., made of paper, must be transmitted to the spirit-world through fire, thus becoming invisible and so suited to invisible spirits, while food can be immediately partaken in its essence by the spirits. The government of the lower world is the counterpart of that in China, and officials of Hades are open to bribery and look upon the outward appearance, just as in earthly ya-mêns. This not only calls for much paper money, but also for the assistance of a corrupt horde of priests who mercilessly fleece survivors. The system presupposes that disembodied spirits are more powerful than in life, and if their wants are not fully supplied, they can, and probably will, bring varied calamities upon their posterity. Fear thus becomes the all-powerful spur to filial piety toward dead ancestors.

One must admit that *this worship has benefited China* by inculcating a reverence for parents, which has thence reached upward and caused national respect for rulers and emperors. It has also made women honored, especially the wife ; so that but one tablet being allowed for mother, there is only one wife, even in polygamous households, the rest being concubines. Chinese women thus rank higher in domestic position than those of any other Asiatic or heathen race.

On the other hand, *ancestral worship is China's bane*, as well as a sin against God.   It is a useless expense—$151,752,000 per annum, according to Dr. Yates's careful estimate—to a people who sorely need every dollar.   It congests population, instead of allowing colonization to sparsely settled sections of the Empire, since one must be buried near the ancestral hall or among relatives.   For the same reason, it substitutes for love of country in general a love of home, making the people extremely selfish and provincial. Early marriages and polygamy are very largely chargeable to the desire for male offspring to minister to parents after death.   The worship often makes such exorbitant exactions on the poor that pressing wants of the living are neglected in consequence. Individual liberty is apt to be destroyed by the extreme views of parental authority, the son fearing to espouse Christianity, for example, lest death might be the penalty for failure to participate in idolatrous *post-mortem* ceremonies.   Its doctrine of parental divinities of great power drives out all theories of divine retribution, thus substituting parental likes and dislikes for eternal principles.   And, most serious of all, dead ancestors are put in the place of the one Father and Judge of all men.

5. By an extension of the above worship, China has come by many *deified heroes*, who commonly become gods through Imperial decree.   Happily, those thus promoted are not personifications of the vices deified by ancient Greece, Rome, and India, though they are often men of blameworthy life.

6. In the first mention of religious worship found in Chinese history, we read of the Emperor Shun, "Thereafter he sacrificed specially, but with the ordinary forms, to Shang Ti ; sacrificed with purity to the Six Honored Ones ; offered appropriate sacrifices

to the hills and rivers, and extended his worship to the host of spirits." Probably in the earliest times this *Shang Ti*, or Supreme Ruler, often called Heaven, was regarded as a personal, supreme Being. Though His worship still survives, it can be engaged in only by the Emperor, who, as Son of Heaven, periodically offers up solemn sacrifices, especially at the winter solstice. It is the prevalent opinion of Western scholars that no idea of personality has been attached to the names Heaven—T'ien—and Shang Ti for many centuries, though a few recent native writers are shaking off the trammels of Chu Fu-tzŭ and assert personality of those terms. So far as Heaven is regarded as the material vault of azure, Chinese native worship reaches its zenith in the impressive Imperial ceremonies at the Altar of Heaven in Peking.

Taoism.—1. *Its founder*, Lao-tzŭ, the Venerable Philosopher, owes his title quite largely to Confucius's use of it after their famous interview in 517 B.C. His surname was Li, or Plum, his name Erh, or Ear, and his birthplace in the eastern corner of Ho-nan province. Here Li first saw the light about 604 B.C., fifty-three years before the birth of Confucius. After one has run the gauntlet of legend-mongers, the possible facts are left that he was Keeper of Archives at the Imperial Court, was interviewed by Confucius, foresaw the inevitable downfall of the Chou dynasty, and went into retirement in consequence, and later departed to a far country of the West, stopping on his way with the keeper of the northwestern pass, at whose request he dictated the original canon of Taoism, the Tao-tê Ching. He has been likened to the Greek Zeno and the French Rousseau, and he certainly was a protestant against the evils of his age, like Luther. Eminently practical in some of his views, he was on the whole a transcendental dreamer, as well as China's first great philosopher.

2. The Scripture of Lao-tzŭ, *the Tao-tê Ching*, or Canon of Reason and Virtue, contains only 5,320 characters, which can be read in thirty-six minutes.

It is thus the shortest of Sacred Canons, being less than half the length of St. Mark's Gospel. The difficulty of interpreting the book may be guessed from the perplexity of translators concerning the equivalent for Tao, which has been rendered Way, Reason, Word, Logos, and Nature, and also from the terms in which the treatise itself speaks of Tao. Professor Douglas, while regarding Way as the best single equivalent, adds: " But Tao is more than the way. It is the way, and the way-goer. It is an eternal road ; along it all beings and things walk ; but no being made it, for it is being itself ; it is everything and nothing, and the cause and effect of all. All things originate from Tao, conform to Tao, and to Tao at last they return." As nearly as one can describe it, Tao seems to be "(1) the Absolute, the totality of being and things ; (2) the phenomenal world and its order ; and (3) the ethical nature of the good man and the principle of his action."

On *its practical side* the Tao-té Ching promulgates a politico-ethical system by which Lao-tzŭ attempts to reform the Empire by wooing the people back to a primitive state of society. Self-abnegation is the cardinal rule for sovereign and subject alike. " I have three precious things which I hold fast and prize, *viz.*, compassion, economy, and humility. Being compassionate I can be brave, being economical I can be liberal, and being humble I can become the chief of men." In the amplification following this quotation, Lao-tzŭ shows himself to be the Christian as opposed to the Confucian Moses, and especially in another injunction " to recompense injury with kindness," to which Confucius stoutly objected.

3. Though Lao-tzŭ was China's Pythagoras, " the first great awakener of thought," *later Taoist leaders* degenerated, until Rationalism, as Taoism has been translated, became the most irrational of beliefs. Lieh and Chuang, two celebrated Taoist writers of the fifth and fourth centuries, B.C.—if indeed Lieh is a historical character—did more than their master

to illustrate and popularize his ideas. The former so far departed from Lao-tzŭ's spirit that he taught Epicureanism. Chuang, on the other hand, after popularizing Taoism, came to doubt differences in motives and the reality of personal existence. Life was merely a series of phantasmata. Thus after dreaming that he was a butterfly, the dazed philosopher asks, "Was the vision that I was a butterfly a dream or a reality? or am I now a butterfly dreaming that I am Chuang-tzŭ?" Another Taoist writer, nameless, though probably of the Sung dynasty, has given to his sect and to China one of the most widely read religious books of the Empire, the Kan Ying P‘ien, or Book of Rewards and Punishments. So far is it from being imaginative or fanciful that it is little else than a list of virtues and vices which are to be cultivated or avoided; since for great faults twelve years are deducted from one's life and a hundred days for small faults. It is thus a system of moral book-keeping between man and the spirits, the spirit of the hearth being a sort of detective to check up the facts.

4. But to other leaders and writers than the above, Taoism owes *its awful degradation.* Before the introduction of Buddhism, it had so captured the Great Wall Builder that he despatched two expeditions, consisting of thousands of girls and young men, to the golden islands of the blest to secure from the genii the draught of immortality. From that time onward it gave itself increasingly to magic, the search for the philosopher's stone, the elixir vitæ and pills of immortality. For high ideals and eternal truths, it gave its followers senseless shibboleths to ward off evil spirits, and no less harmful moral falsehoods in the shape of rituals and sacrifices in honor of a host of newly created gods and goddesses.

5. If one would know *the Taoism of to-day,* one has only to follow men in slate-colored habit, wearing caps out of the top of which project a knot of hair, to their temples or communal homes, and note there

the many gods ranging from Lao-tzŭ and his companions in the trinity of The Three Pure Ones, through the powerful Pearly Emperor, the Bushel Mother of the North Star, the Chinese Mars, Kuan Ti, the no less noted God of Literature, the everywhere-present God of Wealth,—Buddhism also claims him,—down to the most common and potent deity of all, the cheap paper kitchen god, found near the hearth of nearly every family of the Empire. Hardly less than a living deity is the pope of Taoism, who has his abode in the picturesque Lung Hu Shan—Dragon and Tiger mountains—of Chiang-hsi, whence, by Imperial permission, he rules the Taoist world.

Other proofs of the power of this faith are seen in magic scrawls on houses, gates, and people, in Taoist fortune-tellers, in Cagliostros not a few, who will furnish purchasers with pills of immortality, and in ten thousand superstitions, most of them Taoist in origin, which harass millions "who through fear of death were all their lifetime subject to bondage." Spirits above and spirits below, demons on the right hand and on the left, fears in life and terrors at death, drive the superstition-ridden victim to the supposed saviour, the Taoist priest, whose costly ministrations leave one to despairingly cry, with Queen Katherine,

" Spirits of peace, where are ye? are ye all gone?
And leave me here in wretchedness behind ye? "

Confucianism, the Sect of the Lettered.—Confucius—the Latinized form of K'ung Fu-tzŭ, the Master K'ung—is the " Throneless King " of nearly twenty-five centuries, and of one-fourth the human race. No other mere man, Buddha not excepted, has had so extensive an influence as he, nor set such an ineffaceable stamp upon a race.

1. Some *items from his life* will help the reader to understand his marvellous power. K'ung, whose adult name was Chung-ni, was born in 551 B.C., in a village near the centre of what is now Shan-tung

province. His father was a military officer distinguished for bravery and physical strength, figuring in one story as a Samson raising a closed portcullis, thus allowing his imprisoned soldiers to escape. He died when his son was three years old, and his mother, in spite of straitened circumstances, took charge of his education. As a boy he delighted to " play at the arrangement of vessels and at postures of ceremony."

At fifteen he " bent his mind to learning," and became an earnest student and admirer of the great characters of Chinese history, especially Yao and Shun. Marrying at nineteen, one son and two daughters were born to him, whose descendants now constitute a fair-sized city in the home of their great ancestor. Poverty caused the young man to fill a number of petty offices, but at twenty-two he was able to begin his career as teacher, surrounded by a band of admiring and earnest students. A year later his mother died, and Confucius went into a three years' mourning, which he devoted to study and meditation. Later we see him and his disciples in his native state, except for short intervals, till 517 B.C., when he fled, as did his Duke, on account of political disorders.

Sixteen years more elapsed before his great opportunity came to put into practical execution those theories of government that he had so enthusiastically taught his 3,000 followers. Then, at the age of fifty, he became governor of the town of Chung-tu, a year later was made Minister of Works for the State, and also Minister of Crime, and for three years so conducted affairs that we are told, " He strengthened the ruling house, and weakened the ministers and chiefs. A transforming government went abroad. Dishonesty and dissoluteness were ashamed, and hid their heads. Loyalty and good faith became the characteristics of the men, and chastity and docility those of the women. Strangers flocked to Lu from other states." The jealousy of neighboring principalities soon invaded this Utopia, and a lure of beautiful courtesans and fine horses, sent by a plotting marquis, caused a breach between the Sage and his ruler. Accordingly he left his beloved Lu to roam among neighboring states, accompanied by his disciples. Courted by some, assailed by others, he journeyed on, a mystery to princelets, who were too small to perceive in him a seer and sage.

In his sixty-fifth year he was recalled to his native state, where he spent the remaining years of his life in putting finishing touches to his edition of the ancient writings, in digesting the odes and reforming the music with which they were accompanied, and in composing his only surviving original work, the Ch'un Ch'iu, or Spring and Autumn Annals.

But the pitcher was soon to break at the fountain. Confucius had ceased to dream of his great hero, Duke Chou, and one spring morning, as he walked before his door, he was heard crooning over another presage of his end,

> " The great mountain must crumble;
> The strong beam must break;
> And the wise man withers away like a plant."

The last recorded speech and dream of the Sage had to do with the funeral ceremonies of ancient dynasties, after which he took to his bed, where he died a few days later, in 479 or 478 B.C. His weeping disciples buried him beneath the tumulus which to-day survives as the Mecca of Confucianism, surrounded by sombre cypresses, regal halls and courts, eulogistic monuments of marble, and the graves of more than seventy generations of his posterity. His own generation knew not Joseph, but later centuries have not ceased to do him highest reverence.

2. Only a word can be said of *Confucius's character*. His family life, though somewhat more fortunate than that of Socrates, was not very commendable, and he apparently rejoiced when she died. His son also was so sternly and scornfully dealt with by the father, that one can believe that he had failed in the matter of

paternal duty.   While the charge of untruthfulness and insincerity can be supported, he usually had a high regard for truth and righteousness.

His attitude toward the past, as described by himself, is found in the words, "A transmitter and not a maker, believing in and loving the ancients." This meant the restoration of ancient life and ceremonial in person, family, and state, and to accomplish this object he gave himself with a perseverance, courage, and lack of compromise that are phenomenal.   He felt that Heaven had committed to him the right way, and that he was immortal till his work was done.   The student desirous of getting a comprehensive view of the Sage's life and character should read Book VII. of the Analects, where he is seen in the varied relations of life.

His disciples tell us that "there were four things from which he was free, foregone conclusions, arbitrary determinations, obstinacy, and egoism ; that there were four subjects which he avoided in talking with them, extraordinary things, feats of strength, rebellious disorder, and spirits ; that there were four things which he taught them, letters, ethics, lealheartedness, and truthfulness ; that there were three things of which he seldom spoke, profitableness, the appointments [of Heaven], and perfect virtue ; and that there were three things in regard to which he thought the greatest caution should be exercised, fasting [as preliminary to sacrifice], war, and [the treatment of] disease."

3. *Confucian literature* is popularly said to consist of Thirteen Canons, the "Four Books" and "Five Classics" being most important.   The most widely known of these are the *Ssŭ Shu*—Four Books.   The Ta Hsüeh, or *Great Learning,* and the Chung Yung, or *Doctrine of the Mean,* were taken from the Li Chi by Chu Hsi to form two of the Shu.   The first chapter of the former contains Confucius's words as handed down by Tsêng, and the remainder is made up of quotations selected by him and Chu Hsi.   The Chung

Yung, the most philosophic of the Four Books, was composed by Confucius's grandson, and its object is to illustrate the nature of virtue and the character of the princely man.   The Lun Yü, or *Analects*, is a collection of reminiscences of the Master, recalled by various disciples, thus resembling Luther's " Tischreden," or Boswell's " Life of Johnson."   The fourth section of the Four Books, and more than half of the whole collection, is made up of the *writings of Mêng-tzŭ*, or Mencius, who was a keener philosopher than his master, though he lived more than a century later, from 371 to 288 B.C.   After his death his disciples collected his conversations and exhortations and published them in this form.

The *Wu Ching*—Five Classics—are as follows : Yi Ching, *Book of Changes*, ranking first or third in antiquity among the Classics, and sometimes ascribed even to the legendary Fu Hsi.   Though commonly regarded as a cosmological and ethical treatise, some modern Orientalists claim that it is in its fundamental form an Accadian syllabary.   The Shu Ching, *Book of History*, may have been originally compiled by Confucius from the historical remains of dynasties previous to his time, and contains much of a didactic nature.   It is probably first in age of all the Classics, and contains the "seeds of all things that are valuable in the eyes of the Chinese."   The Shih Ching, *Book of Odes*, contains three hundred and eleven ballads, used by the people of China's ancient petty states, which were selected and arranged by Confucius, who attached great value to them as a means of moulding the national character.   The Rituals are three in number, only one of which, the Li Chi, *Record of Rites*, a sort of digest of other collections, is officially recognized as canonical.   M. Callery says of it : " Ceremony epitomizes the entire Chinese mind ; and, in my opinion, the Li Chi is *per se* the most exact and complete monograph that China has been able to give of itself to other nations."   The Ch'un Ch'iu, *Spring and Autumn* [*Annals*], was prepared by Confucius, aided by his disciples, as a supplement to the Shu Ching, in order to continue the history of his own state down to the year 480 or 484 B.C. The above five works, though less known than the more commonly studied Four Books, are regarded as more valuable to the state.

4. The *teachings of Confucius*—more strictly, the teachings of ancient history, Mencius and Chu Hsi —are ethical rather than religious, and look to the state rather than to the individual, though self-culture is fundamental in his system. This latter point is evidenced by Confucius's "House that Jack Built," found in the Great Learning : "The ancients, wishing to illustrate illustrious virtue throughout the Empire, first ordered well their own states. Wishing to order well their states, they first regulated their families. Wishing to regulate their families, they first cultivated their persons. Wishing to cultivate their persons, they first rectified their hearts. Wishing to rectify their hearts, they first sought to be sincere in their thoughts. Wishing to be sincere in their thoughts, they first extended to the utmost their knowledge. Such extension of knowledge lay in the investigation of things."

The *five relations* underlying the Confucian state —existing between prince and minister, father and son, husband and wife, elder and younger brothers, and between friends—are thus described in a primer that has been committed to memory by more boys than any other in existence : "Affection between father and son ; concord between husband and wife ; kindness on the part of the elder brother, and deference on the part of the younger ; order between seniors and juniors ; sincerity between friends and associates ; respect on the part of the ruler, and loyalty on that of the minister :—these are the ten righteous courses equally binding on all men." "The five regular constituents of our moral nature," known as the *wu ch'ang*, are benevolence, righteousness, propriety, knowledge, and truth, or faithfulness, while

5

the *five blessings*, or happiness, as named in the Shu Ching, are long life, wealth, tranquillity, desire for virtue, and a natural death. A study of these relations, virtues, and blessings, together with that of the *chün-tzŭ jên*, or princely man, and of the individual as related to the state, will acquaint one with the prevalent Confucian ideas.

While *Confucianism is atheistic in tendency*, and often in fact, it cannot be strictly so called. Heaven is spoken of as conferring the nature of man. Filial piety, so characteristic of the system, demands the worship of spirits of the dead. Imperial worship is actually paid to Heaven and the Supreme Ruler; and lest the worship of Heaven and earth should be considered a worship of natural forces merely, Confucius said, "The ceremonies of the sacrifices to Heaven and earth are those by which we serve the Supreme Ruler." Yet it must be confessed that while the materialism of Chu Fu-tzŭ dominates Chinese scholarship, and the literati can quote Confucius's reticence concerning spirits and the future life, it is hopeless to think of deriving much leverage from Confucianism as the missionary tries to introduce the idea of God. The word Reciprocity and the Confucian form of the Golden Rule, "Self what not desire, do not do to men," may be helps to teaching Christian ethics, but the spirit and content of Christianity must be imported *de novo*.

5. *Modern Confucian doctrine* is summed up in the "Sacred Edicts," issued three centuries ago by the celebrated Emperor K'ang Hsi, and wrongly supposed to be read and explained by officials twice each month to an eagerly listening populace. The sixteen precepts inculcate filial piety and brotherly submission, generosity to kindred, cultivation of peace toward neighbors, importance of husbandry, economy, education, banishment of strange doctrines, explanation of the laws, propriety and courtesy, diligence in labor, instruction of sons and younger brothers in right doing, protection against false accusation, warning against

aiding deserters, prompt payment of taxes, combination against thieves and robbers, and the removal of resentment and angry feelings.

. 6. *The worship* of " The Perfect Sage, the Ancient Teacher Confucius," is performed in its simplest form by every school-boy before his tablet, and by officials in 1,500 provincial temples, where twice each year 38,306 animals are sacrificed and 27,600 pieces of silk are offered at his shrine. While the most elaborate temple is found at his Shan-tung home, his worship reaches its acme in the Confucian Temple at Peking, where the Emperor goes in state semi-annually to worship, sacrifice, and pray to the " Teacher, in virtue equal to Heaven and earth, whose doctrines embrace the past times and the present," as well as to Mencius and three other hardly less famous disciples of the Sage, Yen, Tsêng, and Tzŭ Ssŭ.

Buddhism, or Sect of Fo.—The last to enter of the three great sects, Buddhism satisfied, as the other two did not, longings of the soul as to the future, and consequently largely modified Taoism and to some extent influenced Confucianism.

1. This most popular of Chinese religions may have been *introduced into China* about 250 B.C. ; though, as opinions without sufficient evidence are valueless, this traditional entrance may be rejected and the usual date in the seventh decade of the first Christian century, about the time of St. Paul's death, be accepted. Not that Buddhism was then heard of for the first time—for at the date of our Saviour's advent China certainly had become acquainted with the Buddhist canons and images—but not till then did the superstitious Emperor Ming dream that a golden man had flown into the audience hall. A courtier suggesting that it might point to Buddha, the Emperor sent an under-secretary to India to try and get it. Forty-two chapters of the Buddhist canon and a standing image of Buddha were obtained, a monastery was prepared near the capital, and translation of the canon and preaching began. Thereafter for

seven centuries zealous Buddhist missionaries of India
came and went in a ceaseless stream, "joining the
caravans entering the northwestern marts and ships
trading at southern ports."

2. The *spread of Buddhism* was rapid at times, as
during the Sui dynasty when it reached its zenith ;
and at others persecution almost wiped out the faith,
as when, in A.D. 845, 4,600 monasteries and 40,000
smaller religious houses were destroyed, their copper
bells and images made into cash, and 260,000 monks
and nuns forced to return to secular life.   To-day,
in spite of K'ang Hsi's seventh edict, " Discounten-
ance and banish strange doctrines, in order to exalt
the correct doctrine "—aimed especially at Buddhism
as opposed to Confucianism—Buddhist temples are
on all " the hills and under every green tree," and
Buddhist monks and nuns greatly outnumber those
of the Taoists.

3. *Popular Buddhistic doctrines* in China are of
the northern type, as opposed to the cold and cheerless faith of Ceylon, Burma, and Siam.   While there
are two great divisions and thirteen Buddhist sects in
the Empire, they differ little in popular estimation ;
and as they have borrowed from Confucianism "its
reverence for ancestors and for state, and from Taoism
its demigods and its geomantic superstitions," men of
every creed rejoice in its banyan-like shade.

Their *belief concerning Buddha* is almost identical
with that found in Asvaghosha's " Life of Buddha,"
and thus resembles what is found in Arnold's " Light
of Asia."

Theoretically the great *laws of Buddha* are eight :
" Right views," including the faculty for discerning
the truth; "equal and unvarying wisdom," *i.e.*, absence of evil or pernicious thoughts ; "right speech,"
excluding idle or pernicious language ; " correct conduct," or purity ; "right life," or that of a religious
mendicant ; " right endeavor," or the use of proper
expedients ; "right recollection," or repeating from
a true memory Buddha's law and the formulæ of wor-

ship; and "right meditation," or the exercise of a mental abstraction that leaves the mind vacant for the entrance of truth. "These are the eight roads, even and level, by which to avoid the sorrow of repeated birth and death." Practically, however, the Chinese Buddhist cares more for a work called "The Rules of Merit and Transgression" than for such abstract teachings. Thus he is careful to do good deeds, the most meritorious of which are to marry, when rich, a deformed girl to whom betrothed when poor, to publish a part of the Classics, and to forgive a debt, each netting him one hundred credits; to destroy the stereotype plates of immoral books, three hundred credits, and to seek to be pure through life, credit 1,000. Similarly the pious Buddhist will avoid loving a wife more than father and mother, being guilty of usury, cooking beef or dog-meat, digging up a coffin, and drowning an infant, all of which inflict one hundred demerits, and will especially avoid publishing an obscene book, the penalty for which is measureless.

The *doctrine of metempsychosis*, which underlies all Buddhistic teaching, and which was incorporated from Buddhism into the later Taoism, makes life desirable or undesirable, according to one's present lot and one's balance of merit or demerit. The wheel of transmigration ceaselessly turning in Hades with its six ranks or spokes—insects, fish, birds, animals, poor men, and mandarins—renders the death-bed a place of curious and awful dread. Yet this is the firm belief of almost every man, woman, and child in China—even of the learned Confucianist, who, with his exaltation of filial piety, sometimes yields before Buddha's reason for not eating flesh, *viz.*, that in so doing one might very likely eat an ancestor, reborn in animal form.

The *Buddhist heaven* was a new idea to the Chinese. They care little, however, for the heavens described in Sanskrit phrases—the lower ones admitting of sensuous pleasures, and the superior heavens where

happiness consists in thought or pure being ; still less
do they care for the highest heavens, which " admit of
no thought, nor do they exclude it; the condition
here is purely transcendental." What millions long
for, and only thousands can reasonably hope to attain,
is the Western Paradise. "This happy region is ex-
quisitely adorned with gold and silver and precious
gems. There are pure waters with golden sands, surrounded by pleasant walks, and covered with large
lotus flowers. . . . Again, heavenly music is
ever heard in this abode ; flowers rain down each day
three times. . . . Again, there are in this paradise birds of every kind, . . . which during the
six watches raise their notes in concert to sing the
praises of religion. . . . Again, the name of hell
is there an unknown word ; there is no birth in ' an
evil way,' no fear of such births. . . . And living there is a multitude of purified and venerable
persons, difficult to count, innumerable, incalculable.
And therefore all beings ought to make fervent prayer
for that country."

Over against this ineffable glory must be put the
Buddhist hells, or earth-prisons, which, however, are
not often distinguished one from another in the popular mind. The ordinary conception is gained from
the hell found in some Buddhist temples, where,
set forth with all the plastic or pictorial arts, are
seen the horrors of the damned, most of whom are
women. The ten kings of hell, infernal lictors, black,
white, and blue devils, the mortar, mill, chopping-
knife, caldron of boiling oil, cylinder, village of wild
dogs, lake of blood, bridge of snakes, hill of knives
—all with their suffering victims—demons sawing
women asunder or pulling out their tongues, men
wandering aimlessly up rugged heights with decapi-
tated head in hand, are all so grewsomely depicted or
sculptured in that chamber of horrors, that even foreigners cannot sleep after visiting one because of
troubled dreams.

And what is *the Buddhist's salvation ?* The Nirvana

of the books, gained in Buddha's way; but straight is that gate, and only a pitiful few of China's millions are seen agonizing to enter in thereat. As for the rest, if they live a compassionate, benevolent life, and have a large credit on their moral ledger, a better transmigration may be expected—a woman be born a man, if she has been surpassingly saintly, and a poor man be reborn as a scholar with a sure chance of growing rich from the spoils of office. There are also saviours among the gods who can aid mortals, thanks to the attempt of Northern Buddhism to meet an inborn need of every human soul.

4. The *Buddhist priesthood* is too ignorant and inactive to merit special mention. Monks and nuns are scarcely distinguishable, as both sexes have un-bound feet, loose socks and trousers, yellow robes, made flowing to allow for spiritual influences, and clean-shaven pates. Begging alms in the street, raising funds for temple repairs by various nerve-moving austerities, and their numerous and noisy presence at the prolonged wake preceding funerals, constitute their main extra-temple functions.

5. *Temples and pagodas* are the architectural contributions of Buddhism to the community, though Confucianism and Taoism claim the latter as super-lative instruments for bringing to earth the celestial influences so essential to geomancy. Except in cities, temples are always beautifully situated, usually in some quiet or picturesque spot. Their generous courts and capacious buildings are the resort of visitors, as well as the dwelling-place of many gods and of their human attendants.

6. *The worship* at these temples is largely liturgical and hence incomprehensible, as the liturgy is in Sanskrit, which is only imperfectly represented by Chinese sounds. The portly abbot supported by his retinue of monks, candles and burning incense, the monotonous droning of liturgies, the repetition of merit-bringing phrases and prayers accompanied by the rattle of rosaries, the measured beating of wooden

fish-heads, and prostrations in an atmosphere heavy with pent-up smoke, are the prevailing impressions brought away by the visitor.

7. *The gods* in whose honor this worship is performed are too numerous to name, since Chinese Buddhism has adopted a most catholic pantheon of deities. Prominent among them are the Triad of Past, Present, and Future Buddhas,—known as the Three Precious Ones,—Amita and Kuan Yin. The latter, formerly considered a god, has for centuries been a goddess, and is the most common object of veneration among Chinese Buddhists. Her fuller name means " the Sovereign who regards the prayers of the world," and she is also known as the " most merciful, most compassionate." She is a Buddhist Saviour who can rescue from earthly ills and demoniacal hosts every sort and condition of men, from the lunatic, whose prayer makes him sane, to the wisest mandarin of the Empire. "Great Mercy, Great Pity, save from misery, save from evil—broad, great, efficacious, responsive Kuan Yin Buddha," is a cry that penetrates the throne room on the Isle of P'u T'o and moves the heart of the Queen of Heaven. "The Giving Sons Kuan Yin," resembling most strikingly the image of the " Madonna and Child," and two other metamorphoses of her are all greatly reverenced.

Associated with Kuan Yin in worship is Amitabha, Amita, or *O-mi-t'o*, as he is called in Chinese. He is the Buddha of " Boundless Light," so called because " his brightness is boundless, and he can illumine all kingdoms. His life, boundless and shoreless, extends through many kalpas." His chief value in Chinese eyes lies in the fact of his being the " guiding Buddha," who directs his worshippers to the greatly desired Western Paradise. Pronounce his magic name as many times as possible in one breath, and some 25,000 times a day, concentrate the thought on Amita like a thread running through beads, call on his name for seven days with fixed heart, and at death Amita with his holy throng will appear before you ; your heart will not be turned upside down, but, as candidate for the lily-birth, you will be born in the Pure Land.

Chinese Geomancy.—This is known as fêng-shui—literally wind and water—and is everywhere a powerful factor in Chinese life. While it may owe most to the Taoists for its development, it is the product of superstition-mongers of all the sects. Though founded on one of the most ancient Classics, the Yi Ching, it became systematized only in the twelfth century ; yet in seven hundred years it has become " one of the most gigantic systems of delusion that ever gained prevalence among men."

1. The original *objects of care* giving rise to the systems were the spirits of departed ancestors. Made powerful by the act of death, their mediatorship was greatly sought by the living. Naturally their sepul-chre-home was of great importance, and only " wind and water doctors " could properly locate this.

Later, however, the sites of houses, shops, pagodas, and cities came to be determined by these doctors, and their science broadened out until it included "cosmogony, natural philosophy, spiritualism, and biology, so far as they have these sciences."

2. Spirits of the dead are but media through whom survivors can influence *the real power,* which is nature. Nature is regarded as a living organism, over which hover invisible hosts of malignant beings that need to be propitiated. " If a tomb is placed so that the spirit dwelling therein is comfortable, the inference is that the deceased will grant those who supply its wants all that the spirit world can grant. A tomb located where no star on high or dragon be-low, no breath of nature or malign configuration of hills, can disturb the peace of the dead, must there-fore be lucky, and worth great effort to secure."

3. " The *principles of geomancy* depend much on two supposed currents running through the earth, known as the dragon and the tiger ; a propitious site has

these on its left and right. A skilful observer can
detect and describe them, with the help of the compass, direction of the water-courses, shapes of the
male and female ground and their proportions, color
of the soil, and the permutation of the elements."

4. Evidences of *the power of this system* are seen
almost everywhere. Graves with their armchair configuration in the south, crooked streets, blank walls
and screens to prevent spirits from gaining impetus
through rectilinear motion, pagodas and temples
erected to improve fêng-shui, the location of Peking
and of the mausolea of grandees and emperors, theories about the height of new buildings near older ones,
hostility to two-storied houses of foreigners and spires
of Christian churches, and the prevalent dread of
telegraphs, railroads, and mines, so fearfully inimical
to good luck—these are a few samples of many. In
a word, the universal fear of bad fêng-shui is expressed in their proverb, " A real man would rather
die than to have his eyebrows inverted," *i.e.*, lose his
luck. And the key to this most enthralling system
of superstition is held in the itching palm of the
crafty geomancer, usually of Buddhistic or Taoist
faith.

V

BEFORE considering the work of modern missions in the Empire, it will be well to note those movements that have been in a sense a preparation for the coming of the present-day missionary.

Ancient Moral and Religious Conditions.— Those already described have had their value in the way of indicating China's need. *Confucianism* had given to her a code of ethics second only to the Christian system in the opinion of many. There was also embedded in its ancient records, like a fly in amber, intimations of a Supreme Being who ruled in the affairs of men. When Buddhism in our first century had crystallized the cloudlike metaphysics and alchemistic vaporings of *Taoism* into a religion, a change in emphasis as to the ground of virtue appeared. Right for right's sake and filial piety were still believed in, but the Taoist said, " There are in heaven and on earth spirits whose duty it is to search out the faults of men, and who, according to the lightness or gravity of their offences, reduce the length of their lives by periods of a hundred days." Retribution and ever-present spirits thus filled the thought of the duty-doer. *Buddhism* brought to China the emphasis of suffering and its alleviation, its doctrine of Karma which could be accumulated merit, and the sunset glory of its Western Paradise. The loveliness of the unselfish life, the hideous lineaments of lust and passion, arch-enemies of the human race, and the reality of the invisible spiritual world, which might be one's own possession, were also India's gift to China.

The Secret Sects.—1. But another source has been experimentally proven more truly preparatory to the reception of the gospel message than the best elements in the established faiths. This is found in the beliefs held by many of the proscribed and hence secret sects. These tenets have proven helpful, not so much because they are wholly new—since most of their doctrines are a composite of views already current in the Empire—but because the holders of these doctrines are such from conviction and so are prepared to endure much hardship in consequence, while believers in orthodox views are usually mere formalists of jellyfish character. Their number and distribution—it is estimated that there are from 20,000 to 200,000 sect members in each province—are also a source of strength to the Christian movement in that everywhere are found men who have the courage of their convictions, though they are not the views of their neighbors, *an object lesson* of the greatest value to the would-be Christian.

2. As to *the doctrines* taught by these sects, some societies exist for the propagation of political theories, often of a revolutionary character; others propitiate evil powers, and others still hold the symbols of reproduction in reverence, as in India. Most of them, happily, are mainly moral and religious. Thus the Tsai-li Society is one of the most extensive temperance organizations in the world, its members pledging themselves to abstain from gambling, tobacco, wine, and opium, and carrying on a crusade against these evils by means of most realistic representations, through clay figures clothed in rags, of the evils of intemperance. Several sects advocate vegetarianism "as a means of rectifying the heart, accumulating merit, avoiding calamities in this life and retributive pains in the next." Another sect "tries to persuade men to be chaste, to eliminate all passion, and by meditation and study to attain a state of perfect repose and self-control, so that every impulse may be followed without the least risk of falling into sin." The duty of maintaining a patient spirit under injury

and of meeting reviling with silence is the chief teaching of another society. Many a sect member is seen who is really seeking truth and trying to relieve needy and suffering neighbors. The Chin-tan Chiao, or Pill of Immortality Sect, which in 1891 lost 15,000 members through the false charge of being rebels, uses terms and prayers that are essentially Christian, and many of its membership declare after joining the Christian Church that Chin-tan doctrines closely resemble those of Christianity.

3. Mr. James, a Shanting missionary, who has made a special study of the secret sects, thus testifies to the *character of sect converts:* "Some of the best and most consistent Christians I know were once the devoted followers of these societies. And in spite of all the suspicion cast on them by the officials, and the fact that numbers of their leaders and adherents have been punished for seditious practices, it is certain that a large number, perhaps a majority of the most thoughtful, decent, and earnest seekers after God are contained in these sects. With such people it is no political matter, but a strenuous endeavor to do the utmost in their power to eradicate sinful habits, to do good, obtain rest for their souls, and immortal life."

The Jews in China.—Turning from these dim gropings after God, one would expect to find in Judaism and Mohammedanism, with their doctrine of the true God, a more helpful element in preparing the Chinese mind for Christian teachings. It is a question, however, whether this is so. The Jewish leaven has been too small to affect the populous lump, while Mohammedans bring reproach by their lax morality on the God whom they worship.

1. Formerly *the Jews* called their faith the Religion of India, in allusion, Dr. Martin thinks, to the principal land of their sojourn on their way to China; later they were known by their heathen neighbors as the T'iao-chin Chiao, or Sinew Picking Sect, since they pick out the sinews from the flesh before eating (Gen. xxxii. 32).

On a stone in K'ai-fêng Fu, the capital of Ho-nan, are inscribed these *salient facts of their history*: " With respect to the religion of Israel, we find that our first ancestor was Adam. The founder of the religion was Abraham ; then came Moses, who established the Law and handed down the Sacred Writings. During the dynasty of Han [B.C. 206–A.D. 264] this religion entered China. In the second year of Hsiao Tsung of the Sung dynasty [A.D. 1164], a synagogue was erected in K'ai-fêng Fu. Those who attempt to represent God by images or pictures do but vainly occupy themselves with empty forms. Those who honor and obey the Sacred Writings know the origin of all things ; and eternal reason and the Sacred Writings mutually sustain each other in testifying whence men derived their being. All those who profess this religion aim at the practice of goodness and avoid the commission of vice." This stone of witness makes no mention of any great influence exerted by their race in China, though in the fourteenth century they appear to have been quite numerous and to have been scattered over the northern portion of the Empire. A Russian author, Professor Vasil'ev, claims that " they held employments under the Government and were in possession of large estates, but by the close of the seventeenth century a great part of them had been converted to Islam."

3. *Their present condition* is pitiable. A mere remnant confined to K'ai-fêng Fu apparently, in numbers less than 400 in all, unable to read the Hebrew of their ancient scrolls, their synagogue in ruins and the religious assembly given up, and circumcision among the younger generation no longer performed, Dr. Martin's words fitly describe their present prospects : " A rock rent from the sides of Mount Zion by some great national catastrophe, and projected into the central plain of China, it has stood there while the centuries rolled by, sublime in its antiquity and solitude. It is now on the verge of being swallowed up by the flood of paganism, and the

spectacle is a mournful one. The Jews themselves are deeply conscious of their sad situation, and the shadow of an inevitable destiny seems to be resting upon them."

Chinese Mohammedanism. — The Hui-hui Chino, as Chinese Mohammedans call themselves, variously explain the character *hui*. Professor Arnold's belief is that as it may mean either "return" or "submission," their name signifies "a return to God by the straight path, and submission to the will of the Almighty." A Chinese Mohammedan author holds that it is "once" twice repeated, men being born once and dying once, and that no doctrine is of importance that does not deal with the Two Ways of Birth and Death. Dr. Edkins, on the other hand, makes it merely the representation by Chinese characters of a Turkish race-name applied to tribes in Kashgar.

1. Their *entrance into China* was by caravans in the north and by sea from the south. The first mosque in North China was built in 742 at Hsi-an Fu, Shen-hsi. Making its way into Kan-su, a khan was converted about the middle of the tenth century, and endeavored to force all his subjects to become believers. Later, Mongol conquests resulted in "a vast immigration of Mussulmans, Syrians, Arabs, Persians, and others into the Chinese Empire. . . . A great number of them settled in the country, and developed into a populous and flourishing community, gradually losing their racial peculiarities by their marriage with Chinese women."

Their traditions say that they first came to Canton in the sixth year of the Hegira, A.D. 628—known as the Year of Missions—under the leadership of a maternal uncle of Mohammed, whose tomb is still an object of reverence for all Chinese Moslems. In 758 there were added to their number 4,000 Arab soldiers who came, like the Manchus, to assist in quelling rebellion, and who, like them, declined to withdraw after it was accomplished. This and the immigra-

tion under the Mongols are the only large accessions
coming in from without.

2. *Their increase* to some thirty millions—M. de
Thiersant's estimate, based on data furnished some
twenty years ago by Chinese officials, was twenty millions for the Empire, while Dr. Jessup's estimate of
four millions is evidently too low—is a matter of interest to the missionary.   If this is the only result of
twelve centuries of propagandism within the Empire,
can Christianity expect any greater conquests ?

Their growth in numbers is not due to any such
missionary zeal as was displayed by the Buddhists or
by Protestant missions, for very little of it has ever
been shown.   It has rather resulted from natural increase of the Mohammedan section of the population,
aided by compromise in objectionable religious views,
the purchase of children of poor parents in time of
famine, and the instruction of even the humblest by
means of metrical primers in Islamic doctrine.   That
this growth would have been still larger had they not
been proverbially rebellious, and so subject to constant
decimation—the Panthay rebellion of 1855–74 resulted in the death of more than two millions of their
number—is perfectly evident.   With more than half
the population of Kan-su and Yün-nan Mohammedan,
one can see the possibilities of even a false faith.

3. *The present status and practices* of Mohammedanism will also help to account for its slow increase.
Moslems go by the appellation "Mohammedan
thieves," are regarded by the people as responsible for
most of the counterfeiting, and are in demand when a
deed of blood, such as slaughtering animals or execut-
ing criminals, is to be done. "The Chinese recognize
in their physiognomy, especially in the nose, a proof of
the violent temper popularly ascribed to them.   Jests
at their expense are common," and the proverb runs,
"I said Mohammedans are thieves, but according to
you they are dogs." So far as the literati are concerned, their rigid rule that the Koran must not be
translated has kept it from being known to scholars,

even to those of their own faith. The prohibition of
the flesh of " the black beast " is a serious one to a people who, in many cases, must eat pork or refrain from
meat altogether, while the inhibition of wine is not
relished by a temperate people who wish to imbibe on
important occasions.

4. Yet this faith is not without *its advantage* to
the Christian missionary. The two great features of
Mohammedanism, its proclamation of the one true
God and its denunciation of idolatry, have come to
the ears of many in the Mohammedan provinces of
the north, northwest, south, and southwest. The
nominal observance of Friday as worship-day and
the use of certain theological terms have imparted an
inkling of Christian life and truth to other few of the
people. Yet when all has been said, most missionaries of Mohammedan experience would probably pre-
fer to work in a field where they are not found.

Nestorian Christianity.—Though its entrance
into the Empire probably antedates that of Mohammedanism, it has been reserved until now because of
its higher teachings.

1. Traditions of some importance assert that " the
Christian faith was carried to China, if not by the
apostle Thomas, by the first teachers of Christianity." As early as 300 A.D., Arnobius speaks of the
Christian deeds done among the Seres. The heretical
leader, Mani, also very probably visited the country
in the third century.

Yet the *entrance of the Nestorians*, as early as 505
A.D. perhaps, constitutes the first Chinese Christian
movement of which we possess certain and comparatively full evidence. Driven out of the Roman Empire, Nestorian monks penetrated into western China
and thence spread eastward to the ocean.

2. Built into a brick wall, where it had once stood,
outside of the ancient capital of Hsi-an Fu, Shen-hsi
is the oldest Christian monument in the Empire, and
perhaps the most ancient one in all Asia, the birth-
continent of our faith. A fierce controversy has been

6

waged about that tablet since its discovery in 1625, but the general opinion is that it is a genuine record of the Nestorian Church, dating from the T'ang dynasty and the year 781 A.D.

From its florid and genuinely Chinese periods one can gather these apparent facts concerning the *heyday of Chinese Nestorianism.* The most virtuous Olopun came from Syria, and after "beholding the direction of the wind he braved difficulties and dangers," arriving in the Empire A.D. 635. The illustrious T'ai Tsung, who then occupied the throne, conducted his guest into the interior, "the sacred books were translated in the imperial library, the sovereign investigated the subject in his private apartments; when, becoming deeply impressed with the rectitude and truth of the religion, he gave special orders for its dissemination." If the record can be believed, later emperors favored the new faith and caused Illustrious Churches to be erected in every province. "While this doctrine pervaded every channel, the State became enriched and tranquillity abounded. Every city was full of churches and the royal family enjoyed lustre and happiness." The machinations of opposing Buddhists seem to have come to naught, and the faith spread in spite of all opposition.

3. If the Nestorian monument truly reflects the *doctrines taught,* China must have been much benefited, though in their enunciation there is an evident accommodation to Chinese beliefs. The great truths of Christianity, with the exception of the Crucifixion and the Atonement, were proclaimed, and the Emperor T'ai Tsung himself, on the Incarnation day, is said to have "bestowed celestial incense and ordered the performance of a service of merit." Better still, the lives of the propagators of the Illustrious Religion, as Nestorianism was called, were apparently consistent with their assertion, "Now without holy men principles cannot become expanded; without principles holy men cannot become magnified; but with holy

men and right principles, united as the two parts of a signet, the world becomes civilized and enlightened."

4. *Later Nestorianism* in China ill deserved the name of Illustrious Religion. An imperial edict of the year 845 commands 3,000 of its priests to retire to private life, while Arabian travellers, a century later, report the death of many Christians in the siege of Canfu. Marco Polo speaks of them as being both numerous and respected in the thirteenth century. Barring that *ignis fatuus* of mediæval history, Prester John, who bears many Nestorian features, and who was the fabled Christian priest-king of Asia, the Nestorian faith can boast of nothing in later centuries. They "suffered much, but maintained a precarious footing in China during the time of the Yüan dynasty, having been cut off from all help and intercourse from the mother Church since the rise of the Moslems. They had ceased long before this period to maintain the purity of the faith, however, and had apparently done nothing to teach and diffuse the Bible, which the tablet intimates was in part or in whole translated by Olopun, under the Emperor's auspices." To-day Nestorian churches, books, and Christians are no longer to be found in China, and even the noble monument of those apostles of an earlier and purer faith was found in 1893 to be laid low, and part of the inscription was defaced, the work of malicious hands, apparently.

5. The Christian Church in China may perhaps *owe to Nestorianism* its first translation of the Word of God, though it has long since perished. It certainly has conferred upon the Church these benefits. One appeals to the Chinese because of its antiquity, viz., the historic testimony concerning the early introduction of Christianity into the Empire. A rubbing of the Nestorian tablet, or a reduced photograph of the same hung in Christian chapels and explained to the people, would do much to remove the charge of its being a novel and strange doctrine recently foisted upon a credulous few by designing foreigners. This

inscription, with a copy of the contemporaneous edict
of their famous T'ai Tsung, quoted from on the monument, is a witness from the past of the utmost value
to men who almost worship antiquity.   A second benefit coming to the Chinese Church from the vanished
glory of the Illustrious Religion is the warning against
compromise, which is the apparent secret of its utter
decay.   As Dr. George Smith has said of Indian Nestorianism : "Nestorius is the representative of those
who preach a Christ less than divine, and who have,
therefore, ever failed to convert mankind.   .   .   .
This fact of compromise must be remembered when
we proceed to look at the otherwise bright missionary
progress of Nestorian Christianity in Asia, central,
east, and south."   The third one is also a word of
warning.   Their aim seemed to be to gain first the
rulers of the land, and they boasted much of imperial
favor, while little was said of work among the common people.   This reversal of Christ's law, "To the
poor the gospel is preached," may largely account for
their ultimate failure.

A further possible benefit conferred by this faith is
found in the suggestion that the creeds of Christian
truth taught by men of the secret sects may have
been derived from Nestorian teaching.   Though not
proven, it is possible that Christian phrases, used by
certain of the sects, and fragments of Nestorian
prayers, are to-day being uttered in secret by their
members in many a city and province of China, thus
perpetuating the real life of these ancient Chinese
Christians, long after their Church has perished.

Catholicism's First Stadium in China.—1.
Rome's first great apostle to the Chinese was *John of
Montecorvino*, who arrived in India in 1291, preached
there successfully for a year, and thence proceeded
with a caravan to the court of Kublai Khan.   In
spite of Nestorian opposition he had, at the expira-
tion of eleven years, a baptized following of nearly
6,000 persons, a church at Peking with "a steeple
and belfry with three bells that were rung every hour

to summon the new converts to prayer," and he had bought one hundred and fifty children, whom he instructed in Greek and Latin and composed for them several devotional books. The story of his missionary life he thus gave : " It is now twelve years since I have heard any news from the West. I am become old and grayheaded, but it is rather through labors and tribulations than through age, for I am only fifty-eight years old. I have learned the Tartar language and literature, into which I have translated the whole New Testament and the Psalms of David, and have caused them to be transcribed with the utmost care. I write and read and preach openly and freely the testimony of the law of Christ." If Catholic historians truly depict this hero of the faith, one can well believe that at his death in 1328, " after having converted more than 30,000 infidels," "all the inhabitants of Cambaluc [Peking], without distinction, mourned for the man of God, and both Christians and Pagans were present at the funeral ceremonies, the latter rending their garments in token of grief."

2. The *labors of his successor*, Nicholas, and his twenty-four Franciscan assistants seem to have been almost wholly for the Mongol tribes instead of for the Chinese, over whom the Mongol emperors ruled. If this is correct, it largely accounts for the fact that after the overthrow of the Mongols by the Ming dynasty, both Nestorians and Catholics sink out of sight, having, it is supposed, "lapsed into ignorance and thence easily into Mohammedanism and Buddhism." The Pope's order to have " the mysteries of the Bible represented by pictures in all the churches, for the purpose of captivating the barbarians," may have served a temporary purpose, but such thin soil was incapable of supporting the plant after the fierce sun of persecution arose upon it.

3. As one roams over the Mongolian plateau and sees everywhere evidence of the mighty grasp of Tibetan Buddhism, which holds in its sway not only the oldest son of each family as a priest of Buddha, but

which dominates every member of the family as well, one cannot but mourn over a possible "*it might have been*" of Christian history. Professor Douglas, in writing of Kublai Khan, says: "Had his endeavor to procure European priests for the instruction of his people, of which we know through Marco Polo, prospered, the Roman Catholic Church, which did gain some ground under his successors, might have taken stronger root in China. Failing this momentary effort, Kublai probably saw in the organized force of Tibetan Buddhism the readiest instrument in the civilization of his countrymen, and that system received his special countenance." A similar crisis now confronts Protestant Christianity. Is the future historian to write against her fair name a similar charge?

The Second Catholic Entrance.—After Xavier, the St. Paul of Roman missionaries, had fallen on sleep beside the sleepless China Sea, his successor, Valignani, exclaimed in sadness as he gazed on the mountains of China, "O, mighty fortress! when shall these impenetrable brazen gates of thine be broken through?" The key to those gates was placed in the hands of the Italian Jesuit, Matteo Ricci, and they were unlocked and stood ajar until one hundred and fifty years later, when the decree of the Emperor Yung Chêng closed them again.

1. *The hero* of the first part of this period was a man who stands foremost among Catholic missionaries "for skill, perseverance, learning, and tact." Ricci came first to the Portuguese settlement of Macao, but soon gained entrance to China itself by a proceeding characteristic of the man and of Rome's methods in the Empire. He and his companion applied to the Governor of Kuang-tung for permission to build on the mainland, since "they had at last ascertained with their own eyes that the Celestial Empire was even superior to its brilliant renown. They therefore desired to end their days in it, and wished to obtain a little land to construct a house and a church where they might pass their time in prayer

and study, in solitude and meditation." With similar duplicity he posed in turn as Buddhist priest, as scholar, as philosopher, and as official, as seemed most expedient, but always with his eyes fixed on Peking and the occupant of the Dragon Throne. His indomitable energy finally brought him within Peking's tunnel-like portals on July 4, 1601. Once in the capital, his learning, pleasing manners, and judicious distribution of presents gained him favor among those in authority and won for the Church many adherents.

His extremely busy *life in Peking* was filled with manifold labors. Visitors, who were never turned away, and new converts who were to be warmly welcomed, thronged his residence. As head of the China mission with its four stations, an exhausting correspondence must be carried on. His relation to the Court and high officials and scholars entailed a grievous burden upon him. A still more trying ordeal was the correspondence arising from inquiries coming from all parts of the Empire concerning the doctrines taught by him and the books which he had published.

His *literary labors* were extremely important to the work. Rarely has a foreigner succeeded so well as he in clothing foreign and Christian ideas in so attractive a Chinese dress. In the topics chosen he also adapted himself to the taste of the literati. Themes such as Friendship, Years Past no Longer Ours, Man a Sojourner on Earth, Advantage of Frequent Contemplation of Eternity, Future Reward and Punishment, Prying into Futurity Hastens Calamity, etc., were pleasingly discussed. His *Hsi-kuo Fa*, or "Art of Memory as Practiced in the West," was especially popular, the more so since Ricci was himself an expert in mnemonics. A map of his, which was prepared on a peculiar projection to give the Chinese an idea that their land was indeed the middle kingdom, was widely used and did much to remove the disgust occasioned by ordinary maps in which China appears only as a little corner of the world. His religious

writings, the best of which is perhaps the "Veritable
Doctrine of the Lord of Heaven," are not aggressively
Christian, and naturally the doctrine of faith in
Christ is but slightly touched upon, while he gives
much space to parallels between Christianity and the
teachings of Confucianism.

Decisions as to certain questions, which were mainly due to Ricci, kindled a fierce controversy which
was waged for a century by the Jesuits and other
Catholic orders. Colonel Yule thus summarizes them :
"The chief points of controversy were (1) the lawful-
ness and expediency of certain terms employed by the
Jesuits in naming God Almighty, such as T'ien,
Heaven, and Shang Ti, Supreme Ruler or Emperor,
instead of T'ien Chu, Lord of Heaven, and in particular the erection of inscribed tablets in the churches,
on which these terms were made use of ; (2) in respect
to the ceremonial offerings made in honor of Confucius and of personal ancestors, which Ricci had recognized as merely civil observances ; (3) the erection of
tablets in honor of ancestors in private houses; and (4),
more generally, sanction and favor accorded to ancient
Chinese sacred books and philosophical doctrine, as
not really trespassing on Christian faith." While
Ricci and the other Jesuits favored compromise measures, and consequently were supported by the Chinese
and even the great Emperor K'ang Hsi, as well as by
one of the popes, the other orders held to the Christian view of allegiance to truth rather than to expediency, and with the support of another papal decree, their views finally prevailed.

Catholic writers, usually his opposers, have given
Ricci rather a hard *character*. One can agree with
them when they write : "Being more a politician than
a theologian, he discovered the secret of remaining
peacefully in China. The kings found in him a man
full of complaisance ; the pagans, a minister who ac-
commodated himself to their superstitions ; the mandarins, a polite courtier skilled in all the trickery of
courts." An impartial student of his life would

hardly venture to assent, however, to their assertion that he was a faithful servant of the devil, " who, far from destroying, established his reign among the heathen, and even extended it to the Christians."

2. *Later Catholic leaders* of this early period were men of great ability, though less open to criticism than the crafty Ricci. The talented and learned German Jesuit, Schall, at one time tutor of the Emperor K'ang Hsi; Faber, the miracle-working saint of Shenhsi, and Verbiest, of whom a competent witness says, " No foreigner has ever enjoyed so great power and confidence from the rulers of China as this priest," were men who did much for China as well as for their Church.

But worldly favor speedily changes its "Hosanna!" to "Crucify him!" and Catholicism gradually became much *hampered in its work*. Persecution in the provinces affected both missionary and convert; and though at court Catholic scholars were tolerated, it was mainly because of their secular services as astronomers, scientists, surveyors of the Empire, etc., that they were held in esteem. Finally, the rivalries and opposition of popes and priests to one another, and to the opinion of K'ang Hsi caused Yung Chêng to issue his order of 1724, strictly prohibiting the propagation of the T'ien Chu Chiao, or Lord of Heaven Sect.

3. A *period of eclipse* followed, which practically lasted until the treaties of 1858 inaugurated a new era. During these thirteen decades persecution, exile, imprisonment, and death were common experiences, and some of the most heroic and devoted deeds are recorded of both missionaries and their converts. At risk of life converts stood by the Church and its leaders in a way that is a prophecy full of hope for the time when the Protestant Church shall be subjected to similar trials. In spite of all opposition 400,000 converts were enrolled in the Church in 1846 and eighty foreign missionaries ministered to their scattered flocks.

4. *Since 1858* Catholic missions have prospered. Old occasions of much friction have been removed by the apportionment of the different orders to sections by themselves, so that Jesuit and Dominican no longer need war each upon the other. Diplomacy of European Catholic powers has by means not always beyond criticism gained for Catholicism—and hence, by the "most favored nation clause," for Protestants also—toleration and protection. Church property, practically sequestered during the decades of eclipse, has been again restored, often with most astonishing and dubious enlargement, and lay brothers of keen business instincts have dealt in property desired by foreigners in a way that renders some missions self-supporting. Imposing churches have been built, in one case with a roof of imperial tiles surreptitiously secured and painted, so that their real character would become only slowly apparent, and progress is evident all along the line.

5. A word about *Catholic methods* must suffice. From the outset they have sought to adapt themselves to the people and to the popular need. If curiosity filled the mind of officials and the Court, curious clocks and other Western novelties were used. Science being demanded, they were mathematicians, surveyors, and astronomers. They may have gone too far in becoming all things to all men, but their idea is worthy of careful consideration in our day of national transformation and new needs.

Practical charity has never been forgotten, and the labors of a consecrated company of Sisters of Charity must not be forgotten. Orphan asylums and the work of teaching girls those arts which are needed in the Christian home, as well as branches of learning that will be useful, have been of great value to the Church.

The *native convert* has not been forgotten in his relation to his family and the native Church. The raising of European vegetables, and arts, such as those of watch-repairing, electro-plating, etc., have been taught by the missionaries, thus enabling converts to be self-

supporting. Tidiness and self-respect, as well as devotion to the Church, are assiduously inculcated.

Nor is the convert's *usefulness to the Church* forgotten. From the day that the noble Hsü and his daughter Candida were won by Ricci to the present time,
they have been used. While few have approached
the usefulness of Candida, who built "thirty-nine
churches in different provinces and printed 130
Christian books for her countrymen," as well as set
blind story-tellers at work telling the Gospel story,
they have been used by the priests for the good of
Mother Church in many ways.

Other features have not been so praiseworthy.
Thus one cannot rejoice with the many Catholic writers who have told of the great accessions, won by
women mainly, who figure as amateur doctors and
visit homes where children lie at the point of death,
and who, by this *pieuse ruse*, baptize "seven or eight
thousand infants every year." Nor can one approve
of the activity of the foreign priests in supporting
converts who have law-suits, though this practice se-
cures many accessions.

Père Ripa has brought against his *missionary brethren* charges that still largely lay at their door. He
accounts for their lack of wide influence by their
feeble attempts to gain an accurate use of the language, their imitation of officials in their dress, their
mode of travel, their haughty isolation from the
common people, and their relegation of preaching and
the main care of converts to the native catechists.

6. *Catholicism's relation to Protestant missionaries*
and their work is a blot on the name of the Church,
from which one would gladly turn away. Until comparatively recently their policy was simply that of
"let alone," but at present it is quite otherwise. Beginning first as a system of proselyting among Protestant Chinese, it has proceeded to most active opposition, amounting often to bitter persecution of
Chinese Christians. Being fearless of law-suits because of Catholic protection, and unscrupulous as to

method if only the Church is the gainer, they have
repeatedly attempted to blot out weak Protestant communities. While this has been mainly confined to
three or four provinces, and has probably been little
encouraged by the missionaries themselves, the evil is
a growing one, and must be reckoned with in fore-
casting Protestantism's future in China. It should
be added that most of the criticisms of missions made
by the Chinese and by anti-missionary foreigners, including nearly every item of any validity, are charge-
able to the policy and work of Catholic missions,
though these critics do not discriminate between
Catholics and Protestants in their accusations.

7. While it is believed that the above strictures
would be agreed to by any impartial writer cognizant
of the facts, *the other side of the case* should be borne
in mind. Drs. Milne and Medhurst, early Protestant
missionaries of catholicity and candor, thus testify to
the merits of these first modern occupants of the
field.

Dr. Milne wrote : " The learning, personal virtues, and ardent zeal of some of them, deserve to be
imitated by all future missionaries ; will be equalled
by few, and, perhaps, rarely exceeded by any. Their
steadfastness and triumph in the midst of persecutions, even to blood and death, in all imaginable
forms, show that the questionable Christianity which
they taught is to be ascribed to the effect of education, not design, and affords good reason to believe
that they have long since joined the army of martyrs, and are now wearing the crown of those who
spared not their lives unto the death, but overcame
by the blood of the Lamb and the word of His testimony. It is not to be doubted that many sinners
were, through their labors, turned from sin to holi-
ness, and they will finally have due praise from God
as fellow-workers in His Kingdom."

Dr. Medhurst further testified : " Some idea of
their doctrines may be gathered from the books
which they have published in the Chinese language.

Many of these are written in a lucid and elegant style, and discuss the points at issue between Christians and Confucians in a masterly and conclusive manner. Their doctrinal and devotional works are clear on the Trinity and the Incarnation, while the perfections of the Deity, the corruption of human nature, and redemption by Christ are fully stated ; and though some unscriptural notions are now and then introduced, yet, all things considered, it is quite possible for humble and patient learners to discover by such teaching their sinful condition, and trace out the way of salvation through a Redeemer. It must not be forgotten, also, that the Catholics translated the major part of the New Testament into Chinese, and though there is no evidence of its having been published, yet large portions of the gospels and epistles were inserted in the lessons printed for the congregations. As it regards the sciences, the Catholics have done much to develop them to the Chinese ; and a native who had been instructed by them lately published a treatise on astronomy and geography which has been highly esteemed and widely circulated. The Romish missionaries have not been remiss in preparing works for the elucidation of the Chinese language to Europeans." He might also have added that nearly all of value that was known concerning China in the Occident until this century came from Catholic sources.

With any disadvantage to the cause of Protestant missions arising from the presence of Catholic Christians, it certainly means considerable for the Kingdom of God that in sixteen of the provinces, including hostile Hu-nan, as well as in Manchuria and Mongolia, are European missionaries and Catholic converts, estimated to number in 1898 about one million.

The Greek Church in China.—The bare fact only needs to be mentioned that this communion gained an entrance in 1685 into Peking, where it has since had its chief seat. A treaty made with Russia four years later permitted the establishment of a college for Greek priests. It has had some scholars of note, like the Archimandrite Palladius, but their literary work has been confined mainly to Chinese and Russian, and so has done little for modern missions. Considerable assistance has, however, been derived from their Chinese versions by Protestant Bible translators. In recent years this Church has again given itself with some earnestness, but with little success, to the gaining of converts. What effect the growing influence of Russia will have upon their Church can only be surmised.

VI

ALL the religious movements, detailed in the previous chapter, were to a greater or less degree preparatory for the work of Protestantism. Yet, as has been suggested, every one of them, the work of Rome not excepted, had also sown many tares in the field, which have proven a greater embarrassment in many cases than the good seed has been of help. The beginning of the Protestant enterprise was accordingly beset with difficulties. The edict of 1724 was still in force, and the few Catholic missionaries in the country were mainly in hiding.

Protestantism's Pioneer.—Notwithstanding the extensive work of Catholicism in the Empire and its inculcation of most of the great truths of Revelation, Dr. Williams, in his sketch of Robert Morrison, regards him, rather than Rome, as having laid the foundations of the Church of Christ in China.

1. This last and boot-tree maker of Newcastle-upon-Tyne journeyed from England to China via America, and during his early career lived with the Americans at Canton. Morrison had been planning to go to Timbuctoo, but in being sent to China God had answered his prayer that He "would station him in that part of the missionary field where the difficulties were the greatest, and, to all human appearance, the most insurmountable." He arrived not only with a letter from our Secretary of State to the United States consul, but also with a preparation unusually complete for that day. He had whetted his memory to attack Chinese by a use of the 119th Psalm and other mnemonic tests, and had further prepared him-

self for his future field by the acquisition of a theological education and a fair acquaintance with medicine and astronomy, and he had transcribed two manuscripts, one a Chinese translation of the New Testament as far as Hebrews—probably by a Catholic missionary—the other a Latin and Chinese dictionary. He had also begun in London and continued on shipboard the study of the spoken language under a Cantonese teacher named Yang.

2. His *twenty-seven years of Chinese service* are thus summarized in the inscription upon his tomb in the resting-place for the Protestant dead at Macao : "Sacred to the memory of Robert Morrison, D.D., the first Protestant missionary to China, where, after a service of twenty-seven years cheerfully spent in extending the Kingdom of the Blessed Redeemer, during which period he compiled and published a Dictionary of the Chinese Language, founded the Anglo-Chinese College at Malacca, and for several years labored alone on a Chinese version of the Holy Scriptures, which he was spared to see completed and widely circulated among those for whom it was destined, he sweetly slept in Jesus. He was born at Morpeth, in Northumberland, January 5, 1782, was sent to China by the London Missionary Society in 1807, was for twenty-five years Chinese translator in the employ of the East India Company, and died at Canton August 1, 1834."

One must read many things between the lines of this inscription. His service under the Company, besides being a necessity, if he would remain in the Empire instead of laboring on its fringe, as did his early associates, was also the means of securing a liberal salary with which he greatly aided other missionary schemes, the Malacca Anglo-Chinese College in particular. The difficulty of obtaining a teacher was so great that when he secured a Pekingese of the Catholic faith, this man carried about poison with which to commit suicide, if his countrymen detected him in his unlawful employment. Weary and as-

siduous private labors secured Morrison his first convert, Tsai Ako, in 1814, but as he was never suffered
to preach in public, he won only a few during his
entire career.   Schemes of various sorts, calculated
to benefit foreigners and the Chinese, found in him
their cordial supporter, though it must be confessed
that a few of these were somewhat visionary.   While
Morrison possessed none of those charms which made
Ricci so acceptable to the Chinese, unlike the latter,
he never stooped to compromise, but laboriously laid
those strong and deep foundations that have ever
since characterized the work of Protestant missions.
In a word, he was to China very much what Carey
was to India.

War and Missions.—The Protestant beginnings
had been made, but missions at Morrison's death were
greatly hampered.   How were these restrictions to
be removed?   The answer can partly be found in
the Hebrew statement, "The Lord is a man of war,"
and though these wars were in some cases without
justification, He caused good to spring from the evil
doing of men.

1. *The Opium War*, as it is called, grew out of
what the Chinese regarded as an undoubted right
and duty, while the English could with some justice
take the stringent measures employed by them.   The
destruction by the Chinese of 20,283 chests of opium, brought to their shores in foreign bottoms, and
their haughty and unwise conduct accompanying
this action, led to a war lasting from July 5, 1841, to
September 15, 1842, when the Nanking treaty was
ratified.

While much can be said in defence of Britain's
action, and though Queen Victoria's order recites
that "satisfaction and reparation for the late inju-
rious proceedings of certain officers of the Emperor
of China against certain of our officers and subjects
shall be demanded of the Chinese Government,"
still. when the broad issue at stake is considered,
which was the attempt by the Emperor to root out

7

a vice fatal to his people, one can hardly escape the conviction that the war was at once " unjust " and " immoral." Whatever may be the reader's opinion, the Chinese have always looked upon it as a stigma upon the British name and a valid objection against Christianity.

The second article of the treaty granted the *right of residence* in Canton, Amoy, Fu-chow, Ningpo, and Shanghai—a right eagerly embraced by waiting missionary boards—and Hongkong became British territory.   Two years later France and America concluded treaties with China, which included the right to erect houses of worship in the ports.   The French treaty led the way in procuring the revocation of the persecuting edicts of 1724 and later, and the issue of a decree of toleration.   These provisions were partly a dead letter, however, until 1860.   Dr. Williams says of the outcome of this war which opened up part of China to the world: " Looked at in any point of view, political, commercial, moral, or intellectual, it will always be considered as one of the turning-points in the history of mankind, involving the welfare of all nations in its wide-reaching consequences."

2. Though missionaries could now enter strategic cities, it was reserved for a native rebellion to advertise in a general, though unfortunate way, the leading features of Christianity.   The leader of this T'ai P'ing—*Great Peace*—*Rebellion* was a student named Hung Hsin-ch'uan, who had met Liang, one of Milne's converts, and read several tracts composed by that venerable Chinese Christian.   These books, sickness and a series of cataleptic visions, and some instruction from missionaries, notably an American, I. J. Roberts, finally resulted in Hung's beginning a quiet movement of instruction and religious reform. So large a following soon gathered about him that ambition was aroused and he headed a rebellion which rapidly spread until it had reached from the South to within little more than one hundred miles of Peking.   Some of China's fairest provinces were laid

waste, for nearly fifteen years the evils of internal strife scourged the Empire, and fully 20,000,000 of Chinese perished. It was finally crushed out in 1865 by the Imperialists, aided most powerfully by "Chinese Gordon" and his Ever Victorious Army, which owed its origin and early strength to an American named Ward.

This rebellion will appear *most significant* when it is remembered that it was a movement managed by Chinese, the leaders of whom were the student, Hung, and two of his converts who were schoolteachers. Its progress from 1844 to 1851—when it became a rebellion—was promising for Christianity. Hung established communities called Churches of God. "A strictly moral conduct and the keeping of the Sabbath were enjoined on the congregations; all idolatrous practises and the use of opium were forbidden; proffers of union from leaders of the Great Triad Society, pledged to the restoration of a native Chinese dynasty, were rejected." As the movement which Hung and his followers, later called T'ien Kuo —Kingdom of Heaven—developed, however, its leader became emboldened, and gave forth revelations and decrees as from "the Heavenly Father" and "the Heavenly Elder Brother." Gradually the proclamation of salvation by repentance and faith in Jesus, which had given his preaching such power at the first, was abandoned, and worldly ambition and blasphemy greatly increased. Were it not for this fact, the early religious organization of his army and kingdom would have done credit to Cromwell. While the T'ai P'ings are execrated for their deeds of blood, they carried throughout the eastern provinces Christian phrases and some corrupted Christian ideas. The rebellion had shown that a Christian basis could underlie a great movement, and it had brought China's future great statesman, Li Hungchang, into vital touch with the saintly Major Gordon, whose influence upon him and other high officials has never been forgotten.

3. The second war with Great Britain occurred
during the T'ai P'ing Rebellion, and was known as
the "*Arrow War*," because a lorcha bearing that
name and flying the British flag—apparently unlaw-
fully—had been seized by the Chinese and the flag
hauled down. This conflict, which began in 1857,
when Canton was captured, was not finally concluded
until in 1860 war was carried to the very gates of
Peking. The treaties, which were then made with
England, Russia, France, and the United States,
permitted residence and trade in six additional cities
in China and one in Shêng-ching. "It conceded
the right to travel with passports throughout the
eighteen provinces, and contained also a special
clause giving protection to foreigners and natives in
the propagation and adoption of the Christian religion. . . . The moral effect of this war was
very great. The superiority of Western nations, at
least in this one art, could no longer be questioned,
and a much more favorable impression was made by
the moderation, magnanimity, and clemency of the
victors than by their military power." Previous to
this time, William Burns was the only one who syste-
matically disregarded the limitation of evangelization
to the five ports; henceforth every missionary was
free to roam at will throughout the land.

Missionary work could not be permanent if it
could only be carried on through itineration, and except in the ports and at Peking this was all that the
treaties allowed. The additional right of residence
was gained through the French treaty, which, in
Article VI. of the Chinese text, though not in the
French original, which was the final authority, contained this provision : "It is, in addition, permitted
to French missionaries to *rent and purchase land* in
all the provinces, and to erect buildings thereon at
pleasure." Strange to say, the Chinese have never
made serious objection to this most questionable
piece of diplomacy, probably because the clause was
in their own version of the treaty, and so was ac-

cepted consciously by them. The advantage coming to French Catholic missionaries accrued as well to Protestant missionaries of other treaty-making Powers, because of the clause extending to all Powers the advantages granted to the most favored nation; hence every missionary legally possesses the right to secure residences and erect mission buildings where desired.

A new obstacle to missions soon arose from the fact that it was understood that missionaries should first secure the consent of the officials before purchasing property, and that often caused delay or failure. Though the French minister in 1865 obtained a convention making this permission unnecessary, it was not until the French and United States ministers revived the clause thirty years later that it became practically operative.

4. Wars and rumors of war have effected other helpful features in mission work. Thus the *massacre at Tientsin* of twenty French and Russian subjects in 1870, largely as the result of fancied abuses in the orphanage of the Sisters of Charity, led to a concentration of the naval forces of the Powers in the North. War was finally averted, but it gave rise to the first Chinese state paper discussing the difficulties connected with Christian missions, and some of the evils of Catholic mission policy were condemned, with the result that the missionaries of that confession have partly given up their questionable practices. A further result of this threatened war was the use of unexpended military appropriations in establishing the Chinese Educational Commission, under the leadership of a Chinese graduate of Yale, Yung Wing. Though the young men sent to America for education were recalled before they were fully prepared for national service, many bright students, some of whom are in influential positions in China to-day, have personal acquaintance with Christian institutions, and a few of them are earnest Christians.

The threatening attitude of Great Britain because of the *murder of Margary* in 1875 caused the officials to realize the sacredness of the individual life, and most of them are anxious, as never before that event, to protect the missionaries from all violence.

The *French war* of 1883–85 in Tong-king and southern China did more than any other thing to cause the Chinese to distinguish between the Catholic missionaries and the Protestants, a distinction of great importance to Protestantism.

Riots—more than a score of which have occurred in recent years, attended by the death of a few missionaries—have so aroused foreign powers, that increasing vigilance is exercised in the official protection of foreigners. Germany's vigorous action in 1897 because of the murder of German Catholic missionaries, and especially her seizure of Kiao-chou, only increases this solicitude for the missionary's safety.

Stages of Missionary Progress.—While Chinese missionaries have never vitally depended upon the mailed hand of war to lead them into fields of usefulness, their opportunities and efficiency have, nevertheless, very largely expanded with the power and influence of the secular arm. Hence epochs of missionary progress correspond partially with the events just outlined.

1. The first stage was preparatory in character, and extended from Morrison's arrival in 1807 to the Treaty of Nanking in 1842.

Preparatory *efforts within the Empire* were these : The publication of a dictionary and grammar ; the translation of the entire Bible, published in 1818 ; the composition of several valuable tracts, notable among which is the very popular and useful one by Milne, entitled "The Two Friends" ; the opening of China to medical missions by Dr. Peter Parker, who was her first great medical missionary ; the establishment of the American Board's Mission Press by S. Wells Williams ; and the founding of the *Chinese*

Repository, which to the present time, though under a different name, has done so much to acquaint the Christian world with China.

Most of the workers during this period labored *outside China Proper,* in the Malay Peninsula and on adjacent islands, where Chinese colonists were found in great numbers, and where access to them was possible. Preaching, tract and Scripture distribution, the preparation of books and periodicals in English and Chinese, and education, of a primary character mostly, though the Anglo-Chinese College, founded at Malacca in 1818, did excellent work, were the lines followed. Gützlaff and Medhurst were especially zealous in their efforts to distribute books and preach along the coast. The former reached Tientsin even, while Medhurst went as far as Shan-tung. Williams desired to enter Japan through some shipwrecked Japanese. Though this was not possible, some of them were converted, and he prepared in their tongue a translation of Genesis and Matthew.

By 1842 these *results* were evident : Three British societies and four American organizations had some twenty representatives in the Empire and in the Chinese colonies adjacent. Macao, Canton, Hongkong and Amoy had had for a longer or shorter time resident missionaries, and six converts constituted the entire Protestant Chinese church.

2. From 1842 to 1860 constitutes the *years of entrance,* though very little could yet be done outside the treaty ports.

The *field of labor* included the populous cities of Canton, Amoy, Fu-chou, Ningpo, and Shanghai. While the vices of the West came in with commerce, these cities were *entrepôts* of extensive districts, and hence were strategic. Hongkong, being under British control, was also a very important centre of missionary effort at this time.

The *nature of the work* was now somewhat broader. Revised translations of the Bible, and new and better Christian literature were steps forward. Though

STATISTICS OF PROTESTANT MISSIONS IN CHINA, 1898.

NAME OF SOCIETY.	Year of entrance.	Ordained missionaries.	Laymen.	Missionaries' wives.	Unmarried women.	Number of these who are male physicians.	Number of these who are female physicians.	Total foreign workers.	Native laborers of both sexes.	Number of stations.	Out stations.	Communicants.	Number of day schools.	Number of pupils.	Higher educational institutions.	Number of students.	Total in schools.
I. American Societies.																	
American Board	1830	36	11	42	23	12	4	112	329	15	116	3,740	122	2,276	19	696	2,962
American Baptist Missionary Union	1834	24	7	32	15	5	1	76	135	14	77	2,238	34	573	1	8	681
Protestant Episcopal Board	1835	14	3	10	4	3	..	31	97	5	45	1,134	54	1,239	1	337	1,576
Presbyterian Board (North)	1838	58	18	68	40	16	.9	184	527	19	304	8,317	201	2,490	11	685	3,125
Reformed Church in America	1842	5	..	4	8	1	..	17	45	3	33	1,304	15	264	8	265	529
Methodist Episcopal Church (North)	1847	41	9	48	54	12	12	152	696	15	180	20,326	474	6,623	22	1,206	7,829
Seventh-Day Baptist	1847	1	..	1	2	..	..	4	5	1	1	55	2	58	2	32	90
Southern Baptist Convention	1847	15	1	15	10	..	2	40	43	10	50	1,499	31	516	2	..	516
Methodist Episcopal Church (South)	1848	13	..	12	9	3	2	44	62	6	18	751	58	1,310	.6	552	1,862
Presbyterian Church (South)	1867	21	8	23	14	6	5	66	53	11	6	370	18	300	1	..	300
Woman's Union Missionary Society	1859	..	..	..	18	..	1	18	13	1	..	..	6	..	1	..	..
Presbyterian Church, Canada	1871	.9	.2	5	2	..	..	6	87	2	4	9	..	..	..	..	..
American Bible Society	1876	1	5	..	..	..	2	24	8	4	6	204	7	113	2	48	161
Foreign Christian Missionary Society	1886	9	..	10	3	1	..	10	..	5	6	19	..	..	..	..	..
Christian and Missionary Alliance	1888	5	53	28	35	1	..	121	18	34	1	1	4	148	1	..	143
United Brethren in Christ	1889	3	3	2	3	1	2	10	..	1	1	1	..	..	..	..	..
Swedish-American Mission	1890	3	..	1	..	..	..	*5	18	1	..	50	6	100	1	..	100
American Friends' Board	1891	1	..	..	.6	..	..	*6	.7	1	..	10	.6	100	..	..	..
Methodist Episcopal Church, Canada	1891	6	3	3	..	3	.2	6	..	2	.2	..	..	..	..	..	..
Gospel Baptist Mission	1892	8	..	3	1	..	..	12	..	.3	..	..	..	..	..	..	..
Y. M. C. A. in Foreign Lands	1895	.2	.3	3	..	.3	..	6	..	1	..	..	..	..	..	..	..
Reformed Presbyterians	1896	1	..	2	..	..	..	4	..	1	..	..	..	..	..	..	..
Cumberland Presbyterian	1897	1	1	1	..	1	..	3	..	1	..	..	..	..	..	..	..

Society	Year																
London Missionary Society	1807	45	3	36	24	12	3	108	291	16	140	7,097	117	2,580	…	…	2,530
British Bible Society	1836	4	11	12	…	…	…	27	270	10	…	…	17	400	…	…	…
Female Education Society	1837	40	23	43	6	12	…	6	16	2	8	…	250	3,823	…	…	400
Church Missionary Society	1845	12	6	60	6	12	1	166	510	26	122	4,911	250	3,823	6	62	3,885
English Presbyterians	1847	13	…	18	18	3	1	48	112	18	37	3,790	31	174	5	44	218
Wesleyan Missionary Society||	1852	26	…	18	7	1	…	30	129	…	2·7	4,088	31	896	4	…	896
Baptist Missionary Society	1859	…	7	…	3	1	…	51	188	6	94	2,125	2·7	1,128	…	…	1,128
Methodist New Connection	1860	10	12	10	2	2	…	14	92	6	94	2,125	37	489	2	41	580
Scotch United Presbyterian	1862	4	7	7	5	5	4	36	158	4	63	5,183	55	652	…	…	652
Scotch Bible Society	1863	8	…	…	…	…	…	16	170	6	…	…	…	…	…	…	…
Society for Propagation of the Gospel	1863	4	…	5	5	2	1	17	7	2	…	400	14	77	…	…	95
Methodist Free Church‡	1864	8	7	3	3	4	…	9	63	7	49	996	5	77	1	18	127
Irish Presbyterians	1867	4	3	4	4	1	1	23	105	2	49	911	11	127	…	…	127
Church of Scotland	1878	2	…	3	3	1	…	9	12	7	3	110	3	150	…	…	150
Zenana Missionary Society	1884	…	…	37	37	…	1	37	25	1	…	…	2	…	…	…	…
Bible Christians†	1885	7	4	3	3	1	…	14	4	3	3	28	2	70	…	…	70
Friends' F. M. Association	1886	6	5	3	3	1	…	14	7	2	3	5	2	162	…	…	162
British Totals		174	85	166	183	50	12	625	2,159	133	866	29,644	547	10,678	18	165	10,843

III. CONTINENTAL SOCIETIES.

Society	Year																
Basel Missionary Society	1847	21	2	13	…	1	…	36	127	13	49	3,000	47	1,121	2	55	1,176
Rhenish Missionary Society	1847	9	2	6	2	2	…	19	10	5	8	375	4	66	2	8	74
Berlin Woman's China Society§	1856	1	1	4	4	…	…	6	…	1	…	…	…	…	…	…	…
Berlin Missionary Society*	1882	3	2	…	…	2	…	6	50	5	29	479	18	270	5	81	351
Gen'l Evang. Prot. Mis. Ass'n‡	1885	1	…	…	…	…	…	3	…	1	…	…	…	…	…	…	…
Swedish Mission†	1887	8	8	14	14	2	…	29	14	4	60	60	4	82	…	…	82
Congregational Church of Sweden‡	1890	…	9	4	4	…	…	13	…	2	…	9	3	…	…	…	…
German China Alliance†	1891	…	2	5	5	2	…	16	4	6	3	45	…	32	…	…	…
Norwegian Lutheran	1891	1	1	2	2	1	…	8	…	3	3	25	3	…	…	…	…
Danish Mission Society	1892	5	2	2	2	1	…	9	7	3	2	4	…	…	…	…	…
Continental Totals		52	28	32	33	5	…	145	205	43	91	3,997	79	1,539	9	144	1,683

IV. INTERNATIONAL SOCIETIES.

Society	Year																
China Inland Mission	1865	30	296	176	274	16	1	776	605	149	169	7,147	114	1,589	3	137	1,726
Chinese Blind Mission§	1887	1	1	1	…	1	…	2	…	1	…	…	…	…	1	20	20
Diffusion of Christian Knowledge	1887	1	…	1	…	…	…	2	…	1	…	…	…	…	…	…	…
International Totals		32	296	178	274	16	1	780	605	151	169	7,147	114	1,589	4	157	1,546
Totals of all Societies		534	535	686	746	139	56	2,517	5,093	482	1,975	80,815	1,772	30,116	105	4,425	34,401
Less statistics inserted twice‡		8	17	12	22	3	…	59	22	13	6	133	6	70	…	…	70
Net Totals for China		526	518	674	724	136	56	2,458	5,071	469	1,969	80,682	1,766	30,046	105	4,285	34,331

* Totals correct, though not fully explained. † These societies associated with China Inland Mission. ‡ Statistics from "China Mission Handbook," 1896. § Dean Vahl's "Missions to the Heathen," 1897. || Society's Report for 1896; it includes statistics of missionaries only of the Central China Lay Mission and of the Joyful News Mission.

evangelization was nominally permitted, it was a difficult process. One of the missionaries, Dr. Ashmore, says of it : " We were mobbed in the fu city, mobbed in the district cities, mobbed in the large towns. We got so used to being pelted with mud and gravel and bits of broken pottery that things seemed strange if we escaped the regular dose. . . . We went out from our homes bedewed with the tears and benedictions of dear ones, and we came back plastered over, metaphorically speaking, with curses and objurgations from top to bottom. . . . It went badly with our chapels that we rented. They were often assailed ; roofs were broken up, doors were battered in, and furniture was carried off. There was nothing else to do but to keep at it. Driven out of one place, we betook ourselves to another, according to instructions. But we did not leave the country as the literati desired, and we did not intend to. We wore them out, as an anvil sometimes wears out a hammer."

Converts of such troublous times were naturally men of strong convictions, and though usually ignorant, they bravely endured the anathemas and petty persecutions of neighbors and nearest friends. Isolated and ostracized, they clung with tenacious grip to the truth, and the grace of God did not fail them.

The *missionaries* were for the same reason men and women of great strength of character, and were perforce of the heroic mould. During these years Protestantism's fiercest battles over the "Term Question " were waged. In lieu of any clear conception and name for God among the Chinese, the missionaries, like the Romanists of early days, strenuously advocated the use of whichever of the terms, Shang Ti, T'ien Chu, Shên, etc., seemed to them least open to objection and most honoring to Jehovah. Though this controversy practically died away soon after, it is still a dangerous topic to introduce in a missionary gathering.

Tangible results were not numerous. Though the

word of truth had sounded forth from the missionary centres into the four populous littoral provinces of Kuang-tung, Fu-chien, Chê-chiang, and Chiang-su, and though the boards had increased from seven to nineteen, with some 160 missionaries, each of them could on an average point to only six converts as the reward of his self-denying toil. Judged by other than statistical standards, these years were very fruitful in many directions.

3. Seventeen years intervened between 1860 and the first great missionary conference of China, which met at Shanghai in 1877. They were years of *development and wider entrance* into new fields. Carstairs Douglas could report at the conference that Chih-li, Shan-tung, An-hui, Chiang-hsi, Hu-pei, and Shêng-ching, or Southern Manchuria, had been occupied ; but of the nine provinces still unentered, only the merest Protestant beginning had been made, and darkness still reigned, except for the flickering and smoking lights of Catholicism.

Some of the *advances noted* are the wide development of educational and medical work, the practical inauguration of woman's work, which had only been begun in the previous period, the establishment of several strong churches in place of the isolation of believers in the earlier days, and above all the establishment of the China Inland Mission in 1865. Its emphasis of inland occupation and new fields was of the utmost importance to the Empire, though naturally pioneering and evangelistic work are not statistically so successful as older and more diversified labors.

Some of the statistics of the 1877 conference are worth repeating. Missionaries resided at ninety-one centres, had organized three hundred and twelve churches, and Chinese communicants numbered 13,-035. In all, twenty-nine societies—twelve American, fifteen British, and two Continental—were on the field, with four hundred and seventy-three missionaries, including seven unconnected.

4. Thirteen years more elapsed before the missionaries again gathered at the Second Shanghai Conference of 1890. The communion of missionaries of different denominations and sections, and the free interchange of views in 1877, were most helpful. *Two key-words* of that gathering were systematic co-operation and the earnest appeal for more laborers. In both these directions gratifying progress was made.

Two additional features of the period should likewise be mentioned. *Famines*, particularly that of 1877–78, gave foreigners and the missionaries, both Catholic and Protestant, who were their almoners, an opportunity to show their love to those who had hitherto been their enemies. In the years 1877-78 it is estimated that from " nine and a half to thirteen millions " perished, mainly in the three northern provinces of Shan-tung, Shan-hsi, and Shen-hsi. Foreigners contributed nearly half a million dollars toward their relief, and of those personally engaged in distributing aid four died from exposure and overwork. Naturally distrust and opposition gave way before the good-will, affection, and gratitude evoked by this charitable beneficence. But while doors were thus opened and many were won thereby, it gave to the Church some who entered it for motives of gratitude or cupidity, and hence gave rise to a form of the old " rice Christian " problem. Primarily for this reason, but largely as a result of the enlargement of the native church, the question of *self-support* came to the front during this period.

The 1890 *statistics* revealed these facts among many others : The twenty-nine societies of 1877 had become forty-two, and the missionaries numbered 1,296, an increase of nearly three-fold. A striking advance in the number of women missionaries was noted. " In 1877 they formed little over one-eighth of the whole force ; in 1890 they were nearly one-fourth the entire number, showing the rapid development in the work of women for women." Native communicants numbered 37,287, an increase of about

one hundred per cent. for each four years since 1877.
Among the natives 522 organized churches existed,
and 1,657 Chinese were engaged in Christian work.
Education was fitting for Christian usefulness 16,836
Chinese children and youths.

5. *The eight years since* the last conference have
been largely lived in the inspiration and strength
arising from that gathering. The Union Bible in
three different literary styles, which was decided on
then, "after forty years of separation," and which
caused the delegates to rise and sing the Doxology
when the report was presented, is proceeding rapidly,
as is the work of the Committee to prepare an anno-
tated Bible. The four appeals issued by that body
came like a bugle-call to Christendom, and have met
with a fair response. Though their request for 1,000
men within five years was not quite responded to,
in that only 481 of the 1,153 missionaries who entered
the Empire during that period were males, God saw
what was needed, and the appeal of the women was
more than met, 672 having reached China. The
fuller discussion of methods by persons from so many
centres has given rise to more thoughtful work, and
the deepening of the spiritual life has never before
received such emphasis as within the past eight years.

Other characteristics of this period are these : The
missionary entrance into Hu-nan, the last and most
hostile province of the Empire ; the various attempts
to snuff out by mob violence Chinese missions ; the
sifting of the Church by the fires of a persecution
which has led to the death of a few missionaries, but
which has also wonderfully enlarged its membership ;
the necessity laid upon congregations unwilling to do
their duty in the matter of self-support, because of
the financial depression in the home lands, thus leading to greater independence ; the possession of the
field by two organizations that had previously only
been initiated, viz., the Young People's Societies and
the National organization of the Young Men's Christian Association among students ; the Chinese En-

deavor Conventions, and four conferences held by
Mr. J. R. Mott and others in the fall of 1896, attended
by 2,883 delegates, among whom were 999 Chinese
students ; the presentation to the Empress Dowager
in 1894 by the Christian women of China of a magnificent copy of the New Testament, one of the most
costly single volumes ever printed ; the consequent
purchase by the Emperor of copies of the Scripture
and many other religious and scientific books ; the
presentation to the Emperor in November, 1895, of
a Protestant Memorial, in connection with which a
full discussion of Protestant missionaries' aims and
methods was had with the Tsung-li Ya-mên ; and
the use of the Bible in one case as the basis of a question asked in one of the government examinations.
Such events are a foreshadowing, perhaps, of the
period prophesied by Dr. Martin, " when the Church
of Christ shall be favored by the Imperial power as
the best, if not the only hope of national regeneration."

Missionary Geography.—A study of the accompanying map will indicate the present distribution
of the missionary force. It should be said, by way of
explanation, that this is a distinctively missionary
map, and for the sake of clearness very few cities
have been entered upon it which do not contain
resident missioners. The few cities not containing
missionaries are easily distinguished by the style of
type used. It should also be noted that a number of
stations occupied by missionaries are not found on
the map, as their location could not be determined
by the compiler, and in most cases the board did not
know their situation.

1. *Every province* has been entered, though Hu-
nan has only one station, and the missionaries there
are so persecuted that for a time it may be that itineration will be the best method of accustoming the
hostile gentry to the foreigner's presence among
them. Shan-hsi has the largest number of mission
stations, both absolutely and in proportion to the

number of square miles ; but even here each station
would have 1,285 square miles of territory to care
for, if they were equally distributed. It is as if only
one town in Rhode Island contained a church, whose
pastor and members were responsible for the evangelization of the entire State and a considerable fringe
of Connecticut besides. Hu-nan's one station has
territory equivalent to that of Maryland and the two
Virginias to cover ; while Kan-su has but one station
to 10,454 square miles, Kuei-chou, one to 12,911
square miles, Yün-nan, one to 17,995 square miles,
and Kuang-hsi, one to 19,562 square miles. Surely the territory is not yet occupied for Jesus Christ,
and there is still much land to be possessed.

2. The *character of the places occupied* by missionaries should be noted. They are marked to indicate
their rank as fu cities, tings, chous, and hsiens.
These and the provincial capitals are all walled cities,
and 247 of them are marked on the map as being
mission stations. Yet in the eighteen provinces
there are 1,746 such walled cities, including Formosa ; hence about one-seventh of these important
centres of life have foreign missionaries resident
within their walls. When it is recalled that these
cities are deemed influential in the order of hsien,
chou, ting, fu and provincial capital, and that in
them are held the examinations for all but the highest degree, thus assembling in them toward a million students each year, their occupancy is manifestly
called for.

Yet the *smaller towns*, which are missionary residences to the number of eighty-eight, are usually
chosen because of an especially inviting opening, and
so are often more fruitful than larger places.

3. As the provinces on the map have been colored
to indicate *density of population*, it will be seen that
stations are planted without reference to this fact,
for the reason that the force is still so small in proportion to the population and size of territory that
this factor has not needed to be considered. Yet in

general the littoral and Yang-tzŭ provinces, where population is most dense, are fairly well cared for, Hu-nan excepted. Future operations in the Empire will doubtless have regard for this important factor of density where accessibility coincides with populousness.

4. *Unoccupied territory* is everywhere found, even where stations are most numerous. Thus in the district that the writer labored in, of the more than six hundred towns and villages properly belonging to his station's field, probably not more than one-third had ever been visited by preachers. A glance at the map will show what provinces and parts of provinces are least able to reach Christian books and the servants of Christ. Hu-nan, Kuang-hsi, Kuei-chou, Yünnan, and large sections of Ssŭ-ch'nan are very remote from the bearers of truth.

Some Statistics.—Those found on pages 104, 105 are as accurate as any of recent date, though it has been impossible to get returns from all societies, and so such data as was obtainable from earlier reports have been used. Those taken from the 1896 edition of the "China Mission Hand-book" are mainly for the year 1893 ; hence the totals are too small.

1. It will be seen that fifty-three *organizations* have their representatives in China. Had those women's and other societies, working in co-operation with boards whose names are mentioned, been entered, the number would be still larger, of course. Twenty-three of the societies listed are American, including Canada, seventeen are British, ten are Continental societies, and three are international—*i. e.*, receive their support and missionaries from more than one country. The only one of importance is the China Inland Mission, mainly British, but having in its membership 112 sent out from America, besides a number from the Continent.

2. *The force* sent out by all these organizations numbers 2,458 missionaries, of whom 967 belong to American societies, 625 to British organizations, 145

are Continentals, and 780 are members of international societies. It should be said that an injustice is done all national totals, save the American, in this enumeration, since they are the only ones that, without exception, mention the entire force, including wives of missionaries, as some European societies do not.

So far as given, 526 of these, or 21.5 per cent., were ordained ; 518, or 21.2 per cent., were laymen ; 674, or 27.6 per cent., were wives of missionaries, and 724, or 29.7 per cent., were unmarried women. A medical force was reported of 192, of whom 136 were men and 56 women. A native contingent of 5,071 faithful Chinese men and women were engaged in various forms of Christian activity. With the missionaries added, the entire Protestant working force numbers 7,529, an average of one worker to every 51,701 of China's population. If foreign workers are alone considered, each man and woman has a parish to care for of 158,362 souls !

3. These agents are located at 335 *main stations,* whence they go forth to regular appointments at 1,969 outstations, not to mention the far larger number of cities and villages where the gospel has been proclaimed, but which are not reported in the statistics. As a result of these efforts, 80,682 converts are found in Protestant churches, an average of one Christian to 4,824 of his fellow-countrymen. Connected with these centres of light are 1,766 day-schools with 30,046 boys and girls under Christian instruction, and 105 institutions of higher learning attended by 4,285 young men and women. This total of 34,331 under instruction is a most hopeful feature in Chinese work, and if those who attend station-classes or who are taught at their homes by Bible women and missionaries were added, the results accomplished through teaching would be still more gratifying.

Additional Agencies.—In the tables no place has been given to organizations which do not commis-

8

sion special foreign agents to do their work in the
Empire, but which do a most important work for the
people.

1. First among these efforts may be placed the aid
furnished by the *Tract Societies* of the West, which
nobly co-operate with the Tract Societies of China.
The main societies working in the Empire are the
North China Tract Society, with Peking as its head-
quarters, the Chinese Tract Society of Shanghai,
the Central China Religious Tract Society of Han-
k'ou, the North Fuhkien Tract Society of Fu-chou,
and the Kiukiang Tract Society. Aided by the
American Tract Society and the Religious Tract Society of London, they are yearly issuing myriads of
tracts adapted to the dialects of the regions occupied, besides periodicals of great value in mission
work. Most of these sell their product to the natives at a greatly reduced price, or even donate
them where thought desirable.

The Society for the Diffusion of Christian and
General Knowledge has a somewhat different object
in view. Its publications are intended for general
enlightenment and for the higher classes not reached
by ordinary efforts. The books and periodicals are
accordingly more apologetic and scientific in character than those of the Tract Societies, and are usually
sold at cost price.

Book-lending Societies among the native Christians
are intended to make these publications accessible to
hitherto unreached classes, such as school-teachers,
local officials, and gentry. Calls and conversation
lead to the loan of books, and this gives opportunity
to call again, extend the acquaintance, and make clear
what is misunderstood.

2. The *mission presses* have been most potent
agencies for good, from the first one established by
Drs. Morrison and Milne of the London Mission,
down to the latest one set up. They have not only
furnished valuable books, but have taught China
how to print in modern style and by more economical

methods. The two largest, and among the most important mission presses of the world, are those of the American Presbyterians at Shanghai and of the American Methodists at Fu-chou. Other most helpful ones are the American Board's at Peking, the Church Missionary Society's at Ningpo, the English Presbyterians' at Swatau, the National Bible Society of Scotland's at Han-k'ou, the Methodist Central China Press at Kiukiang, that of the China Island Mission at T'ai-chou, and smaller establishments at Peking—belonging to the S. P. G. Mission and the American Methodists—one at Nodoa in Hai-nan, and another at Mukden in Shêng-ching.

THE MISSIONARIES AT WORK

MISSIONARIES soon find the need of versatility, since one must be all things to all men as occasion requires. Even sex distinctions are often overlooked, and the woman preaches to men as well as to her sisters. In general, however, women devote themselves to educational work and evangelism of the house-to-house and less public sort, while a small proportion of them are physicians or devote themselves to the preparation of literature. In the brief summary following, it is understood that women adapt the methods mentioned to their special constituency, rather than adopt entirely different methods.

The Human Agent in Missions.—As much depends upon him, humanly speaking, it is manifest that self-culture must occupy much of his time.

1. The possibilities of error in a monosyllabic *language*, with its important tonal distinctions, are so great and vital that missionaries in no other country need to be so conscientious and thorough as those in China in their language study. One can readily prepare himself to be misunderstood in a few months; few, except physicians, can so far master Chinese as to do satisfactory work in less than a year or a year and a half, and none will be so foolish as to ever cease delving at the language.

2. Meanwhile the missionary can be *useful in other ways*. If stationed with colleagues, he can relieve them of many secular details, such as the care of the premises, the station treasurership in some cases, and after a few months he can have general charge of the station book-room. He can also be

useful in drawing a crowd for native preachers, if he sings or is willing to be a "sign-board," which in new regions is tantamount to being a menagerie for the curious, gaping crowd. But he can be something more ; for with the help of one's teacher a brief sermonette can be prepared and memorized, and this may be repeated indefinitely and added to from day to day.

3. A still more vital matter is *preparation of heart*, which is of the utmost importance in a spiritual work of such difficulty. The hours spent in Bible study, meditation, and prayer will be found a most profitable investment. Daily conduct must be watched with the utmost care, since the Chinese have been trained to imitate their teachers, and native Christians follow the national habit.

4. During these early months the missionary will devote as much time to the *study of the people* as to the language, perhaps. Books will aid in this, but a loquacious teacher or trusted Christian, and constant observation and inquiry, will do more still.

Efforts for China's Physical Alleviation.— 1. *Medicine* has been the wedge used to open doors of hundreds of unfriendly homes. From the first moment of his arrival, the physician is most useful, and though the natives may not realize the priceless worth of the gospel message, release from pain, and from many diseases which Chinese practitioners cannot heal, is appreciated most gratefully. An iron will is needed to make physicians take time to learn anything more than the vocabulary required by professional demands ; for this reason and because of heavy clinics, doctors are always tempted to leave to others the ministration to soul-needs.

While dispensaries are far more common than hospitals, the latter are apt to yield more encouraging spiritual results. Leisure to learn through oral instruction the gist of the gospel is there afforded, and hundreds have also embraced the opportunity to learn to read, through the medium of Christian tracts, which are carried later to their homes as a silent leaven.

The Chinese have a proverb that a woman cannot avoid the doctor and her husband ; yet in spite of this unwilling consent, *women physicians* are gladly welcomed by Chinese women for themselves and children.   Very many invitations to visit homes come from this source.

2. *Famine relief,* as we have seen, is a conciliating agency of great value.   Seldom are missionaries called upon to distribute aid in the afflicted districts, but frequently refugees from local famines come to the mission compound.   This is a favorable opportunity for gaining friends, but it involves one in many per-plexities arising from their willingness to continue in dependence upon the foreigner, and " rice Chris-tians " are apt to be the fruitage of such efforts.

3. *Reforms* of a thousand kinds await the Church of the future in China ; but seductive as is their ap-peal to the missionary, only two thus far have re-ceived much attention.   The *opium curse,* which so threatens China's life, fills the great cities with thin-faced, wretchedly ragged victims.   Naturally opium refuges have been extensively opened, in spite of the fact that so few, who are enabled to give up the drug, persist in their determination after leaving the refuge.

Far more hopeful is the attempt to induce women of the Church to abandon the cruel custom of *foot-binding.*   While comparatively few of them have been willing to unbind their own feet and thus un-dergo once more an agony little less severe than that of their childhood, very many have unbound those of their daughters.   Persistent agitation has led to the formation of native anti-foot-binding societies, and Chinese Christian scholars have written some litera-ture upon its evils.

4. *Defectives* have scarcely been touched thus far by Protestant missionaries.   Mr. Murray in Peking has elaborated a system for teaching *the blind* to read,

and the extreme ease of learning the art has caused it to be adapted for sight readers. He has, also, a sort of blind asylum there, and another school has been opened in the heart of the Empire. A very small beginning has been made in Shan-tung in the direction of instructing *deaf mutes*, but they are so few compared with the many blind that little emphasis is laid upon this effort. Thus far not a single *insane* asylum has been attempted, though it has been strongly agitated by the missionaries in the South.

An excellent *foundling asylum* is conducted at Hongkong by the Berlin ladies, and other less extensive ones are found here and there among the other missions.

Educational Work.—While evangelistic work almost always precedes any other variety of effort, and though it always has the pre-eminence, education in one form or another soon becomes a strategic necessity which most boards recognize.

1. *Day-schools*, usually for pupils of one sex—though sometimes mixed schools are opened for very young children—are the commonest sort of educational institutions. Boys and girls, mainly from poor Christian families, whose parents could not afford to have them go to an ordinary school, make very rapid progress in their studies, thanks to a rational system of instruction and to heredity. Reading, writing, and a beginning in Western learning are imparted, but the staple of instruction is the Bible. Hundreds of pupils in day-schools memorize the gospels, and many the entire New Testament. Better still, they are taught to look upon it as a divine seed, and in many a child's heart it has germinated and brought forth fruit in heathen court-yards.

In some of these schools the pupils need to be induced to come by the gift of a few cash, picture-cards, etc., but in older communities Christians so much appreciate them, that their partial or entire *support* is often obtained. Native teachers, many of them trained in mission schools of a higher grade, are usually in charge, though foreign supervision is always helpful.

2. *Boarding-schools* are attended by a comparatively few picked students; but the close contact with the missionaries, and with a community of Christians isolated from the heathen mass, has been an inestimable benefit to the leaders of the Church, who would otherwise have had no definite conception of what Christianity can effect in associated life. This advantage more than offsets the objection that a hot-house atmosphere, which unfits them for sterner experiences of service, is the penalty of such schools. These institutions are especially valuable for the young women, the future wives and mothers of the Christian community, who there learn lessons in home-making that will prove invaluable.

The studies pursued in such schools are disappointingly limited in range in the opinion of the newly arrived foreigner; yet in many cases they are such as are best adapted to the peculiar needs of the Chinese. Ancient and modern languages—except English along the coast and in the ports—are not worth learning, as dense ignorance on more vital topics exists, and the study of their own Classics is indispensable as an element of Chinese culture, and as a mental discipline is almost as valuable as Greek and Latin to the student of the West.

3. Comparatively few genuine *colleges* exist. Yet the pressing need of the near future is that of a body of well-trained natives who can enter the vast fields opening to the civil engineer, the mining expert, the electrician, and the topographical engineer. Astronomy and mathematics, which have previously been desired, must also be taught. It can be said with perfect truth that thus far the missionaries have been China's best, and almost only, instructors, and in the higher institutions students are being trained who receive a moral education second to that imparted in no Western college, and a mental develop-

ment that compares favorably with that of our students.

The Chinese are settling for themselves the mooted question of *English study*. The new demand for a knowledge of our language has drawn to mission colleges young men of a higher social standing than have ordinarily been reached, and they have gladly paid the required fees. As a mere matter of acquiring knowledge, more accurate information could be gained through Chinese, and in a far less time than is necessary when English is the medium of instruction. But the question of keeping up with the progress in the sciences is a most serious one, if Chinese text-books and periodicals are the sole dependences. Moreover, English is the only possibility of communicating with most Western merchants and promoters of various sorts, and as pidgin English is wofully meagre, a full-fledged variety is a necessity. Thus far the chief difficulty connected with its study has been the fact that English-speaking compradores, etc., are in such demand that students are drafted off as soon as they get a fair command of the tongue, and often fall before the temptation to "squeeze" the foreigner. With few honorable exceptions, such men are of little use to the native church thereafter.

Another charge brought against English instruction and Western education in general is that so much time is required for such studies that the student cannot acquire his own classical language, thus failing to have influence as a writer over the powerful literary element of the Empire. Yet, if Western ideas are modified enough to permit the memorization of the Classics, in part at least, and of study aloud, so that tones can be corrected by the teacher, it is quite possible for the student, aided by modern ideas of education, to gain much knowledge from the West, as well as Chinese culture, in the same number of years required for taking the Chinese degrees.

4. *Industrial education* has its advocates in some missions, both as a means of discipline and as a preparation for usefulness and self-support in later life. It has its value, also, in ennobling the native conception of labor and in living down the current conviction that the moment the scholar's gown is donned the finger-nails may grow and no manual labor be undertaken—a curse of China's present situation. The growing demand for technical schools will also aid in this direction.

5. *Education for Christian service* is an endeavor that even those boards approve of which do not encourage a general educational work. *Station-classes* for men and women—separate, of course—bring together for a few weeks or months, usually in the winter season, when people are least busy, a company of interested Christians or inquirers anxious to be fitted for usefulness in their homes. It is a rare privilege to have in charge such a class. Some are stupid, but all are eager learners ; for, as they often say, " This is heaven," and such heavenly privileges are never undervalued or misimproved. Hundreds every year gain information and inspiration in these classes that enable them to stand alone in the midst of persecution, and become a savor of life unto life among unbelieving multitudes.

The few *theological schools* established attempt to do more thoroughly for chosen young men of the Church what station-classes accomplish for the uneducated many in more advanced life. Though Formosa missions must now be considered as belonging to Japan, Dr. Mackay's class of theological students receive there a training as nearly ideal as can be found for Chinese helpers. On the Chinese mainland seminary students are most thoroughly educated in all that pertains to the work of evangelization and the regular ministry, and in these institutions are men some of whom have mastered the contents and drunk in the spirit of the Bible as no seminary students of the Occident have done.

Literature in Chinese Missions.—As no other missionary country honors literature so highly as China, so literary work has had a correspondingly large amount of attention given it.

1. *The preparation of literature* of every variety, Bibles, religious treatises, educational works, and periodicals both secular and religious, has fallen almost entirely on the shoulders of missionaries, as did, in the earlier days, the writing of philological works. Many have become authors who have no gifts in that direction, but it is probably true that no country has had so large a number of competent translators and authors as China. Bible translators, like Morrison, Medhurst, Bridgman, Blodget, Burdon, and Schereschewsky, and the present Committees working on revised versions, are men to be grateful for, even if some of the earlier generation aimed at perspicuity and elegance of diction, rather than at rigid faithfulness in translating the sometimes ambiguous, and to the Chinese, distasteful statements of the Scripture writers. Milne was the forerunner of authors like Burns, Martin, and Griffith John, who could so sink themselves in the Chinese environment and "get their stomachs so full" of choice and attractive forms of expression, that the Chinese read on in spite of themselves, after once tasting the "flavor" of their writings. Mateer, Sheffield, Hunter, and other missionaries have rendered a hardly less important service in text-book preparation than those in government employ, like Edkins, and Fryer; while Faber and Legge have done invaluable work in making Chinese writings accessible to the Western reader. Yates, Allen, and Richard are a few missionaries among many who have made the periodical literature of China an agency of illumination and regeneration.

2. The *manufacture* of books is an effort which mission presses have undertaken in spite of the fact that this meant competition with thousands of native presses, the entire outfit of almost any one of which might be packed in a hand-satchel. The experiment

of Pi, made nearly 900 years ago, has become effective in the elegant movable type of to-day, and though the mission-press compositor may be bewildered at first as he stands, like a man in a museum, in the midst of the 6,000 and more compartments of his gigantic type-cases, he can far outstrip the block-cutter, both in speed of composition and beauty of type.   Native firms have adopted the idea of photo-engraving and reproduce at a low price volumes formerly inaccessible, as well as pirate recent missionary productions, thus underselling the works of foreign presses.   Though the production of mission presses is very large, yet this is but a foretaste of the demands to be laid upon them and upon authors in the awakening that is now beginning.

3.   Practically every Protestant missionary and native Christian worker in China aids in the *distribution of this literature.*   Inquirers are taught to read through books ; schools and training-classes cannot exist without them ; and they are the best and almost only agency through which to reach the gentry and officials of the Empire, from local Nicodemuses, to the occupant of the Dragon Throne.   Missionaries and colporteurs sell books or judiciously loan or give them away in chapels and tea-shops, at fairs and near the gates of government examination-halls.   Books are a legitimate excuse for the foreigner's presence in a hostile district, and the native Book-lending Societies of the South gain an entrance for Christian truth by their means into country schools and the homes of grandees.

Evangelistic Work.—Highly as the missionary esteems efforts for the bodily and mental well-being of men, he never forgets that his primary object is to preach the gospel of an all-powerful Saviour, and a loving Father in heaven.   This is the thread of scarlet that runs through the web of his royal weaving.

1.   Perhaps the most profitable efforts on the China field are those in which the missionary labors with individuals, as did Jesus at the Samaritan well.   When

masses are addressed, one cannot tell whether the strange message is understood ; but let one sit down and talk with a man, as to a brother, and not only are misunderstandings cleared away, but a personal relation of friendliness and respect is established. It is this *private work* that gives one an opportunity with men of the higher classes, and in general it is so profitable that Romanists confine themselves almost entirely to it, encouraging converts to bring such inquirers to them.

Timid *women of the better classes* can often be reached through visits at the missionary lady's home. It is a curious, new world to the visitor, and in a life with very few outings it forms the staple of conversation in her home for months after. Christian women also grow much in their spiritual life through personal visits at the mission compound. Mothers' meetings are a more public form of the same beautiful and helpful service. Colored Scripture pictures are very useful in such a connection, and many have been placed in the homes of women otherwise inaccessible to Christianity.

2. If most of the work thus far described resembles that done in missions at home, *chapel preaching* presents some unique features. These buildings are usually rented shops, located on a frequented city street, and open to all comers. Though the place is a cheerless one, and provided with rude, backless seats and only doubtful means of warmth in the winter, a respectable audience, or even a crowd, soon gathers to gaze at the "foreign devil," or to hear singing which is so unorthodox, because not falsetto in character.

The singing over, and politeness having overcome their prejudices, they are now seated. In new districts it will hardly do to offer prayer, as this method of proceeding might be mistaken for a magic incantation to entrap them, and so cause a stampede. Few can hope to hold an audience if a long passage of Scripture is read. Beginning immediately, there-

fore, the missionary, by conversation or in simple address, attempts to bring before his auditors the great
facts of God, sin, and salvation. Interruptions are
numerous : peanut-venders may shout their wares ;
old friends recognize each other across the room, and
start an animated conversation ; an opium-smoker
attempts to create a disturbance ; an intermittent
procession of smokers circulate about the stove or in-
cense-spiral to light their pipes ; a passing mandarin
or a street brawl calls out the entire audience to " behold the hot racket," etc., etc. But they soon return,
and comers and goers keep the chapel supplied all day
long. Preaching alternates with tea-drinking, conversations with groups, reading, and the sale of books
and Scriptures, and instruction of any inquirers
present. So few have ever heard the gospel before,
and so rarely come again, that this agency is useful
in scattering broadcast an inkling of the truth, rather
than in direct conversion.

3. *Itineration* requires some nerve and great powers of adaptation. Journeying on foot, by wheelbarrow, cart, sedan-chair, or boat, a walled-city is visited,
usually on a day when a fair is being held. Armed
with books and Scriptures, the itinerant takes up his
position on the side of the narrow, crowded street,
and amid the bedlam of shouting sellers of all kinds
of commodities he speaks his message as he is able.
Very rarely is one stoned out of the city, and work
can be continued till nightfall, if lungs and throat
permit. The curious crowd tenders an evening reception at the inn, but this is compensated for at its
close, when not infrequently an awakened searcher
after Truth remains to continue till midnight, perhaps, a conversation that angels might rejoice to
hear.

In *villages* this itineration is much less taxing and
more fruitful. Seated beside the village well, or
standing on the steps of the dingy temple, groups of
farmers just in from the fields, and often women—
who rarely appear in public in the cities—gather

round to look on and to hear the stranger's words. A talk-sermon, general friendliness, catechisms or tracts bought, and perhaps a few simple characters written on the hard earth of the highway or thresh-ing-floor to testify to the truth of the gospel, are the means used by the Spirit to regenerate lives.

Where such itineration is *systematic*, and progress can be made, as in the field of the American Presby-terians and English Baptists in Shan-tung, this work is exceedingly valuable. The German missionaries in Kuang-tung are also great believers in country work, as contrasted with the more unfavorable efforts made in Chinese cities. The late Dr. Nevius was the leading advocate of the fully developed village-circuit system, and it can be found described in his " Methods of Mission Work." In a word, his plan is to interest vil-lages through itineration, and as soon as inquirers ap-pear, make the ablest of them the leader of the group. These meet periodically for the study of a graduated series of lessons and for worship. These leaders are themselves instructed through station-classes at the missionaries' home. Rev. A. G. Jones's modification of this system is, however, more productive of per-manent desirable results, perhaps.

The Native Church.—This is the natural out-come of mission schools, Christian literature, and an oral proclamation of the gospel. Upon its purity and activity depends the future of Christianity in China.

1. A traveller *visiting one of these churches* would see little peculiar about them. To be sure it may be only a " church in the house " of some Chinese Aquila and Priscilla, but that is surely apostolic. Then if in a church building, the sexes may be sep-arated by a " middle wall of partition," and creeping babies and unquiet dogs may be much in evidence. He would note the hearty singing, albeit discordant, the kneeling audience engaged in prayer, and would remark the exceedingly simple and scriptural form of the sermon, if he could understand it. At the con-clusion of the service he would see evidences of

apostolicity in the mutual affection or regard shown ; and if he followed inquirers to waiting-rooms and saw the kindliness exhibited and the desire to instruct them in Christian truth and life by the " church-friends "—members—he would believe in missions.

2. A well-regulated *Chinese Sunday-school* is an inspiration. Bright-faced boys, demure girls with " willow gait " and flower-bedecked jet black hair, a few youths and maidens, middle-aged and gray-haired men and women, are keenly enjoying the singing, the lesson-study, in preparation for which consider-able time has been spent, and the blackboard work, or lesson review. Few methods have excited greater in-terest than those of modern Sunday-schools of the West, adapted to conditions in China.

3. Though *young peoples' societies*, both of the Young Men's Christian Association and Endeavor type, are very useful, they are somewhat hampered by the prevalent opinions concerning the inferiority of youth and the relation of the sexes. While mixed young peoples' societies are a success in some mis-sions, a better effect is usually produced on the com-munity if the sexes meet by themselves. The feel-ing of personal responsibility for the religious life of other Christians and for the salvation of neighbors has been a new and much-needed element introduced by these organizations.

The Association has been especially helpful, and in some cases has changed the members from useless hangers-on in the church to being inventive and active unpaid fishers of men. New methods have been so useful that they have overcome in some dis-tricts the prejudice against youthfulness. In places where students are gathered in some numbers, it has been most successful. The conventions arising from these young peoples' societies have given the native Christians a greater sense of solidarity than any other fact perhaps.

4. The condition of the churches is further apos-tolic in that some of their saints are of the seamy sort,

just as in Corinth. This makes *discipline* a matter of much importance and anxiety to the missionary. The mutual suspicion and fear of petty revenge which has before conversion filled their life, operates to make them conceal evils until an explosion occurs, and then in the midst of mutual recriminations facts are hard to ferret out. In older communities, where a substratum of faithful Christians is present, these evils are few and do not bring serious reproach on the Church. Polygamy in some cases has caused much trouble, and in others opium - smokers and "rice Christians" have been the source of mischief. Impurity, strange to say, has occasioned remarkably few lapses from the faith. One of the great needs of the Chinese Christian is that of a stronger conviction of the unity of the Church of Christ, and of the fact that all suffer in the sin of one.

5. As already intimated, *self-support* is a perplexing problem in the present missionary situation. Church members are few in most congregations; almost all of them are from the poorest class in society and find it difficult to make ends meet since they must keep the Sabbath, and thus suffer in the keen competition of populous China; and they live in a climate and on soil which are less friendly than those of Burma, where such wonders in self-support have been seen. For these and other reasons, most missionaries have asked their boards to assume the expenses, or most of them, until the church should become strong enough to bear them.

Some of the *evils of this policy* are thus stated by Dr. Nevius : "It weakens and may break up new stations by removing from them their most intelligent and influential members in order to use them as evangelists elsewhere; it presents Christianity too much as an alien system, supplied by foreign funds and propagated for the foreigner's benefit; it has a tendency to attract applicants for baptism influenced by mercenary motives, and to retain in the church persons who seek mainly worldly advantages; it in-

9

volves the necessity of a large amount of money and
of a great deal of machinery and supervision ; it cre-
ates dissatisfaction and discussion in the native
Church, arising from supposed partiality in the distribution of favors ; by appealing largely to temporal
rather than to spiritual motives, it vitiates the character of Christianity and diminishes its power ; the
worldly or mercenary element, which at first promotes
a rapid and abnormal growth, is very apt to be the
cause at no distant period of an equally rapid decline
and disintegration." Though his advocacy of a system to avoid these evils has great favor in America,
Chinese missionaries, while acknowledging the evils
mentioned, are far from regarding his system of pre-
vention as successful, mainly because it is too superficial. In a word, this problem admits of no one solu-
tion, and all boards are endeavoring to create a spirit
of independence as rapidly as possible.

6. Closely allied with the problem just mentioned,
is that of *self-propagation* by the older established
churches that may have already come to the position
of self-support. A strong Christian Association or
Endeavor Society can do much in this direction, especially if the former is made up of the members of
a single church. Another method that has been
adopted in a few cases is to have the church appoint
members to itinerate during the less busy season, pay-
ing their light travelling expenses where necessary.
In the Nevius system, the infant church exists for
others as well as for itself, and the work of teaching
neighbors proceeds from the very beginning. In
southeastern China, both self-support and self-propagation have advanced quite satisfactorily, as it has
in many stations of the China Island Mission.

7. Writers in Christian lands have bewailed as an
even greater evil threatening the mission churches
the existence of *denominationalism*. Whatever may
be true of Japan, this has not proven a serious evil
thus far in China, except within limited areas, and
in the case of two or three boards. As a matter of

fact, very many Christians do not even know the name of the denomination to which they belong. Chang-lao Hui, Kung-li Hui, Chien-tu Hui, etc., mean about as much to them as to the reader. They do know that they belong to the Yeh-su Chiao, Jesus Sect, as opposed to the T'ien Chu Chiao, or Lord of Heaven Sect—Catholics—but beyond this many have not gone in denominationalism. It is true that some time and money may be unwisely expended in carrying on two higher educational institutions, for instance, when one would do for several boards in that locality ; but as a rule comity is carefully regarded and most stations exist in a field of their own with Christians of no other denomination near. Each year more attention is being paid to economy of men and means, and denominationalism causes almost no harm in the Empire.

Occasional Efforts.—Under this head may be placed items which do not constitute the programme of most boards, or which are only occasionally operative.

1. *Conventions and conferences* are growing in number and are being recognized as a profitable investment of mission funds. Spiritual power and wise direction of effort are consequent upon these gatherings, and they mark distinct epochs in the history of Chinese missions. As India and Japan have begun the system of annual conferences for the promotion of the spiritual life, so the decennial conferences at Shanghai for the discussion of methods and administrative details, are being supplemented by more frequent sectional gatherings for spiritual purposes. Perhaps no fact promises more of blessing in the future than this assembling together of the missionaries of China.

2. Efforts for *the literati* of the Empire are increasingly important with the entry of China into the wider world-brotherhood. It is a thankless task, and one from which little good can be expected, beyond that of removing ignorance and creating friendliness. High officials cannot be Christians and

hold office, since their position requires idolatrous acts of worship, and at present almost necessitates dishonest actions, unless officials were men of independent fortunes.

Lectures have been very slightly useful and will probably continue to be so, until literary men cease to fear one another and are willing to come in numbers to such meetings. Private interviews and visitation are far more effective in imparting a knowledge of Christianity and Western progress.

Museums in connection with private work are undoubtedly helpful and have been successfully used in three or four centres. With the coming of Western manufactures and industrial reforms, advocates of this sort of service confidently expect the leaders of China to take an increasing interest in such collections of products of Occidental skill.

Far more promising is the attempt to interest the higher classes through *specially prepared literature.* The backbone of Hu-nan's opposition to Christianity has been injured, if not broken, by this weapon, and the Emperor himself seems to be open to this method of approach. Periodicals and the translation of such volumes as Mackenzie's "Nineteenth Century" have already furnished material for discussion in sporadic and short-lived reform clubs.

The Need.—More than methods new and old, China needs a mighty outpouring of the Spirit of God. Missionaries, cumbered with much serving, acknowledge this all-important lack ; Chinese helpers, who read their Bibles aright, are sighing for the power of Pentecost ; the great body of church members needs to be brought face to face with spiritual things, until they long for the vivifying breath which, coming upon the vast valley of dry bones, will make their brethren and companions live once more, and for the first time breathe the breath of God. If the 80,000 Protestant church members of China were Spirit-filled men and women, the problem of China's conversion would be an easy one. The two needs of nearly 400,-

000,000, which a distinguished Chinese missionary says, are "character and conscience ; nay they are but one, for conscience is character," can be supplied only by God Himself.   But as Abraham wrestled and would have prevailed for Sodom, had God's condition been fulfilled, so these faithful ones, if enabled to live a spotless, useful, loving life, and if clothed with the power of prevailing prayer, would be the ten righteous for whose sake this mighty Empire might be saved from death.

VIII

Signs of Dawn.—1. A recent British writer has asserted that, in spite of the remarkable article attributed to the late Marquis Tsêng, in which that eminent Chinese statesman pointed out some evidences of China's awakening, there is, in reality, no such thing in that somnolent Empire. China has simply been roused from her slumber by the disturbing rattle of a window-shutter, and having adjusted that, she will soon sleep again. It is doubtful whether he would have so written had he penned this statement within the past two years. Those who have been too willing to join in the smile created by the hitherto truthful illustration of India's Viceroy-elect, are agreed that China can never again indulge in "her ancestral sleep," but has arisen because bursting dawn has driven slumber from her eyelids.

2. That she has actually *opened her doors* and windows to the light is attested by something more substantial than the few ports formerly accessible to Western commerce, and the permission granted missionaries to enter her populous provinces by the treaty of 1860. The recent opening of additional inland water-routes of China to foreign vessels and native steamers will be appreciated if one remembers Minister Denby's words: "Imagine every railroad in America removed, and a canal substituted, and one will form some idea of the magnitude of the system in this vast Empire." The *North China Daily News* of February 26, 1898, in commenting upon it, says: "From the foreign point of view, the concession should mean an enormous increase in the trade; and

from the Chinese, it should mean not only increased wealth and enlightenment, but also the safeguarding of the integrity of the Empire." To this the Christion may add as a prophecy the words of the apocalyptic Seer : "On this side of the river and on that was the tree of life, bearing twelve manner of fruits, yielding its fruit every month : and the leaves of the tree were for the healing of the nations." Not only are the Empire's water-gates open to the missionary as at no previous time, but imperial decree has gone forth that they shall not be closed any more, and that foreigners entering them must be protected from all assault and interference. Thus has the Gospel free course as never before in China.

3. Opening doors mean also the entrance of *the outer world's life and work.* Our daily papers are full of the complications arising among Western Powers about railway concessions, rights of exploitation of various sorts, etc. Telegraphs are threading all the Chinese provinces ; the first railroads are but the beginning of myriads of miles of rails ; provincial governors are negotiating with syndicates for the opening of mines, and all those industries grouped about the pit's mouth ; arsenals and navy yards are springing up ; the whir of the spindle, and the fragrance of tea-drying machines are present in many centres of industry. China, which is essentially an agricultural country, is entering upon the manufacturing stage of her history. Naturally, she is also an increasing buyer in the markets of the world. Thus the Bureau of Statistics at Washington reports exports from the United States to China during the year ending June 30, 1897, to the value of $17,984,-472, as contrasted with $3,978,775 in 1880, an increase of over three hundred per cent. in seventeen years. Her life is accordingly beginning to remotely resemble that of the West, with its new wants and higher ambitions.

4. If these signs of awakening are questioned let a glance at Hu-nan, *China's citadel of darkness,* con-

vince the objector, and be taken as an illustration of
other sections of the Empire. A telegraph line con-
nects its capital with Wu-ch'ang, and even the elec-
tric light is an actuality within its sacred precincts.
In spite of the proud boast of its literati that "the
devil's church should never be planted in the pure
confines of Hu-nan," the London and China Inland
Missions, and the American Presbyterians and Epis-
copalians are laboring in seven Hu-nanese centres ;
while Christian and Missionary Alliance and Cumberland Presbyterian missionaries are residing in one of its
cities. The once notorious writers and publishers of
anti-foreign and grossly obscene attacks upon our religion are now reading Christian books and periodicals, and the Chancellor of Education of the province
more than a year since wrote to the Christian Literature Society at Shanghai, acknowledging that Hu-
nan needed reform, and asking that the Chinese editor of that society become professor in the college of
their provincial capital.

5. Signs of *an awakening mind* are not far to
seek. For some years mathematics have had a place
in government examinations in some of the centres.
Last fall candidates for the M.A. degree at the capital of Chiang-hsi were confronted with the question,
"What do you know of the repeopling of the world
by Noah and his family after the flood ? " an inquiry
which occasioned the sale of Bibles by the score. The
latest copies of Chinese periodicals speak of a change
in the scope of the examinations for the two highest
degrees, whereby the Emperor orders the old system
of essay writing to give place to an examination " on
general subjects, embracing certain branches of modern science and history." Commenting upon this,
one periodical says, "The movement is a bold one,
and one which will find favor with China's progress-
ive men ; but the difficulty presents itself, how is the
necessary knowledge to be acquired before the next
examination, to meet the new requirements?" As
the widely present missionaries are the only teachers

available, they will doubtless be approached by these high Chinese scholars for aid in preparing for the examinations, just as a few interested in reforms have applied to missionaries for help in that direction. These papers also state that in connection with the Imperial University of Peking, a number of colleges are to be opened throughout the Empire. The Chinese Minister in Japan has been instructed to obtain careful plans of the Imperial University at Tokyo, with the expectation that it will be the model for college buildings throughout China. Meanwhile, old imperial palaces or temples will probably be used for the purposes of education.

But *others than the Emperor* are stirring in the matter of better instruction. Rev. H. M. Woods writes that even Hu-nan has established schools for the study of English, mathematics, and the sciences, while in other cities such institutions are being opened under Confucian auspices. One of these requires its students to worship the tablet of Confucius, while at the same time it bears the name of the school "which exalts the real," as if to say that "the empty pretensions of the high-flown poetry and essay-writing of the old Confucian school" was to give place to the real at last. Private study of English with missionaries is not infrequent, even in the interior, a result due, possibly, to the example of the Emperor, who studies our language. The movement has extended even to women, and as the result the National Reform League of China issued, last year, a prospectus of an institution for young women, to be carried on wholly under Chinese control, though some of the teachers were to be foreigners. The plan was an ambitious one, and included instruction in English, mathematics, medicine, and law, as well as a kindergarten and an industrial department. At a meeting held in its interest, a native lady of rank, for the first time in history, perhaps, made a public speech and asked for co-operation in their attempt to found in China an institution akin to the School for

Peeresses, established by the Empress of Japan at Tokyo.

6. Parallel with this movement is the new interest taken in *social reforms*. Though a reform club made up of members of the Han-lin, the highest literary body of the Empire, came to a speedy end at the capital in 1895, the idea has spread somewhat widely throughout the provinces, and a modified form of the organization, with the name of a Book Society, has, as its president, the Emperor's tutor.

Anti-Foot-binding Societies are often found outside of Christian circles. Thus the National Reform League very strongly condemns the practice, as it does that of domestic slavery of woman. One of the strongest utterances on the foot-binding evil is a booklet made up of a ballad prepared by the society at the capital of Hu-nan, and a denunciation of the cruel practice, written by the famous Chang Chih-tung, Viceroy of Hu-pei and Hu-nan.

7. That *a religious awakening* is also evident in China the sixth chapter has shown. But it should be remembered that the rate of progress is greater now than at any previous period in many provinces, as in Fu-chien and in Shêng-ching, amounting to an annual increase of fifty per cent. in a few of the older boards. When the Prussian Güttzlaff had succeeded, somewhat more than half a century ago, in sowing along the coast the seed of Christian literature, the Peking Government issued an edict to the effect that "the Christian religion is the ruin of morals and of the human heart; therefore it is prohibited." To-day, persecutors of the Christians are being punished by imperial order, on the ground that Christian teaching is beneficial to the individual and to the Empire. Surely the Sun of Righteousness has arisen upon Sinim with healing in his wings.

Obscuring Clouds.—Yet the whole truth has not been told. Clouds are upon the horizon, and in some sections they are so thick that one can hardly believe that dawn has really come.

1. One such cloud is the hostility felt by many in high positions, because this rude and real awakening has come against the nation's will, and by reason of the greed or unrighteousness of Western Powers. With Celestial suavity progress is acknowledged and perhaps lauded, but in the heart is bitter enmity against every hated foreigner. Could Might perch on Imperial banners, every Occidental would be thrust out immediately, and progress would soon cease. While such sentiments are felt by comparatively few, they constitute an influential minority.

2. Many another official will do all in his power to circumscribe the missionary in his work, because of the interference of foreign governments—notably France in earlier times, and Germany, and, to a less extent, Russia at the present—in the interests of mission converts. The Governor of Shan-tung, degraded at the demand of Germany after the murder of two German missionaries, was most bitter in his denunciation of foreigners. He protested against everything Western and missionary, using the classic phrase, "Barbarians should not be used to change China," very largely because the province had been obliged to yield in previous cases before the power of foreign ministers at Peking. Undoubtedly, Germany's recent action, no matter what justification it has, will embitter Peking officials as nothing else, for is it not the missionary who has brought upon the Empire its present cataclysm of woes? If there is ever a covert opportunity to embarrass missions, why should it not be embraced?

3. Thousands of *the literati* and of the scholars of the first degree looking for promotion through successive examinations, are naturally opposed to Western education, brought so largely to China by the missionaries. When men have striven for years to attain official position and have almost gained the coveted degrees through their faithful acquisition of the native Classics, they are incensed to learn that a new line of education has been introduced, and that they

must begin, often in middle life, to acquire the learning of the West, the key to which in some cases is
the English tongue. Young men who have not expended half the years that they have in study, grasp
the golden prizes, and the efforts of a life-time avail
nothing. As missionaries will do much to aid their
younger competitors in stripping them of their lau-
rels, they will receive their full share of the consequent animosity.

Officials have *another grudge* against foreigners.
Accustomed as they have been to a life of dishonesty
in office, they hate men like those in the customs
service, because foreign ideas of honesty—absent in
this service so often in the West—have set an object-
lesson of which the Government highly approves.
Will further intercourse with the Occident disturb
still more the present system, and make it necessary
to give up corrupt methods of administration ? If
so, all hope of gain is gone, and foreigners, especially
the honest missionary, are responsible for this serious
loss.

4. Other prevalent evils among the people greatly
obscure the morning sky. The *opium habit*—so universal among those who can afford to indulge in the
drug that in some provinces the people will tell the in-
quirer that "eleven out of every ten" are opium-users
—is an obstacle to Christian missions of the greatest
moment. The harmful effects of its use are undoubtedly less evident among those who can afford the
time to smoke, and the money to keep their strength
up, as apologist for the traffic claim. It is also largely
true that death is oftener occasioned by starvation
and other causes connected with opium-eating than
by opium *per se*. Yet when every careful observer
will testify that these accessory evils are practically
unavoidable, save among the well-to-do, and further
bear witness to the baneful effects of the drug under
the most favorable circumstances, one can see how
indefensible the position of opium-apologists is, and
how harmful it may be in mission work. Some

boards will not admit to church-membership opium-smokers, even if they have reformed, for the reason that opium blunts or destroys not only the will, but also the moral susceptibilities. No one will deny that the Gospel has power to heal every moral disease, but one would be slow to assert that the presence of opium in a community is anything but a serious detriment to missionary effort.

Ancestral worship is so much more difficult an obstacle to overcome than any other form of Chinese darkness, that it alone is deemed insurmountable by some. One of the most prominent foreigners in China, formerly a missionary, presented at the last Shanghai Conference a paper in which he pleaded for toleration in this one particular, if Christianity was to make any progress in the Empire. While the delegates were willing to admit the seriousness of the obstacle, they indignantly protested against such vital compromise with a species of idolatry, even if their attitude diminished the possibility, which Ricci found realized, of large accessions, because converts were allowed this privilege.

5. Another cloud which broods over the entire non-Christian world is the fact that *men love darkness* rather than light. With the coming of a pure religion to China, every form of impurity and evil is rebuked and sometimes antagonized. Humble men and women are so shrouded in moral darkness and surrounded by practical difficulties threatening their comfort or life even, if they break with heathenism, that thousands shrink back at the prospect. Here is a business man whom the missionary would win for Christ. He objects that a Christian cannot lie, and that no Chinese can do business who does not use falsehood as an indispensable aid, as well as false weights and measures. Do Occidental Christians long to see the official class and the scholars of China enter the Church? But how is this possible when every official of sufficient rank must participate in idolatry as an essential part of his duty. When the

Emperor is required to fast sixty-four days in each year and offer up forty-three different sacrifices in honor of deities ranging from Shang Ti, through the higher powers of nature, down to roads, gates, cannon, etc., the subordinate official must follow his high example. When the difficulties with Germany were at their height last year, the *Peking Gazette* placed more emphasis upon the number of incense sticks to be burned and the new names to be given local deities which had prevented serious overflow of rivers, or caused the death of insects that threatened to destroy the foliage in the imperial mausoleum, than it did to the grave matters threatening the very existence of the Empire. Truly "the whole head is sick, and the whole heart faint. From the sole of the foot even unto the head there is no soundness in it ; but wounds and bruises and festering sores." But there is balm in Gilead and a Great Physician there, and the promise is that "at evening-time there shall be light."

6. A sixth obstacle which prevents the dawning of a better day is the *opposition of Romanism*. If its representatives would allow Protestantism to do its work, the presence in the Empire of two Christian bodies holding such variant views of life and doctrine would be a serious objection against Christianity. But when Rome does all in her power to thwart and destroy the work of Protestantism, even to the extent of involving Western Powers in Chinese politics, the harm is still greater. Perhaps one of the most serious struggles of the near future will be between the promoters of this faith, both missionaries and governments, and those identified with Protestantism.

7. Sad to say, the most pitiable occasion for regret at this time of unprecedented opportunity is found in the *apathy of the Church of God*. Hard times have so occupied her thoughts that the manifest beckonings of His hand are not seen. Men and means are demanded as never before, and never before have most boards been so unable to enter the

splendid openings that Providence has thrust before them. Where are the men of vision who can see the field in all its magnitude, and who, possessed of the compassion of the Master for the multitude scattered as sheep having no shepherd, and fired with the zeal of a Peter the Hermit, will preach in the pulpits of Christendom a nineteenth-century crusade, not to rescue from unbelievers the sepulchre of a Risen Saviour, but to save from graves of despair and hopelessness the unbelieving millions who stand upon their brink.

Rival Forces.—As the myth of Osiris and Isis was suggestive to the ancient Egyptian of the struggle of the sun with the powers of darkness in the heaven above, and "of the parallel on the earth beneath in the perennial conflict between the beneficent Nile with the sands of the desert," so the light and dark principles in Chinese Dualism suggest the present-day rivalry for the supreme place in China. Is the dawn to shine "more and more unto the perfect day," or is the shadow on the dial to turn backward and darkness brood once more over the face of China?

1. The first principle which strives to win away from the light this newly awakened nation is *materialism*. Perhaps no land so far advanced in civilization as China has so little imagination and is dominated so wholly by a gross materialism. In this very matter of dualism, so common in the Orient, Dr. Martin has shown that while the Persian, for instance, makes light and darkness the symbols of moral ideas, China regards them as physical agents. Listen to the conversations of guests at Chinese inns, as they come to the ear; an actual stenographic report and later calculation have shown the writer that a large proportion of it—possibly eighty per cent. under ordinary circumstances—has to do with money, bodily comfort, and other items pertaining to the earth, and hence earthy. Note how assiduously the laundryman gives himself to his business and how little else than creature-needs enter into the calculation. He will go anywhere and

endure anything for the sake of money, the means of ministering to animal necessities and of acquiring sensuous luxuries.

Now that the new possibilities of gaining a living or a competence have entered the Empire, there is a moral certainty that the tendency will be to make its inhabitants more materialistic than ever. Atheism will find a god to most devoutly worship in this Crœsus of the West. Even the higher elements of Western life are apt to be sacrificed to lower ends. Thus our language will be studied for the sake of commercial or scholastic promotion, rather than for the broader life which can be drawn from the well of English. As openings in business or secular teaching become increasingly lucrative, the temptation, already present, will increase among our Christian Chinese to enter these doors, rather than to minister educationally and spiritually to their countrymen, when only a meagre pittance can be gained therefrom. The Church is thus threatened with a loss which will prove almost fatal to independent growth and usefulness.

2. Another rival for the hand of the New China is found in all the great courts of Europe, *alien domination.* Thus far it has been no lover's wooing. As the Chinese ideogram for marriage is made up of an ear, a hand, and a woman—alluding possibly to the ancient practice of leading captured maidens to the marriage by the ear—so the Powers have thus far striven to win China by this barbaric method. But the failure of Occidental rivals in their suit, and the Czar's recent call for a general disarmament, point to the time when coquetry will fill the Chinese court with insinuating candidates for China's hand. While one Power may urge commercial advantage, another internal development, a third protection against the power and spite of other rivals, what one of them will strive to gain China's friendship and love for the sake of her reformation and soul's betterment?

Positive disadvantage may come to the cause of

righteousness in that land if she becomes the victim of
foreign domination. Russia's recent action concerning
the Stundists is a foretaste of what may happen to
Protestant institutions in the Empire, if she gains
the ascendancy, while France has uniformly shown a
zeal for Catholic missions there which bodes ill to
Protestant effort. Worse still, what can the Confucianist think of a religion professed by enlightened
nations which exhibits such fruits of palpable injustice, and such an absence of that love and good-will
which the Prince of Peace came to usher into the
world ? So long as Christian Powers continue to
wrangle and fight over what they deem their deserved
spoil, simply because they hold the right of might,
just so long is the bright shining of the sun eclipsed
by political and commercial shadows.

3. Is *Confucianism*, then, to come to China's relief,
in this struggle between light and darkness ? One
who reads that panegyric of the system, presented at
the Parliament of Religions by the Chinese Minister
at Washington, would imagine that only in Confucianism could the Empire find its saviour. As the
reader remembers the revival of the teachings of the
Chinese Sage in the strivings after light which swept
over Japan a few years since, and as one notes the
strongly moral life of Japanese Confucianists of the
generation just passing away, it may seem more than
a possibility that a reformed Confucianism will take
possession of the nation's heart, as it comes to reflect
upon its corruption in the past and the ethical needs
of the New China. Many a missionary has noticed
the blush come to the cheek of his Confucian teacher
as he has read some portions of the Old Testament,
and some of them are bold enough to assert that in
the Classics there is not a line that will occasion an
impure thought. It is quite possible, then, that the
struggle which is now on will bring out as one of
Christianity's strongest rivals this hoary system of the
past, even though Buddhism and Taoism may be cast
aside in consequence.

10

4. That He whose right it is shall reign, and that ultimately *Christ* will gain the victory over every rival to His peaceful sway in China, no Christian can doubt. But while our Lord postpones His personal coming to that Empire and to the world, His disciples have no right to delay their going thither. His " Go ye " is a categorical imperative, and admits of no tarrying. The conquest of China is the storming of heathenism's Gibraltar, and demands corresponding forces and prayers. The Church should be as awake to the priceless value of this populous territory as are earthly powers. If India is " the rudder of Asia," China is her gigantic hull, filled with teeming life, and threatened with awful shipwreck, unless guided into waters of quietness ; worse still, if left to her own awakened steersmen, she may become a menace to the world. What she needs is a prize crew to take possession of her in the name of humanity and of Christ, and make her a vital factor in Asia and for the Kingdom of God.

If it be said that this duty is no special concern of Protestantism, but devolves rather upon Romanism with its larger foothold, or upon the Greek Church, in view of Russia's present paramount influence, let it be remembered that what China sorely demands is not so much a better system of belief, but rather a living Saviour and national regeneration. Without being bigoted, it can be safely asserted that in neither of those communions is there such emphasis of these fundamental truths as Protestantism everywhere insists upon. Formalism may delight and please the Chinese, but heart-life and heavenly purity are essential to China's new birth. Have not Protestants been brought to the kingdom for such a time and work as this ? Plainly the responsibility belongs to her to whom heavenly privileges have been granted.

The Morning Summons.—These are already echoing in the Christian's ear, but it may be well to reiterate them once more.

1. Obviously we hear the *call of the multitudes.*

Dr. Paton, the Saint John of the New Hebrides, labored with his colleagues in a hostile territory, speaking different dialects, and rightly has the interest of the world been given to his apostolic story. Hawaii is a part of Christian America to-day, because the missionaries of the American Board gave their lives to her evangelization. The Fijis are the Paradise of the Pacific, for the reason that English Wesleyans were willing to dwell by cannibal ovens, that they might hold up in the midst of demoniacal orgies the banner of the Cross. But numerically considered, these island populations are but as the dust of the balance compared with China's myriads. One's heart goes out in anguish over the overturned skiff with its drowning couple, but the blood turns cold as one thinks of the hundreds of victims of the La Bourgogne. Chinese missionaries have, within two miles of their home, a larger, and often a more approachable, constituency than the African missionary can reach by threading scores of miles of malarious trails. The letters of our Bibles have been marshalled, processions of various ingenious sorts have passed before the spectator's imagination, and in other ways attempts have been made to impress upon the Christian these vast populations, but all in vain. They are a multitude that no man can number, and if anyone longs to preach to the masses, China is certainly the best field.

But on Sinim's shores one hears more than the cry of mere numbers; they are multitudes who are *suffering and dying*. More millions go to bed hungry each night in China than in any other land; more bodies endure torture under the hands of Chinese quacks than under the tender mercies of practitioners of any other race; more women suffer from the limitations of their sex in China than in any other heathen nation; more men pay the penalty of their vices there than anywhere else; more brides commit suicide, and more young men sell themselves to be put to death in China than can be found in any other clime, simply because the sweetness of life is gall, and existence is misery.

This summons is one of *pressing emergency*. The Chinese character for world and for generation is made up of three tens. While we of the West speak of a generation as thirty-three years in duration, this linguistic fossil of past millenniums asserts that in three brief decades the Chinese world comes to birth, lives its cheerless life, and crumbles into dust. Students meet for an hour to study the needs of China ; when this hour is over, 1,325 Chinese have ceased to breathe. Missionary receipts are so insufficient that a board postpones entering China until another year ; that twelve months' delay has removed from the possibility of ministration 11,613,728 who sorely needed help. The Church of God may sleep on for thirty years more, but when it awakes, China's four hundred millions have passed beyond her power to save them. If China is not evangelized in our generation, then the Church can never perform her duty to onefourth of the human race, which she has been commanded to minister unto.

2. The call of China's dawning is one to *heroism*. To be sure, the missionary lives in comparative comfort and among a people who are usually law-abiding. But count the names on China's roll of martyrs, add to the list those whose minds have been shattered because they have lived in the midst of hostile rumors and open opposition ; remember that the statement of one veteran there is true of many others—" I never address a Chinese crowd without feeling that I am standing on the edge of a volcano." It requires heroism to look in the face conditions such as are alluded to in the last issue of *China's Millions*—not an alarmist sheet by any means : " The objects of the hatred of men, as foreigners, deprived of protection of any kind by their position in the interior, defenceless by choice for conscience sake that they may live as well as preach the doctrine of peace—what might not happen if Satan should direct in open acts the rage of

men against our beloved fellow-workers? It is more than a possibility that not a few might be called to lay down their lives at Jesus's feet, as Stephen did. And are the missionaries prepared for this? Have they reckoned the cost in giving themselves to a work whose peril is so great?" While most boards do not hold to a policy of non-resistance, as does that mission, the risks of interior missionaries call for constant bravery and boldness.

Furthermore, it is a summons to *versatility*. Read again the varied scheme of work undertaken by the Church for China's redemption. Every talent can here find its exercise. If one desires to be a specialist, there is certainly considerable opportunity to utilize differing gifts and preferences. To those who say with Paul, "This one thing I do," there will come demands for other service, when a colleague is home on furlough—which averages more than one-tenth of the time—and it is necessary that his work be kept up. There is scarcely an accomplishment or gift which cannot be made useful to China, if one so desires.

It is a call to *privilege* also. While all service is this, there are diversities of glory. The Chinese missionary is permitted to labor among one of the most remarkable races in history, and one of the most potent in its possible influence upon the life of our times. He has to do with the reconstructive forces of the China that is to be while the nation is in its fluid state, ready to receive the impress of foreign minds and hearts. It is also a privilege to take the place of another person whom the Government might summon to aid in reconstruction—were the missionary not there—but who would not care for the moral and spiritual welfare of men. Millions of Mexican dollars, of inferior manufacture and liable to be counterfeit, are found in China, to thousands made in Japan and America of far greater value. Why? Simply because they were first in the market and the people have become accustomed to them as they have

not to the purer coin.   If missionaries and other
Christians do not come to the front at this time of
great demand, and continue to be the nation's edu-
cators and advisers, adventurers of various sorts will
take these places of influence, and a decade hence
they will be the Mexican dollar that will keep out
Christian coinage.

The present-day call is one to men and women of
deepest consecration.   A frequent Hebrew word for
consecration means " with full hands."   The sort most
needed in the Chinese missionary is precisely this.
Come to the Empire with a practical preparation of
various sorts ; bring with you the social qualities of
a Ricci, without his defects ; store the mind with
learning of varied scope, to meet the intellectual
needs of the day ; come with a love that is undying
for those who would perhaps put you to death, if
they dared ; come above all as a manifest child of
God, endued with all those spiritual graces which
spring from the Holy Spirit and which are daily re-
newed in a consecrated closet.   Let every power be
laid upon the altar, and self be sunk in Christ-like
service.

3. The summons of China's dawn are weighty because they come from such a variety of forceful con-
siderations, and appeal to such worthy and Christ-
like ambitions.   Yet the reader should not lay this
little book down without a thought as to the One by
whom these summons are primarily uttered.   Christ
is speaking through current history, and His words
are both winsome and authoritative.   Have we had
much given us? of us He requires correspondingly
much.   If "God's heart then is love"—as "God is
love " is rendered in the Mandarin New Testament—
it is enough to be His children and exhibit this love
in accordance with the corollary to John iii. 16,
found in 1 John iii. 16, 17 : "Hereby know we love,
because He laid down His life for us ; and we ought
to lay down our lives for the brethren.   But whoso
hath the world's goods, and beholdeth his brother in

need, and shutteth up his compassion from him, how doth the love of God abide in him?"

The *investment of a life* is the most momentous of all human decisions. As Jesus before entering upon his active ministry went up to a mountain-top and there beheld the kingdoms of the world and the glory of them, so should every Christian examine the opportunities for a life investment presented by the nations of a weary world. Not led by Satan, but allured by the One "whom not having seen ye love," let the disciples of Jesus gaze long and prayerfully upon the plains and hills of T'ang, with the glad word of surrender upon their lips, "Here am I, send me." Such attitude makes impossible any regrets at that Great Day, when the Judge of all the earth shall utter the words of blissful significance, "Come, ye blessed of my Father, inherit the kingdom prepared for you from the foundation of the world." Then shall the translated missionary realize the royal nature of his service in Sinim. He thought that he was ministering to hostile Chinese who were hungry, thirsty, strangers, naked, sick, and in Satan's prison-house ; but the backward look revealed the blessed fact that "Inasmuch as ye did it unto one of these my brethren, even these least, ye did it unto Me."

APPENDIX A

Provincial Divisions.—China Proper is often called by the Chinese The Eighteen Provinces, but Shêng-ching, in southern Manchuria, may be considered as the nineteenth province. Formosa, since the recent war, belongs to Japan, and the only other considerable island, Hai-nan, constitutes part of Kuang-tung province. A few leading points concerning each of them are given below. For convenience in consulting the map, the order in which they are taken up is that of the thirteen which form boundary provinces—beginning at the northeast and passing southward, westward, northward, and eastward to the starting-point—and later the six interior provinces are described.

1. *Shêng-ching*=Affluent Capital (43,000 square miles, somewhat smaller than Pennsylvania; population, 6,000,000, or 140 per square mile.—Professor R. K. Douglas, in Britannica). Though part of the original realm of the Manchus, this section of Manchuria has always been essentially Chinese, and at the present time is being rapidly colonized by natives of the two provinces to the south of it. It is one of the most fruitful mission fields of China, in spite of the strong opposition of Catholics. Mukden, the capital, gives its name to the province and stands second among the cities of the Empire in official rank. It is the chief centre of Protestant missionary work and is one of the pleasantest cities of residence in China. The southern tongue of this province contains Port Arthur, recently taken possession of by Russia.

2. *Chih-li*=Direct Rule (58,949 square miles, size of Georgia; population, 17,937,000, or 304 per square mile). The name arises from the fact that " from this province the supreme power which governs the Empire proceeds," Peking, the capital—regarded by travellers as the most interesting and unique city of Asia—lying within its boundaries. Mohammedans are quite numerous in this province, especially in the north, where in Peking alone 20,000 families are said to reside. Most of the territory is very flat and low-lying and consequently much of the land along the rivers is subject to yearly devastation. Tientsin, its great port, is the residence of the far-famed Li Hung-chang, who has for many years been China's virtual ruler. It is also an important seat of Western educational institutions, which have been fostered by Viceroy Li.

3. *Shan-tung*=East of the Hills (53,762 square miles, size of Arkansas; population, 36,247,835, or 557 per square mile).

Shan-tung has a maritime border equal to more than half its circuit which includes Wei-hai-wei and Kiao-chou Bay, recently taken possession of by England and Germany respectively. This is the Holy Land of China, as within its borders were born her two greatest philosophers and sages, Confucius and Mencius. Its sacred T'ai Shan, a mountain famous in Chinese history for 4,000 years, is still annually visited by thousands of pilgrims. A French missionary mentions one such party consisting of old ladies from seventy-eight to ninety years of age who had travelled 300 miles to secure a happy transmigration for their souls. Shan-tung is also a very fruitful mission field.

4. *Chiang-su*=River Thyme, a name derived from the first syllables of its capital Chiang-nan—known to the West as Nanking—and of its richest city, Su-chou (44,500 square miles, size of Pennsylvania; population, 20,905,171, or 470 per square mile). Like the two preceding provinces, Chiang-su forms part of the Great Plain. It has few hills and is more abundantly watered than any other province. It contains one of the former capitals of the Empire, Nanking, meaning Southern Capital, as Peking signifies Northern Capital. Shanghai, its great semi-foreign city, ranks first among Chinese ports. Another famous place is Su-chou, reckoned by the Chinese as the luckiest place in which to be born, because it has the handsomest people. Chiang-su was the main centre of the great T'ai l'ing rebellion, Nanking being the rebel capital from 1853 to 1864.

5. *Chê-chiang*=Tidal-bore River, a stream that gives its name to the province (39,150 square miles, size of Virginia; population, 11,588,692, or 296 per square mile). It is hilly throughout and is celebrated for its tea and silk. The capital, Hang-chou, occupies a most picturesque site overlooking the sea, and is so beautiful that with its sister city, Su-chou, it has given rise to the common proverb, "Above there is Paradise, below are Su and Hang." Were it not for its furious tides and famous bore it would monopolize the eastern trade of China. It is one of the strongholds of Mohammedanism in the Empire. Chê-chiang's climate is most healthful, its fruit and forest trees valuable, its manufactures varied and excellent, and its inhabitants comparable in wealth, refinement, and learning with those of other provinces.

6. *Fu-chien*=Happily Established (38,500 square miles, size of Maine and New Hampshire combined; population, 22,190,-556, or 574 per square mile). Though the smallest in the Empire since the island of Formosa has been added to Japan, this province is the most densely settled of all, Shan-tung not excepted. "In the general features of its surface, the islands on the coasts, and its position with reference to the ocean it resembles the region east of New Hampshire." A German writer calls Fu-chien "the Chinese Switzerland." Fu-chou, its capital, and Amoy are important places, both from a commer-

cial and missionary point of view. Since the Ku-ch'êng (Ku-t'ien) massacre of 1895, missionary work in this province has marvellously prospered, proving anew that "the blood of martyrs is the seed of the Church."

7. *Kuang-tung* = Broad East (79,456 square miles, size of Minnesota; population, 29,706,249, or 377 per square mile). The above area includes the island of Hai-nan. From this province, the birthplace of Chinese Protestant missions, most of our early knowledge of China was derived, as it was the only one open to foreign trade; and from it have come to America almost all of our Chinese fellow-citizens. Its capital, Kuang-chou Fu (Canton), is probably the most populous city in the land and its inhabitants have been called the Yankees of China. Hongkong and Macao on this coast are well-known possessions of Great Britain and Portugal, while thirty miles southwest from Macao, on the island of St. John, lie the bones of Rome's most famous missionary, Francis Xavier.

8. *Kuang-hsi* = Broad West (78,250 square miles, size of North and South Carolina combined; population, 5,151,327, or 65 per square mile). This most sparsely settled province has, like Hu-nan, strenuously resisted the coming of missionaries. Few foreigners have visited the country, as its people are poor and its products not very desirable. Several half-subdued tribes live within its boundaries, who, though under their own governors, are subject to Chinese supervision. On the southwest, near Annam, are many descendants of Lao tribes who appear to have come under Chinese authority because of greater security to life and property.

9. *Yün-nan* = Cloudy South, *i.e.*, south of the Yün-ling—Cloudy Mountains (107,969 square miles, size of New England States and Pennsylvania combined; population, 11,721,576, or 108 per square mile). The greater part of Yün-nan consists of a plateau elevated a mile above the sea and containing many valley plains. It is richer in minerals of various sorts than any other province, and its copper mines bid fair to prove of value, now that Japanese engineers have been employed to teach the people modern mining methods. It also supplies to China much of its medicine, including besides "herbs and roots, fossil shells, bones, teeth and various products of the animal kingdom." Colonel Yule says of this section of the Empire that it is an "Ethnological Garden of tribes of various races and in every stage of uncivilization." From 1855 to 1873 much of the province was under the rule of the Panthays, a Mohammedan tribe.

10. *Ssŭ-ch'uan* = Four Streams (166,800 square miles, somewhat larger than the New England and Middle States; population, 67,712,897, or 406 per square mile). This province, containing a greater area and population than any other in the Empire, derives its name from four important rivers which flow south into the Yang-tzŭ. Its western portion is a succession of

mountain-ranges, sparsely settled and unproductive, and inhabited by barbarous tribes. The triangular eastern portion teems with life and is one of the most prosperous sections of the Empire, save in times of unusual drought or flood, when robbery, riots, and even cannibalism add to the general wretchedness. Its brine wells and the natural gas used to evaporate the salt are famous, and have made perhaps the greatest demand on Chinese perseverance and ingenuity. Its abounding clouds and mists and the large quantities of silk and wax exported are other distinguishing features. Catholic missions have flourished here for many decades and recent Protestant effort has proven very successful, in spite of occasional outbreaks and the destruction of mission property.

11. *Kan-su* = Voluntary Reverence—derived, like Chiang-su, from the names of two leading cities (125,450 square miles, somewhat larger than New Mexico; population, 9,285,377, or 74 per square mile). Kan-su is second in size and next to the lowest in sparseness of population among the provinces. Except in the eastern part, it is little else than "a howling wilderness of sand or snow." As its central portion commands the passage into Central Asia, it is of great strategic importance to the Empire. This province was seriously affected by the great Mohammedan rebellion led by Yakub Beg and quelled by General Tso in 1877. Williams thus writes of this conquest: "During the early years of the campaign it appears that the soldiers were made to till the ground as well as construct fortifications. The history of the advance of this 'agricultural army' would, if thoroughly known, constitute one of the most remarkable achievements in the annals of any modern country."

12. *Shen-hsi* = Western Defiles (67,400 square miles, size of Missouri; population, 8,432,193, or 126 per square mile). This purely agricultural province is remarkable as having contained Hsi-an Fu, the capital of the Empire for more than 2,000 years. It is in that city that the famous Nestorian Christian Tablet was erected. It ranks next to Peking in importance, and the valley of the Wei River, in which it stands, has been more closely connected with the fortunes of the Chinese race than any other portion of China.

13. *Shan-hsi* = West of the Hills (56,268 square miles, size of Illinois; population, 12,211,453, or 221 per square mile). More than half this area is a plateau, elevated more than a mile above sea-level, and constituting a vast coal-field. Iron of great purity is also very abundant, so that here are probably found the most remarkable coal and iron regions of the world. It has been estimated that, at the present rate of consumption, Shan-hsi could supply coal to the entire globe for thousands of years. It is further remarkable as being the original seat of the Chinese people, and for sending out into the Empire, and even into Japan and America, a multitude of shrewd bankers. The people

in general, however, are great opium-eaters and are poor. Famine is frequent, owing to lack of moisture. In the north rises the sacred mountain of the Buddhists, Wu-t'ai Shan, a popular resort for the Mongols of the north and west. Mission work is actively prosecuted in the southern half of the province.

14. *Ho-nan* = South of the River, *i.e.*, the Yellow River (66,-913 square miles, size of Washington; population, 22,115,827, or 340 per square mile). Leaving the provinces lying on China's boundary, we take up those of the interior. Some of the most fertile parts of the Great Plain lie within Ho-nan, and for that reason and because of its central position, it was anciently known as the Middle Flowery Land and later as the Middle Kingdom. This is historic territory, and from the earliest times has been the scene of feudal and imperial strife and of literary triumphs as well. On this plain communication is largely dependent on the wheelbarrow, some of them with sails, to which Milton refers in the lines :

> " The barren plains
> Of Sericana, where Chineses drive
> With sails and wind their cany waggons light."

15. *An-hui* = Peace and Plenty—coming from the names of two principal cities (48,461 square miles, size of North Carolina; population, 20,596,288, or 425 per square mile). Though its southern half contains most productive soil and a great quantity of tea is produced, the province suffered so unspeakably during the T'ai P'ing rebellion that years will still be required before it regains its former prosperity. Baron von Richtofen writes : " The exuberant fertility of the soil in the lower portions of the province is not excelled by anything I have seen in temperate climates. . . . I have walked for miles through fields of hemp, the stalks of which were from eleven to thirteen feet high."

16. *Chiang-hsi* = West of the River (72,176 square miles, size of West Virginia and North Carolina combined ; population, 24,-534,118, or 340 per square mile). This mountainous province is said to resemble in sections the north counties of England. Within its borders were the great porcelain manufactories of the Sung dynasty, which as recently as 1850 employed a million workmen and still supply all the fine ware used in the country. The Vale of the White Deer, on the western side of Lake P'o-yang, is a favorite place of pilgrimage for Chinese literati, as in this vale Chu Hsi, the great philosopher and commentator on Confucius, lived and taught in the twelfth century.

17. *Hu-pei*=North of Lake [T'ung-ting] (70,450 square miles, size of North Dakota; population, 34,244,685—" Statesman's Year-Book, 1898 " in error in its number—or 473 per square mile). A plain constitutes a large part of this province, and another noticeable feature is the Han River, flowing from its north-

western boundary to the Yang-tzŭ. At this junction lies a trio of cities, Han-kou, Wu-ch'ang and Han-yang, which are of great importance commercially and otherwise. It is to Han-kou that the first great trunk line railroad is likely to extend from Peking. Some of the most magnificent scenery in the world is found in the Yang-tzŭ gorges between I-ch'ang and the Ssŭ-ch'uan border. In some portions the narrowed river runs over rapids, through canyons, the walls of which rise to a height of more than a thousand feet. While its southwestern prefecture has an illiterate population, it was so powerful a factor in early and feudal history that native scholars regard it very highly.

18. *Hu-nan*=South of Lake [T'ung-ting] (74,320 square miles, somewhat smaller than Ohio and Indiana combined; population, 21,002,604, or 282 per square mile). Mainly a country of hills, which segregate the people into small communities, its population has a reputation for violence and rudeness, especially the boat people and the inhabitants of the southern portion. On the other hand, Hu-nan has an enviable reputation for its men of letters, and the inhabitants in many sections are more prosperous than those of other provinces. A vast anthracite and bituminous coal-field, as extensive as that of Pennsylvania, is a source of prospective wealth. This province has been the hot-bed of anti-foreign sentiment, and the instigator, through its scurrilous publications, of the anti-Christian riots. Only recently have missionaries been allowed to labor there, and already some have sealed their testimony with their blood.

19. *Kuei-chou*=Noble Province (64,554 square miles, size of the two Virginias; population, 7,669,181, or 118 per square mile). In spite of its name, this province "is on the whole the poorest of the eighteen in the character of its inhabitants, amount of its products, and development of its resources." Malaria, caused by stagnant water and impure wells, and the rude races of Miao-tzŭ have brought Kuei-chou into disrepute. Yet it claims to possess the largest quicksilver deposits in the world, and produces an abundance of coarse silk.

APPENDIX B

Prominent Events of the Historic Dynasties.—Instead of attempting to thread the wearisome mazes of Chinese history, only a few outstanding facts concerning the principal dynasties will be given.

1. Though the first two of the historical dynasties do not wholly deserve the name, there are facts connected with the earlier one that should be mentioned. Yü the Great, the founder of the Hsia dynasty, is the hero of an early Chinese flood—probably an unprecedented overflow of the Yellow River. While we need not believe that " Yü was 9.2 cubits high," nor that " at that time heaven rained down gold three days," we must believe that he possessed rare skill as a hydraulic engineer. With him came a change in the principle of succession to the throne, which thenceforth was to be hereditary within the reigning family. Then also arose the feudal state—Yü divided his realm into nine principalities—which existed during three dynasties until 255 B.C. This system was much like that prevailing in Europe during the Middle Ages.

2. *The third dynasty*, and the longest on the throne, the Chou, not only boasted of its great men, King Wu, its founder, Duke Chou, and China's three great philosophers, Lao-tzŭ, Confucius, and Mencius, but it was the time when new emphasis was laid on the five relations of society, when fines leading to bribery became common, when the seal character was invented, and when the state of morals sunk from bad to worse in spite of the persistent efforts of the Empire's greatest reformers. During this period the Tartars began those predatory incursions that were later to prove so serious a menace.

3. Succeeding the Chou came the *Ch'in dynasty*. The feudal state of Ch'in had been prominent for centuries, and toward the close of the preceding dynasty, when seven principalities contended for the supremacy, Ch'in was victorious. Though the family occupied the throne for less than fifty years, it was at this time that the Great Wall was completed, the books burned and scholars slaughtered or exiled, and the feudal states fused into a truly imperial mass. The Empire under this dynasty included nearly all the territory now known as China Proper.

4. An honored designation of the Chinese to-day is Sons or Men of Han, a name derived from the *Han dynasty*, which, with the Eastern and Later Han, reigned two centuries before

the Christian era, and somewhat longer after it. This is the formative period of Chinese polity and institutions, the time when the development of commerce, arts, and literature—especially history and philosophy—advanced with rapid strides, and when good government, based on a penal code, was established. The system of competitive examinations for office began with the founder of the Han, and this is another reason why this dynasty has been the most popular in Chinese history. Buddhism was officially introduced into the Empire during the reign of the sixteenth Han emperor.

5. The period of the *San Kuo*, or three warring states of the third century, has been made very famous, not because of its intrinsic importance, but by reason of a notable historical novel, "The History of the Three States," which, like Scott's writings, "has impressed the events and actors of those days upon the popular mind more than any history in the language."

6. During the 300 years following A.D. 620, occurs one of the most illustrious periods in China's remarkable past. The *T'ang dynasty* is distinguished for having seen the introduction of Nestorian Christianity and Mohammedanism, for being the Golden Age of Chinese poetry, and for its territorial expansion, so that Korea became a national possession on the east, and Persia, in the remote west, asked assistance of the Middle Kingdom. Southern China dates its civilization and incorporation into the Chinese rule from the days of the glorious T'angs.

7. When Europe was experiencing its darkest midnight, in the decades preceding the dread millennial year, the splendors of the *Sung dynasty* burst upon the Orient. If the T'ang writers had been poets, those of Sung might be called philosophers and representatives of China's Augustan Age of Literature; at least it was at this time that Chu Hsi flourished, and a host of other authors who had begun to inquire into the nature and use of things. One result of such inquiry and discussion was the unsuccessful trial of socialistic principles. "It is under the Sung dynasty that the language 'is supposed to reach its acme, to have become complete in all its formal and material equipment, having everything needful to make it an effective instrument for expressing the national mind;' and works on philosophy of great and permanent value were produced." For more than a hundred years preceding their dethronement the Sung emperors were harassed beyond measure by the incursions of the Chins, the ancestors of the present Manchu dynasty. They at one time held the territory north of the Yellow River, and even penetrated to the banks of the Yang-tzŭ.

8. A little more than 600 years ago, after an independent existence of more than 3,000 years, the *Yüan* or *Mongol dynasty* brought the Chinese under their first foreign domination. "That vivacious gossip and prince of travellers, Marco Polo," has made this dynasty most fully known in his story of the famous Kublai

Khan, who deepened and lengthened the Grand Canal. Professor Douglas thus writes concerning Kublai : "Never in the history of China was the nation more illustrious, nor its power more widely felt, than under his sovereignty. . . . At this time his authority was acknowledged from the Frozen Sea almost to the Straits of Malacca. With the exception of Hindustan, Arabia, and the westernmost parts of Asia, all the Mongol princes, as far as the Dnieper, declared themselves his vassals, and brought regularly their tribute."

9. With the overthrow of the Mongols, the throne once more reverted to the Chinese, and the *Ming* or *Bright dynasty* ruled the Empire for nearly three centuries. The first Ming emperor, the son of a laboring man, soon won all hearts by catering to the higher classes through the promotion of literature and the establishment of libraries in great cities, and by a lavish distribution of salt to the poorer classes. The temporary occupation of Nanking as the capital, repairs on the Great Wall, the coming of the Portuguese, and the arrival of the Jesuit missionaries were events of importance in this dynasty, as also the framing of a code of laws that has been the basis of subsequent administration. Northern border invasions increased in violence in the latter part of this period, and internal rebellion led to the capture of Peking by a rebel leader, and the suicide of the Emperor. In despair, a Chinese general in the northeast besought the assistance of the Manchus, with the result that the rebellion was quelled, and the further result that the Manchu camel refused to leave the tent into which he had been encouraged to thrust his nose.

10. Thus it happened that the present *Ta Ch'ing* or *Pure dynasty* came from Manchuria, on the northeast, into China, and have remained its foreign rulers for more than two hundred and fifty years, since 1644. Under the nine Ch'ing emperors China has gradually emerged from her haughty seclusion of ages, and is perforce taking her place in the great family of nations. Some of the important events marking the reigns of this dynasty are the early educational work and the imperial surveys of the Catholic missionaries, the splendid literary monuments left by the famous Emperor, K'ang Hsi, the extension of power in the west and northwest, the wars with Russia, England, and France, and with Mohammedan rebels, the pseudo-Christian T'ai P'ing rebellion, and the inroads in 1897–98 of Western Powers, the ultimate issue of which cannot yet be surely predicted. The most marked characteristic of this century's history, so far as the Kingdom of God is concerned, is the beginning and rapid spread of Protestant missions throughout the Eighteen Provinces and Manchuria.

APPENDIX C

Scheme for Studying Denominational Missionary Work in China.—As some denominational classes have desired to study in connection with each lesson the work of their denomination in China, the following outline for such study is given. Information covering all or most of the points named can be secured from the denominational missionary board, or from the article on the board in the "Encyclopædia of Missions." That these supplementary studies may be most helpful, it is suggested that they be prepared in writing and on paper of uniform size, that the several reports may be bound as a manuscript volume, to be kept as a permanent contribution to the institution's missionary library. Not more than ten minutes need be given at each class session to this supplementary work. The number of minutes following each division in the outlines below denotes the length of each paper, one hundred and fifty words being allowed per minute. If this scheme is followed out, the members of the class will have co-operatively prepared a manuscript supplementary volume equal to nearly two and a half chapters of the text-book.

Supplementary Study I.—Beginnings.

I. Causes leading to the board's entering China, *2 minutes.*

II. The first missionaries sent out, *3 minutes.*

    1. Their names and number.

    2. Previous history and training.

III. Date of establishment of first station.

IV. Its location; description of town, *2 minutes.*

V. View of situation on arrival derived from early letters or reports, *3 minutes.*

Supplementary Study II.—Occupation of the Field.

I. Province or provinces now occupied, *2 minutes.*

    1. Location on sketch map.

    2. Items additional to the provincial descriptions in Appendix A of the text-book.

II. Cities and villages containing stations or outstations, *3 minutes.*

    1. Indicate these on sketch map.

    2. Distinguishing characteristics of cities occupied.

III. The people labored for, *3 minutes.*

    1. Population accessible to missionaries.

    2. Their language or dialects.

    3. Friendliness or hostility to foreigners (avoiding items mentioned in Study VI. below).

IV. The workers.

    1. Number of men and women missionaries employed.

    2. Number of male and female assistants.

V. Other boards occupying same cities, *2 minutes.*

    1. Are relations between these boards helpful or prejudicial to the work ?

    2. If prejudicial, study the province to see what other centres can be properly occupied.

Supplementary Study III.—Present Workers.

I. Roll of all present members, if fifteen or less, with brief characterization of each, *6 minutes.*

II. If more numerous, omit above and select four of the most prominent missionaries, not neglecting the women, and give a minute and a half account of each, reporting only striking characteristics, *6 minutes.*

III. If possible, give a two-minute sketch of most prominent native helper, and one of same length of prominent Bible woman, *4 minutes.*

Supplementary Study IV.—Medical, Educational, and Evangelistic Work.

I. Medical work of the board, *3 minutes.*

    1. Show on sketch map location of dispensaries, hospitals, or opium refuges.

    2. Briefly describe most interesting and fruitful medical case.

II. Educational work, *3 minutes.*

    1. Locate on sketch map the mission's schools.

    2. Character and aim of schools of different grades.

III. Evangelistic labors, *4 minutes.*

    1. Brief description of outside chapels.

    2. Location of churches on map.

    3. Describe briefly and graphically Chinese preaching.

Supplementary Study V.—Woman's Work and Other Special Efforts.

I. Word-picture of home visitation, *2 minutes.*

II. Girls' schools, *2 minutes.*

    1. Description.

    2. Value to the mission.

III. Work of Bible women, *2 minutes.*
    1. What they do.
    2. Why their services are essential for efficiency.
IV. Station classes for women, *2 minutes.*
    1. Studies pursued.
    2. Interesting case from such classes.
V. Other lines of work carried on by mission, *2 minutes.*
    1. Work named and located on map.
    2. Aim of each of these departments of service.

Supplementary Study VI.—Obstacles Encountered.

I. Obstacles in the missionaries' private life, *3 minutes.*
    1. Difficulty of language study.
    2. Lack of harmony or helpfulness among missionaries.
II. Obstacles arising from un-Christian foreigners, *3 minutes.*
    1. Example of sailors and travellers.
    2. Life of un-Christian foreign residents.
    3. Difficulties due to attitude of Western Powers.
III. Obstacles arising from heathen environment, *4 minutes.*
    1. Missionaries tempted by exasperating experiences with natives.
    2. Harmful effect of heathenism upon missionary's spirituality.
    3. Open and subtle temptations besetting native Christians.
    4. Opposition and persecution coming to native Christians and churches.

Supplementary Study VII.—Results of the Board's Work in China.

I. Statistical results, *1 minute.*
II. Character transformations, *4 minutes.*
    1. Case of male convert most remarkable in this respect.
    2. Case of most conspicuous transformation of a woman.
III. Effect of the work upon the community, *5 minutes.*
    1. Material improvement effected.
    2. Social changes becoming apparent.
    3. Effects of board's educational work.
    4. Influence of native churches on the community.

Supplementary Study VIII.—What Can This Class Do to Aid the Work ?

I. Pray for the work, *4 minutes.*
    1. Present important data to stimulate prayer.
    2. Enter definite objects upon prayer list or cycle.

II. Give to its support, *2 minutes.*

    1. Describe special work recommended by the board for class support.

    2. Formulate plan for systematic giving to the board.

III. Champion the interests of China, *2 minutes.*

    1. In churches attended by students at college.

    2. In home church.

    3. In addressing other churches and young peoples' societies.

IV. Reasons for personal devotion to the board's work in China, *2 minutes.*

ANALYTICAL INDEX

BESIDES indicating the location of important topics, this Index is also intended for use in preparing the various studies. Having read over its analytical outline before taking up each chapter, the student sees exactly what ground is covered by the section to be mastered. So, too, after having studied the chapter, its outline can again be used in lieu of questions put by a teacher, thus enabling the student to see what topics have been forgotten. The numerals following each topic and sub-topic refer to the pages where they may be found.

CHAPTER I

THE WORLD OF THE CHINESE

I. Scope o the text-book, 1.
II. Names applied to China, 1–3.
  1. Early Occidental names, 1, 2.
    (1) Names given it by land-route travellers, 2.
    (2) Names derived from the Southern route, 2.
  2. Signification of native names for China, 2, 3.
III. China's place in Asia, 3.
IV. Areas with some comparisons, 3, 4.
  1. Area of Empire, with equivalents, 3, 4.
  2. Area of China Proper and American equivalent as to position, 4.
V. Striking physical features, 4–9.
  1. China's waterways, 5, 6.
    (1) The Huang Ho, 5. (2) The Yang-tzŭ, 5, 6.
  2. Chinese lakes, 6.
  3. Mountain ranges, 6.
  4. The Great Plain, 6, 7.
    (1) Location and size, 6, 7. (2) Its populousness, 7.
  5. Loess formation of China, 7, 8.
    (1) Description, 7, 8. (2) Two drawbacks, 8.
  6. Chinese scenery, 8, 9.
    (1) General characterization, 8. (2) Nearer view, 8, 9.
VI. Climatic conditions, 9, 10.
  1. Temperature and isothermal lines, 9.
  2. Rainfall and Northern winters, 9.
  3. Diseases as related to foreigners, 9, 10.
VII. Wealth of the Empire, 10, 11.
  1. Agricultural resources, 10.
  2. Aquatic wealth, 10.
  3. Mineral productions, 10.
  4. Abundant supply of superior laborers, 11.
VIII. Chinese view of the world, 11–14.
  1. Prevalent ignorance concerning their own country, 11.
  2. The extra-Chinese world, 11, 12.
    (1) Chinese maps, 11, 12. (2) Common ideas about foreign lands, 12.

3. Foreigners at close range, 12, 13.
   (1) Foreign sins, 12. (2) Merchants and diplomats, 12, 13. (3) Missionaries, 13.
4. These prejudices decreasing, 14.

CHAPTER II '

CHINA'S INHERITANCE FROM THE PAST

  I. Character of Chinese historical records, 15, 16.
    1. Credibility of Chinese history, 15.
    2. Sources from which it is derived, 15, 16.
      (1) Bamboo books, 15. (2) Classics, 15. (3) Local annals, 15. (4) Dynastic histories, 16.
    3. Literary character of these writings, 16.
  II. China's prehistoric dawn, 16–19.
    1. The mythological ages, 16, 17.
      (1) Duration, 16. (2) Cosmogony, 17. (3) Five early rulers, 17.
    2. The legendary period, 17, 18.
      (1) Duration, 17. (2) Chinese views of this period, 17. (3) Why Confucius made such large use of its history, 18.
    3. Residuum of fact underlying these two periods, 18, 19.
      (1) Civilization possessed, 18. (2) Origin of the Chinese, 18. (3) Origin of their culture, 18, 19.
 III. Key characters in Chinese history, 19–23.
    1. Some prominent rulers, 19, 20.
    2. Philosophers and literary men, 20, 21.
    3. Illustrious women of China, 21–23.
      (1) Reasons for renown, 21, 22. (2) Examples, 22, 23.
 IV. Present-day survivals of China's past, 23–27.
    1. Survivals in material form, 23, 24.
      (1) Great Wall, 23. (2) Grand Canal, 23, 24. (3) Roads and bridges, 24. (4) Other minor survivals, 24.
    2. Institutions and inventions of early times, 24–26.
      (1) Government, 25. (2) Many arts and trades, 25. (3) Compass, gunpowder, and printing, 25, 26. (4) Silk and porcelain manufactures, 26.
    3. Literary treasures, 26, 27.
      (1) Language and literature, 26, 27. (2) Educational system, 27.
  V. Some secrets of China's protracted existence, 27–31.
    1. Protection from external foes, 27, 28.
      (1) Physical barriers, 27, 28. (2) Isolating language, 28. (3) Masses to be overcome, 28.
    2. National characteristics tending to perpetuity, 28.
    3. Internal resources satisfactory, 28, 29.
    4. Safeguards against internal conflict and decay, 29, 30.
      (1) Duty of warrantable rebellion, 29. (2) Peaceful rewards for ambition, 29. (3) National characteristics hostile to decay, 29, 30.
    5. Government and laws favorable, 30.
    6. God's purpose in China's long existence, 30, 31.
 VI. The dawn of a new era, 31.

CHAPTER III

"THE REAL CHINAMAN"

  I. Numbers and distribution, 32, 33.
      (1) Statistics, 32. (2) Reasons for defective census, 32, 33. (3) Densely populated regions, 33.

II. Characteristics of the Chinese, 33–39.
  1. Physical characteristics, 33–35.
    (1) Tibetans, 33, 34. (2) Mongols, 34. (3) Miao-tzŭ, 34. (4) Manchus, 34. (5) Chinese, 35.
  2. Emotional characters, 35, 36.
  3. Intellectual qualities and products, 36–39.
III. Sociological environment of the Chinese, 39–45.
  1. Home and clan life, 39–42.
    (1) Oriental differentiæ, 39, 40. (2) Villages and their daily routine, 40. (3) Food as affected by poverty, 41. (4) Sumptuary laws; clothing, 41. (5) Birth, marriage, death, 41, 42.
  2. Cities and their life, 42–44.
    (1) Sights and sounds, 42, 43. (2) City interiors, 43. (3) Social parasites, 43. (4) Unfortunates and defectives, 43, 44.
  3. Government and laws, 44, 45.
    (1) Makers of law, 44, 45. (2) Its administration, 45.
IV. Industrial life of the Empire, 45–47.
  1. Gradations in society, 45, 46.
  2. Industries and wages, 46, 47.
  3. Trade organizations, 47.
V. Amusements and festivals, 47–49.
  1. Amusements and sports, 47, 48.
  2. Festivals, 48, 49.
VI. The Chinese as painted by themselves, 49–51.
  1. Children in proverbs, 49.
  2. Looking out into life, 49, 50.
  3. Marriage and family life, 50.
  4. Moral maxims, 50, 51.

CHAPTER IV

RELIGIONS OF THE CHINESE

I. Nature-worship, 52–57.
  1. Fetiches, 52.
  2. Totem worship, 52–54.
  3. Animal worship, 54.
  4. Worship of ancestors, 54–56.
    (1) Its central position, 54, 55. (2) Its basis, 55. (3) Its benefits, 55, 56. (4) Its evils, 56.
  5. Worship of deified heroes, 56.
  6. Worship of Shang Ti, 56, 57.
II. Taoism and its founder, 57–60.
  1. Its founder, Lao-tzŭ, 57.
  2. Its Scripture and its teachings, 57, 58.
  3. Later Taoist leaders, 58, 59.
  4. Its awful degradation, 59.
  5. The Taoism of to-day, 59, 60.
III. Confucius and Confucianism, 60–67.
  1. Items from his life, 60–62.
  2. Character of Confucius, 62, 63.
  3. Confucian literature, 63–65.
    (1) The Four Books, 63, 64. (2) The Five Classics, 64, 65.
  4. Confucian teachings, 65, 66.
    (1) Their general character, 65. (2) The Five Relations, Five Constants, and the Chün-tzŭ Jên, 65, 66. (3) Is Confucianism wholly atheistic? 66.
  5. Modern Confucianism, 66, 67.
  6. The worship of Confucianism, 67.
IV. Buddhism, or the sect of Fo, 67–73.
  1. Introduction into China, 67, 68.
  2. Spread of Buddhism, 68.

3. Popular Buddhistic doctrines, 68–71.
    (1) General character, 68. (2) Belief concerning Buddha, 68. (3) His laws, 68, 69. (4) Metempsychosis, 69. (5) Heaven, 69, 70. (6) Hells, 70. (7) Salvation, 70, 71.
4. The Buddhist priesthood, 71.
5. Their temples and pagodas, 71.
6. The worship, 71, 72.
7. Buddhist deities, 72, 73.
V. Chinese Geomancy, 73, 74.
    1. Its original and later objects of care, 73.
    2. The real power behind it, 73.
    3. Principles of Geomancy, 73, 74.
    4. Evidences of the power of this system, 74.

CHAPTER V

PREPARATION AND BEGINNINGS

I. Ancient moral and religious conditions, 75.
    (1) Confucianism, 75. (2) Taoism, 75. (3) Buddhism, 75.
II. The secret sects, 76, 77.
    1. Reasons for their helpfulness, 76.
    2. Doctrines of various sects, 76, 77.
    3. Character of sect members as converts, 77.
III. The Jews in China, 77–79.
    1. Names, 77.
    2. Facts in their history, 78.
    3. Present number and condition, 78, 79.
IV. Chinese Mohammedanism, 79–81.
    1. Entrance into China, in North and South, 79, 80.
    2. Its increase and reasons therefor, 80.
    3. Present status and practices, 80, 81.
    4. Doubtful value to Christianity, 81.
V. Nestorian Christianity, 81–84.
    1. Entrance into the Empire, 81.
    2. Nestorian Monument and its testimony, 81, 82.
    3. Doctrines taught, 82, 83.
    4. Later history of Nestorianism, 83.
    5. Nestorianism's value to the modern missionary, 83, 84.
VI. Catholicism's first stadium in China, 84–86.
    1. First great Catholic missionary there, 84, 85.
    2. Labors of his successors, 85.
    3. Catholicism's lost opportunity, 85, 86.
VII. The second Catholic entrance, 86–93.
    1. Ricci, Catholicism's most famous Chinese missionary, 86–89.
        (1) Early efforts, 86, 87. (2) Life in Peking, 87. (3) His literary labors, 87, 88. (4) Decision of certain questions, 88. (5) His character, 88, 89.
    2. Later Catholic leaders and rivalries, 89.
    3. Period of eclipse, 89.
    4. History since 1858, 90.
    5. Catholic methods, 90, 91.
        (1) Adaptiveness, 90. (2) Practical charities, 90. (3) Native converts and their use by the Church, 90, 91. (4) Defects of converts and missionaries, 91.
    6. Catholicism's relation to Protestantism, 91, 92.
    7. Strength of Chinese Catholicism, 92, 93.
        (1) Milne's testimony, 92. (2) Dr. Medhurst's, 92, 93. (3) Distribution and numbers, 93.
VIII. The Greek Church in China, 93, 94.

CHAPTER VI

THE PROTESTANT OCCUPATION OF CHINA

I. Morrison, Protestantism's pioneer, 95–97.
   1. Early years and preparation, 95, 96.
   2. Life and services in China, 96, 97.
II. War and Chinese missions, 97–102.
   1. The Opium War, 97, 98.
     (1) Occasion, 97. (2) Character, 97, 98. (3) Results, 98.
   2. The T'ai P'ing Rebellion, 98, 99.
     (1) Its leader and its course, 98, 99. (2) Its significance, 99.
   3. The Arrow War, 100, 101.
     (1) Origin and results, 100. (2) The French Treaty, 100, 101. (3) Obstacles, 101.
   4. Other wars, actual and threatened, 101, 102.
     (1) Tientsin massacre, 101. (2) Margary's murder, 102. (3) French war, 102. (4) Riots, 102.
III. Stages of missionary progress, 102–110.
   1. Preparatory stage, 1807–1842, 102, 103.
     (1) Preparatory efforts, 102, 103. (2) Work outside China Proper, 103. (3) Results, 103.
   2. Years of entrance, 1842–1860, 103–107.
     (1) Field of labor, 103. (2) Nature of work, 103, 106. (3) Converts, 106. (4) Missionaries, 106. (5) Results, 106, 107.
   3. Development and wider entrance, 1860–1877, 107.
     (1) Advances noted, 107. (2) Statistical results, 107.
   4. Between the Conferences of 1877 and 1890, 108.
     (1) Key-words of the period, 108. (2) Famine and self-support, 108. (3) Statistics of 1890, 108, 109.
   5. The eight years since 1890, 109, 110.
     (1) Results of the Conference, 109. (2) Other events, 109, 110.
IV. Missionary geography, 110–112.
   1. How far the provinces have been entered, 110, 111.
   2. Character of places occupied, 111.
   3. Density of population and missionary distribution, 111, 112.
   4. Territory still unoccupied, 112.
V. Some China missionary statistics, 112, 113.
   1. Number and nationality of organizations there, 112.
   2. Missionary force.
     (1) National totals, 112, 113. (2) Analysis of net total, 113.
   3. Stations and the work done in them, 113.
VI. Additional agencies, 113–115.
   1. Tract societies, 114.
     (1) Names and aims, 114. (2) The S. D. C. G. K., 114. (3) Book-lending societies, 114.
   2. Mission presses and their work, 114, 115.

CHAPTER VII

THE MISSIONARIES AT WORK

I. The human agent in missions, 116, 117.
   1. Language preparation, 116.
   2. General usefulness in early months, 116, 117.
   3. Heart preparation for usefulness, 117.
   4. Study of the people, 117.
II. Efforts for China's physical alleviation, 117–119.
   1. Medical work, 117, 118.
     (1) Immediate usefulness, 117. (2) Dispensaries and hospitals, 117, 119. (3) Women physicians, 118.

     2. Famine relief and its consequences, 118.
     3. Missionary agitation of reforms, 118.
        (1) Opium curse, 118.   (2) Foot-binding, 118.
     4. Defectives and foundlings, 118, 119.
III.   Educational work, 119–122.
     1. Day-schools, 119, 120.
        (1) Pupils and instruction, 119.   (2) Support, 119, 120.
     2. Boarding-schools, 120.
        (1) Their advantages, 120.   (2) Studies pursued, 120.
     3. Mission colleges, 120, 121.
        (1) Scope and character, 120, 121.   (2) English study, 121.   (3) Criticism of colleges, 121.
     4. Industrial education and its value, 122.
     5. Education for Christian service, 122.
        (1) Station-classes, 122.   (2) Theological schools, 122.
IV.   Literature in Chinese Missions, 123, 124.
     1. Preparation of literature, 123.
     2. Manufacture of books, 123, 124.
     3. Distribution of Christian books, 124.
  V.   Evangelistic work, 124–127.
     1. Individual work : higher classes ; women, 124, 125.
     2. Chapel preaching, 125, 126.
        (1) Chapels and audience, 125.   (2) Services and results, 125, 126.
     3. Evangelistic itineration, 126, 127.
        (1) Visitation of cities, 126.   (2) Village itineration, 126, 127.
        (3) Systematic attempts, 127.
  VI.   The native Church, 127–131.
     1. Churches and services described, 127, 128.
     2. Chinese Sunday-schools, 128.
     3. Young people's societies and Y. M. C. A., 128.
     4. Discipline and its causes, 128, 129.
     5. Problem of self-support, 129, 130.
        (1) Obstacles in China, 129.   (2) Evils of the old policy, 129, 130.
     6. Self-propagation of the Church, 130.
     7. Question of denominationalism, 130, 131.
  VII.   Occasional efforts, 131, 132.
     1. Value of conventions and conferences, 131.
     2. Efforts for the literati, 131, 132.
        (1) Lectures, 132.   (2) Museums, 132.   (3) Literature, 132.
VIII.   The needs of missionaries, converts, and the masses, 132, 133.

CHAPTER VIII

THE DAWN

  I.   Signs of dawn, 134–138.
     1. The awakening not temporary, 134.
     2. China's open doors, 134, 135.
     3. Entrance of the outer world's life and work, 135.
     4. Hu-nan's awakening a signal proof of dawn, 135, 136.
     5. Signs of an intellectual awakening, 136–138.
        (1) Changes in government examinations, 136, 137.   (2) Non-governmental agitation for better instruction, 137, 138.
     6. The social awakening, 138.
        (1) Reform societies, 138.   (2) Anti-Foot-binding societies, 138.
     7. The religious awakening, 138.
  II.   Obscuring clouds, 138–143.
     1. Hostility due to enforced awakening, 139.
     2. Irritation caused by diplomatic protection of converts, 139.
     3. Opposition of literati and officials, 139, 140.
        (1) The new learning feared, 139, 140.   (2) Hostility to Western ideas of integrity, 140.

4. Obstacles arising from evils peculiar to China, 140, 141.
   (1) Opium and its evils, 140, 141. (2) Ancestral worship, 141.
5. Enmity due to manifold forms of sin, 141, 142.
6. Opposition of Romanism, 142.
7. Apathy of the Church of God, 142, 143.
III. Rival forces striving for China, 143–146.
  1. Materialism, 143, 144.
    (1) Old tendencies, 143, 144. (2) New temptations, 144.
  2. European domination, 144, 145.
    (1) Methods of the Powers, 144. (2) Disadvantages arising therefrom, 144, 145.
  3. Confucianism a possible rival, 145.
  4. Christ the ultimate victor, 146.
    (1) Greatness of the prize, 146. (2) Protestantism's duty, 146.
IV. The morning summons, 146–151.
  1. The call of the multitudes, 146–148.
    (1) China's comparative populousness, 146, 147. (2) These multitudes suffering and dying, 147, 148. (3) Their emergency a pressing one, 148.
  2. What China calls the missionary to, 148–150.
    (1) A call to heroism, 148, 149. (2) A call to versatility, 149. (3) A call to privilege, 149, 150. (4) A call to consecration, 150.
  3. The One who utters these calls, 150, 151.
    (1) His a call of love, 150, 151. (2) The opportunity for a satisfying investment of life, 151.

MAP INDEX

By means of this index all names of cities and towns can be readily found on the map. For hints as to pronunciation see key on page xviii. Note the following directions:

The letters following the names indicate the rank of the place. Thus C. means provincial capital; F. means a fu city; T., a ting city; c., a chou city; h., a hsien city; and m. a market-town or village, or one whose rank could not be ascertained.

Places in Italics are not occupied as missionary stations.

The question mark (?) following some of the places indicates that either their Romanization or rank is unknown to the compiler. Numerals following the names of places indicate the board or boards having resident missionaries there. The numerals are the same as those prefixed to the alphabetical list of missionary societies given below.

The capital letter and numeral following each name at the extreme right of the column indicate the square on the map where the place is located. The capital letters may be found midway between the meridians of longitude at the top and bottom margins of the map; the numerals are midway between the parallels of latitude at the right and left hand margins of the map. In some cases mission stations could not be located on the map, and hence the name of the province in which they are has been placed in the right-hand margin of the column.

Provinces are printed in capital letters, thus, SHAN-TUNG, and the numerals following their names show what missionary societies labor in them.

I. AMERICAN SOCIETIES (CANADA AND THE UNITED STATES).

1. American Baptist Missionary Union.
2. American Bible Society.
3. American Board of Commissioners for Foreign Missions.
4. American Friends' Board of Foreign Missions.
5. Board of Foreign Missions of the Methodist Episcopal Church [South].
6. Board of Foreign Missions of the Presbyterian Church in the United States [South].
7. Board of Foreign Missions of the Presbyterian Church in the United States of America [North].

8. Board of Foreign Missions of the Reformed Church in America.

9. Board of Missions of the Reformed Presbyterian [Covenanter] Church.

10. Christian and Missionary Alliance.

11. Cumberland Presbyterian Board of Missions.

12. Domestic and Foreign Missionary Society in the Protestant Episcopal Church in the United States.

13. Foreign Christian Missionary Society.

14. Foreign Missionary Society of the Seventh-Day Baptists.

15. Foreign Mission Board of the Southern Baptist Convention.

16. Foreign Mission Committee of the Presbyterian Church in Canada.

17. Gospel Baptist Mission.

18. Missionary Society of the Methodist Episcopal Church [North].

19. Missionary Society of the Methodist Episcopal Church, Canada.

20. Student Christian Movement in Mission Lands.

21. Swedish American Mission, Covenant of America.

22. United Brethren in Christ.

23. Woman's Union Missionary Society.

II. BRITISH SOCIETIES (GREAT BRITAIN AND IRELAND).

24. Baptist Missionary Society.

25. Bible Christian Home and Foreign Mission Society.

26. British and Foreign Bible Society.

27. Church Missionary Society for Africa and the East.

28. Church of England Zenana Missionary Society.

29. Church of Scotland Committee for the Propagation of the Gospel in Foreign Parts.

30. Foreign Missions of the Presbyterian Church of England.

31. Friends' Foreign Mission Association.

32. London Missionary Society.

33. Methodist New Connection Missionary Society.

34. National Bible Society of Scotland.

35. Presbyterian Church of Ireland Foreign Mission.

36. Society for Promoting Female Education in the East.

37. Society for the Propagation of the Gospel in Foreign Parts.

38. United Methodist Free Churches Foreign Mission.

39. United Presbyterian Church of Scotland Foreign Mission.

40. Wesleyan Methodist Mission Society.

III. CONTINENTAL SOCIETIES.

41. Berlin Evangelical Missionary Society.
42. Berlin Woman's Society for China.
43. Congregational Church of Sweden.
44. Danish Mission Society.
45. Evangelical Missionary Society, Basel.
46. General Evangelical Protestant Missionary Association.
47. German China Alliance Mission.
48. Norwegian Lutheran China Mission Association.
49. Rhenish Missionary Society.
50. Swedish Mission in China.

IV. INTERNATIONAL SOCIETIES.

51. China Inland Mission.
52. Mission to the Chinese Blind.
53. Society for the Diffusion of Christian and General Knowledge among the Chinese.

Amoy T. (port) 8, 30, 32, 34.......E 5
An h. 27........................B 3
An-ch'ing Fu C. 12, 51 ....E 3
AN-HUI, 10, 12, 13, 18, 31, 51.
An-jên h. 51......................E 4
An-lu F..........................D 3
An-shun F. 51.....................C 4
An-tung h. 51.... ....E 3

Canton Fu C. (port) 3, 7, 15, 22, 27, 32,
40, 41............................D 5
Chai-ch'i h. 51...................F 3
Chan-hua h. 33...................E 2
Chang-chou F. 8, 32 ....E 5
Chang-ch'un m. 35................G 1
Chang-pa m. (?) 27................C 3
Chang-p'u h. 30 ....E 5
Chang-sha Fu C..................D 4
Ch'ang-shan h. 51 ....E 4
Chang-shu m. 51..................E 4
Chang-tê F. 16...................D 2
Ch'ang-tê F. 10, 11............ ..D 4
Ch'ang-wu h. 51..................C 2
Chang-yeh h. 10..................B 2
Chao-chia K'ou m. 26, 51... .....E 3
Ch'ao-chou F. 1, 30..............E 5
Chao-t'ung F. 25, 51.............B 4
Chao-yang h. 32..................F 1
CHÉ-CHIANG, 1, 5, 6, 7, 27, 38, 42, 47,
51.

Chefoo (Chih-fu) (port), 7, 37, 51...F 2
Ch'ên-an F ....C 5
Chên-chiang F. (port), 6, 15, 18, 34,
51.............................E 3
Ch'ên-chou F. 51.................E 3
Ch'êng-ku h. 51..................C 3
Ch'êng-tê (Jé-ho) F............E 1
Chêng-ting F ....D 2
Chêng-tu Fu C. 18, 19, 51........B 3
Chêng-yang Kuan T. 51...........E 3
Chên-yüan h. (Kan-su) 51.........C 2
Chên-yüan F. (Kuei-chou).......C 4
Chi c. 51.........................D 2
Chia c..........................D 2
Chia-hsing F. 6...................F 3
Chi-an F. 51......................E 4
Chiang c. 51................Shan-hsi
CHIANG-HSI, 18, 26, 51.
CHIANG-SU, 2, 4, 5, 6, 7, 12, 13, 14,
15, 18, 20, 23, 26, 27, 32, 34, 46, 51,
53.
Chiang-yin h. 6...................F 3
Chia-ting F. 1, 19, 51............B 4
Chia-ying c. 1, 45................E 5
Chieh c. (?), 50, 51..............D 3
Chieh-hsiu. 51.............Shan-hsi
Ch'ien c. 51......................C 3
Chien-ch'ang F..................E 4
Chien ning F. 27, 28.............E 4
Chien-p'ing h. 51 ....E 3

Chien-tê h. 51.....................E 3
Ch'ieo-yang h. 51................C 3
Ch'ih-chou F. 51.................E 3
CHIII-LI, 2, 3, 7, 10, 18, 20, 26, 32, 33, 34, 37, 51, 52.
Chlu c. 35.........................F 1
Ch'in c. 51........................C 3
Ch'ing-chiang h. (port), 14, 51.....E 3
Ching-tzŭ Kuan, 51..............D 3
Ch'ing-yüan F...................C 5
Chi-nan Fu C. 7..................E 2
Ching c. (Hu-nan)..............C 4
Ching c. (Kan-su) 51............C 2
Ch'ing-chou F. 24................E 2
Ching-ning c. 51.................C 2
Ching-shan h. 32.................D 3
Ch'ing-yang h. 10...............E 3
Ching-yüan m. (?) 42.......Chê-chiang
Chin-hua F. 1, 51................F 4
Chi-ning c. 7.....................E 2
Ch'in-shou Chiang m. 48........D 3
Chiu-chiang F. (port), 18, 26, 51....E 4
Ch'iu-fu h......................E 2
Chiung-chou F. 7.................D 6
Chou-chih h. 51..................C 3
Chou-p'ing h. 24.................E 2
Chou-t'ang-ao, 41................D 5
Ch'u c. 13.........................E 3
Chü c............................E 2
Ch'ù h. 51..................Seň-ch'uan
Chuang-lang T..................B 2
Chu-chi h. 27.....................F 4
Chu-ch'i h......................D 3
Ch'u-chou F. 47..................E 4
Ch'u-hsiung F..................B 4
Chung-ch'ing F. (port), 2, 18, 31, 32, 34, 51......................C 4
Ch'u-wang, 16..................Ho-nan
Ch'üan-chou F. 30...............E 5
Ch'ü-ching F. 51.................B 4
Ch'ü-chou F. 51.................E 4
Ch'ü-wu h. 51....................D 2
Cheng-bau (?), 23................E 4

Dang-seng (?), 28................E 4

Fên-chêng m. 21.................D 3
Fên-chou F. 3.....................D 2
Fêng-chên T. 10.................D 1
Fêng-hsiang F. 51...............C 3
Fêng-hua h. 51...................F 4
Fêng-kang m. 51.................E 4
Fo-kang T.......................D 5
Fo-shan T. 40....................D 5
Fu c.............................C 2
FU-CHIEN, 3, 8, 18, 27, 28, 30, 32, 34, 36.
Fu-ch'ing h. 18, 27..............E 4
Fu-chou Fu C. (port), 3, 18, 27, 28, 36..............................E 4
Fuk-wing (?), 49.................D 5
Fu-mên m. (?), 49...............D 5
Fu-min-fu m. 35..........Shêng-ching
Fu-ning F. 27.....................F 4

Fu-tsuk-phai (?), 45.............D 5
Fu-yin Te'un, 24............Shen-hsi

Hai c...........................E 3
Hai-ch'êng h. 39................F 1
Han-ch'êng h. 50, 51...........D 2
Han-chung F. 26, 51............C 3
Han-ch'uan h. 40...............D 3
Hang-chou Fu C. (port), 6, 7, 27...F 3
Han-k'ou h. (port), 12, 32, 34, 40, 51............................D 3
Han-shan h. 10..................E 3
Han-yang F. 1, 40...............D 3
Hêng-chou F...................D 4
Ho c. 51...........................D 2
Ho-chien F.....................E 2
Ho-ch'ih c......................C 5
Ho-ching h. 51...................D 2
Ho-k'ou m. 51...................E 4
Hok-su-ha (?) 45................E 5
Hu-lin-koh-ri T. (?) 10.........D 1
HO-NAN, 16, 26, 51.
Ho-nan F.......................D 3
Hongkong, 3, 26, 27, 32, 36, 42, 45..D 5
Ho-su-wan (?) 45...............D 5
Hsi c. 51..........................D 2
Hsia h. 50........................D 2
Hsi-an Fu C. 24, 26, 51........C 3
Hsiang-ch'êng h. 51............D 3
Hsiao-chaug m. (?) 32..........E 2
Hsiao-i h. 51.....................D 2
Hsiao-kan h. 32.................D 3
Hsiao-mei m. 47.................E 4
Hsien-yu h. 28...................E 4
Hsi-fêng Chên m. 51............C 2
Hsi-hsiang h. 51.................C 3
Hsin c. 24.........................D 2
Hsin-ch'ang h. 51...............F 4
Hsin-chên, 16...............Ho-nan
Hsin-ch'êng (?) 6................F 3
Hsing-an, 51.................Shen-hsi
Hsing-hua F. 18, 27, 28........E 4
Hsing-i F. 51.....................C 4
Hsing-p'ing h. 51................C 2
Hsin-hua h.....................D 4
Hsin-hsing h. 15................D 5
Hsi-ning F. 51...................B 2
Hsin-tien-tzŭ m. 51............C 3
Hsin-tu h. 27.....................B 3
Hsi-yang (?) 28..................E 4
Hsüan-hua F. 10................D 1
Hsü-ch'ien h. 6..................E 3
Hsü-chou F. (Chiang-su), 6.....E 3
Hsü-chou F. (Seú-ch'uan), 1, 51..B 4
Huai-an F. 6......................E 3
Huai-ching F...................D 2
Huai-lu h. 51.....................D 2
Huang h. 15.......................F 2
Huang-yen h. 1..................F 4
Hu-chou F. 1.....................F 3
Hui-chou F. 51...................E 4
Hui-li c.........................B 4
HU-NAN, 10, 11.
Hung-tung h. 51................D 2

Hun-yüan, 51............ ....Shan-hsi
HU-PEI, 1, 10, 12, 21 29, 32, 34, 40,
   43, 48, 51.
Hu-wei, 41........................D 5

Iang-kao (?), 10.............Shan-hsi
I-ch'ang F. (port), 12, 29, 43, 51...D 3
I-chou F. 7......................E 2
I-ning c........................D 4
I-shih h. 51.....................D 2
I-yang h. 51.................. ...E 4

Jao-chou m. 51.............Chiang-hsi
Jêu-ts'un m. 3..............   D 2
Ju-ning F......................D 3

K'ai-fêng Fu C................D 3
K'ai-hua F.....................B 5
K'ai-yüan h. 39.................F 1
Kalgan (Chang-chia K'ou) T, 3, 10..D 1
Kan-chou F.....................B 2
Kang-hou m. (?) 7...............D 5
Kang-pui (?) 49.................D 5
KAN-SU, 10, 51.
Kao-chou F.....................D 5
Kao-yu c. 51....................E 3
Khi-tshung (?), 45 ....D 5
Kia c..........................F 2
Kirin C. 35.....................G 1
K'o-lan c.....................D 2
Kuan h. 51......................B 3
Kuang c.......................E 3
Kuang-chi, 40.................Hu-pei
Kuang-fêng h. 51................E 4
KUANG-HSI, 10, 15, 26, 40.
Kuang-nan F...................C 5
Kuang-ning h. 35...............F 1
Kuang-tê c. 51.................E 3
KUANG-TUNG, 1, 3, 7, 9, 10, 15, 22,
   26, 27, 30, 32, 36, 40, 41, 42, 45, 49.
Kuang-tzû-kang (?), 40.........Hu-pei
Kuang-yüan h. 51...............C 3
Kuei c........................D 3
Kuei-ch'i h. 51................E 4
KUEI-CHOU, 51.
Kuei-chou F...................D 3
Kuei-hua T. 10.................D 1
Kuei-lin Fu C.................D 4
Kuei-p'ing h. 10...............C 5
Kuei-tê F.....................E 3
Kuei-yang c (Hu-nan)..........D 4
Kuei-yang Fu C. (Kuei-chou), 51..C 4
Kung-ch'ang F.................B 3
Ku-t'ien (Ku-cheng) h. 18, 27, 28...E 4
Ku-yüan c.....................C 2

Lai-an h, 51....................E 3
Lai-chou F....................E 2
Lan-ch'i h. 51..................F 4
Lan-chou Fu C. 51...............B 2
Lan-t'ien h. 51.................C 3
Lao-ho K'ou m. 48, 51...........D 3
Lei-chou F....................D 5

Lê-ling h. 33...................E 2
Lê-t'ing h. 33..................E 2
Li c. (Hu-nan)................D 4
Li h. (Kan-su)................C 3
Liang-chou F. 51................B 2
Liao-yang c. 39.................F 1
Li-chiang F...................B 4
Lien c. 7.......................E 4
Lien-chiang h. 27...............E 4
Lien-hua T....................D 4
Lien-p'ing c..................D 5
Li-long (?), 45.................D 5
Lin-an F......................B 5
Lin-chiang F. 51................E 4
Lin-ch'ing c. 3.................E 2
Ling c........................C 2
Ling-wu (?), 6..................F 3
Li-p'ing F....................C 4
Li-t'ang m....................B 4
Liu-an c. 51....................E 3
Liu-chou F....................C 5
Long-heu (?), 45................D 5
Lo-ting c. 10...................D 5
Lo-yüan h. 27, 28...............F 4
Lu c. 51........................C 4
Lu-an F. 51.....................D 2
Lu-ch'êng h. 51.................E 3
Lu-chou F. 13...................E 3
Lung c. 51......................C 2
Lung-chou T. (port)...........C 5
Lung-ch'üan h. 47...............E 4

Macao (port), 10... ....D 5
Mei h. 51.......................C 3
Mêng-tzû h. (port)............B 5
Mên-k'ou-liang m. 1.............E 5
Mien c. 27......................B 3
Mien-chu h. 27..................B 3
Min c. 10.......................B 3
Min-ch'ing h. 18. ....E 4
Mi-yün h......................E 1
Moi-lim (?), 45.................E 5
Mo-ti-chieh m. 51...............D 3
Mukden C. 26, 35, 39............F 1

Nan-an F......................D 4
Nan-ch'ang Fu C. 51.............E 4
Nan-k'ang F. 51.................E 4
Nanking Fu C. (port), 4, 7, 13. 18..E 3
Nan-ning F....................C 5
Nan-hsiung c. 41................D 4
Nan-ling h. 10..................E 3
Nan-wa h. 27....................E 4
Nan-yang F....................D 3
Ning-hai h. 51 (Chê-chiang).....F 4
Ning-hai c. (Shan-tung) 51......F 2
Ning-hsia h. 10.................C 2
Ning-kuo F. 51..................E 3
Ning-po F. (port), 1, 7, 27, 38, 51..F 4
Ning-tê h. 27...................F 4
Ning-tu c.....................E 4
Ning-wu F.....................D 2
Ning-yüan F. ....B 4
Niu-ch'uang h.'(port).........F 1

Nodoa m. (?) 7 .... C 6
Nyen-hang-li (?), 45 ....E 5

Pa c. 51 ....C 3
Pagoda Anchorage (Lo-hsing-t'a)
　m. 3 .... E 4
P'ang-chuang m. 3 .... E 2
P'ang-hai m. 51 ....C 4
Pao-tê c. ....D 2
Pao-an c. (Chih-li) ....D 1
Pao-an h. (Shen-hsi) ....C 2
Pao-ch'ing F. ....D 4
Pao-ning F. 51 .... C 3
Pao ri-hoh-shao (?) 10 ....Shan-hsi
Pao-shan h. 5 .... F 3
Pao-t'eo (?) 10 ....Shan-hsi
Pao-ting Fu C. 3, 7, 51 ....E 2
P'a-t'ang m. ....A 4
P'ei c. ....E 3
Pei-hai (Pakhoi) (port), 27 ....C 5
Peking (Imperial Capital), 2, 3, 7,
　10, 18, 20, 32, 34, 37, 52 .....E 1
Phyang thong (?), 45 ....E 5
Pih-k'eh ts'i (?) 10 ....Shan-hsi
Pi-k'ou m. 44 ....F 2
Piu c, 51 .... C 2
P'ing-lê F. ....D 5
P'ing-liang F. 51 ....C 2
Ping-lo (?) 10 ....Kan-su
P'ing-nan h. 27 .... E 4
P'ing-tu c. 15 .... E 2
P'ing-yang h. 51 (Chê-chiang) ...F 4
P'ing-yang F. (Shan-hsi), 51 ......D 2
P'ing yao h. 51 .... D 2
Ping-yü (?) 37 ....Shan-tung
P'o-kan m. 51 .... E 4
Po-lo h. 32 ....D 5
Port Arthur, 44 ....F 2
P'u-an T. (?) ....C 4
P'u-êrh F. ....B 5

Sah-la-ts'i (?), 10 ....Shan-hsi
Sang chia Chuang m. 51 .... C 3
San-shui h. 51 .... C 2
San yüan h. 24 ....C 3
Sio-ke (?), 8 ....E 5
So-p'ing F. 51 ....D 1
Shang-ch'ing m. 51 ....E 4
Shanghai h. (port), 2, 5, 7, 12, 14, 15,
　20, 23, 26, 27, 32, 46, 51, 53 ....F 3
SHAN HSI, 3, 10, 24, 26, 50, 51.
SHAN-TUNG, 3, 7, 15, 24, 33, 37, 51.
Shan-yang (?) 28 .... E 4
Shao-chou F. 40 ....D 5
Shao-hsing F. 1, 27, 51 ....F 3
Shao-wu F. 3 ....E 4
Sha-ri-ts'ing (?) 10 ....D 1
Shasi (?) (port) ....D 3
Shê-ch'i Tien m. 51 ....D 3
Shê-hung, 31 ....C 3
Shên c. ....E 2
SHÊNG-CHING, 26, 35, 39, 44.
SHEN-HSI, 24, 26, 50, 51.
Shih ch'ien F. ....C 4

Shih-ch'üan h. 27 ....B 3
Shih-nan F. ....C 3
Shun-ch'ing F. 51 ....C 3
Shun-ning F. ....B 5
Shun-tê F. 51 ....D 2
Ssŭ-ch'êng F. ....C 5
SSŬ CH'UAN, 1, 2, 18, 19, 27, 31, 32, 34,
　51.
Ssŭ-ên F. ....C 5
Ssŭ-mao T. (port) ....B 5
Ssŭ-nan F. ....C 4
Su-chou F. (port) (Chiang-su), 5, 6,
　7, 13, 15 ....F 3
Su-chou F. (Kan-su) ....A 2
Sui-tê c. ....D 2
Sui-ting F. ....C 3
Sung-chiang F. 5 ....F 3
Sung-p'an T. 51 ....B 3
Sung-yang h. 47 ....E 4
Swatau (port), 1, 30 ....E 5

Ta-chien-lu T. 51 ....B 3
T'ai c. ....F 3
T'ai-an F. 37 ....E 2
T'ai-chou F. 27, 51 ....F 4
T'ai-ho h. 51 ....E 3
T'ai-kang h. 51 ....E 3
T'ai-ku h. 3 ....D 2
T'ai-p'ing F. ....C 5
T'ai-ts'ang c. 5 ....F 3
T'ai-yüan Fu C. 24, 26 ....D 2
Ta-ku m. 33 ....E 2
Ta-ku Shan h. 44 ....F 2
Ta-ku-t'ang m. 51 .... E 4
Ta-li F. 51 ....B 4
Ta-ming F. ....E 2
Tan c. ....C 6
Ta-ning h. 51 ....D 2
Ta-ting F. ....C 4
Ta-tung h. 10 ....E 3
Ta-t'ung F. 51 ....D 1
Tê-an F. 40 ....D 3
Tê-ch'ing h. (Chê-chiang), 5 ....F 3
Tê-ch'ing c. (Kuang-tung), 9 ....D 5
Têng-chou F. 7, 15 ....F 2
T'êng-yüeh T. 51 ....A 5
Thong-thau-ha (?), 49 .... D 5
T'ien-chêng (?), 10 ....Shan-hsi
Tientsin F. (port), 3, 10, 18, 20, 26,
　32, 33, 34, 51 ....E 2
T'o-t'o Ch'êng (?) 10 ....D 1
Tsao h. ....E 2
Tsao-chou F. ....E 2
Ts'ing-shui-ho-tsi (?), 10 .....Shan-hsi
Tsong-hang-kung (?), 45 ....D 5
Tsong-shun (?), 45 ....E 5
Tso-yün h. 51 ....D 2
Tsun-hua c. 18 ....E 1
Tsun-i F. ....C 4
T'ung c. 3 ....E 2
Tung-ch'ang F. ....E 2
T'ung-chou F. 50, 51 ....D 3
Tung-ch'uan F. 25, 51 ....B 4
T'ung hsin m. 51 ....F 2

T'ung-jên F..............C 4
Tung-kuau h. 49.................D 5
Tung-tsun (?) 10....... ....Kuang-hsi
Tung-un (?) 10 ....Kan-su
Tu-shan c. 51......................C 4
Tu-yün F.......................C 4

Wan c. (Kuang-tung).........D 6
Wan h. (Ssŭ-ch'uan), 51.. ...C 3
Wan-chi (?) 10...............Kan-su
Wei h. (Shan-tung), 7...........E 2
Wei c. (Ssŭ-ch'uan).............B 3
Wei-hai-wei h....................F 2
Wei-hui F.......................D 2
Wei-ning c......................B 4
Wei-yüan T......................B 5
Wên-chou F. 38, 51.............F 4
Wong-buang (?) 28...............F 4
Wu-ch'ang Fu C. 10, 12, 82, 40, 43..D 3
Wu ching-fu m. 30...............E 5
Wu-chou F. (port), 10, 15, 26, 40....D 5
Wu-hu h. (port), 10, 18, 31, 51.....E 3
Wu-hsüeh m. 40..................E 4

Ya-chou F. 1....................B 3
Yai c.........................C 6
Yang h. 51......................C 3
Yang-chiang T. 7................D 5
Yang-chou F. 15, 18, 51.........E 3
Yang-k'ou m. 51.................E 4
Yen-an F......................C 2
Yen-ch'a T....................C 2

Yen-p'ing F. 27.................E 4
Yen-shan h. 32..................E 2
Yin-chia Wei m. 51..............C 3
Ying c. 51......................D 2
Ying-chou F. 51.................E 3
Ying k'ou, 35...................F 1
Ying-shan, 51..............Ssŭ-ch'uan
Yin-tao c.....................B 2
Yo-chou F.....................D 4
Yü c..........................E 2
Yüan-chou F. (Chiang-hsi).....D 4
Yüan-chou F. (Hu-nan).........C 4
Yüeh-sui T....................B 4
Yüeh-yang h. 51.................D 2
Yü-lin c......................D 5
Yü-liu F......................C 2
Yün-ch'êng m. 51................D 2
Yung-ch'ang F.................A 4
Yung-ch'ing h. 37...............E 2
Yung-chou F...................D 4
Yung-ch'un c. 30................E 4
Yung k'ang h. 51................F 4
Yung-kung m. (?) 1..............E 5
Yung-ning c...................D 2
Yung-p'ing F. 33................E 2
Yung-shun F...................D 4
Yün-ho h. 47....................E 4
YÜN-NAN, 25, 51.
Yün-nan Fu C. 25, 51............B 4
Yün-yang F....................D 3
Yü-shan h. 51...................E 4
Yu-yang c. (?)................C 4
Yü-wu m. 51.....................D 2

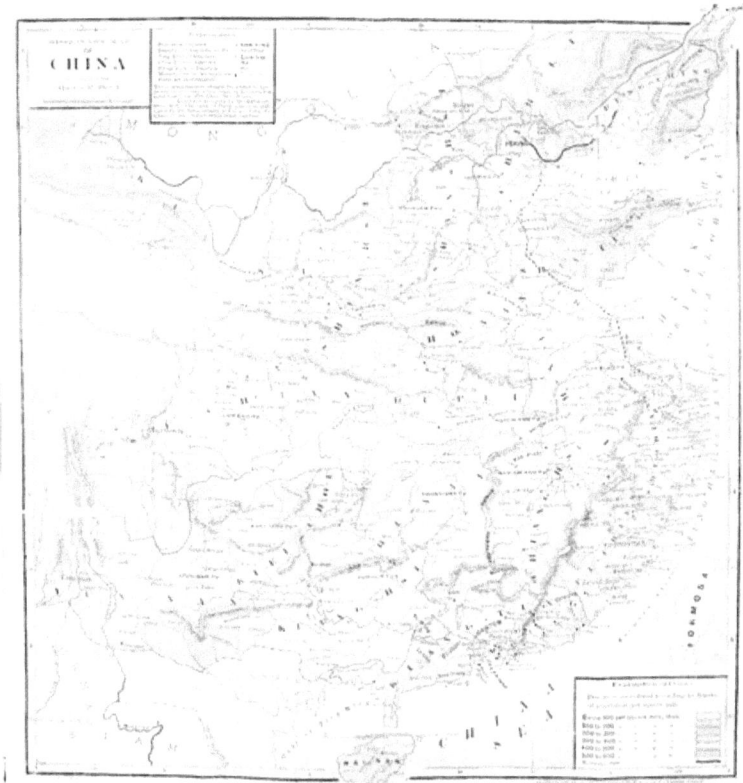

www.ingramcontent.com/pod-product-compliance
Lightning Source LLC
Chambersburg PA
CBHW030829020726
47499CB00006B/2130